BRYAN SINGER AND DEAN DEVLIN'S

THE TRIANGLE

A NOVEL BY STEVEN LYONS

BASED ON A STORY BY BRYAN SINGER
AND DEAN DEVLIN

TELEPLAY BY
ROCKNE S. O'BANNON

ibooks

DISTRIBUTED BY PUBLISHERS GROUP WEST

An ibooks, inc. Book.

Bryan Singer and Dean Devlin's The Triangle
™ and © Electric-Entertainment
All Rights Reserved.
A Novel by Steve Lyons
Teleplay by Rockne S. O'Bannon

Distributed by Publishers Group West
1700 Fourth Street, Berkeley, CA 94710

First ibooks trade paperback printing December 2005

ISBN: 1-59687-161-X

10 9 8 7 6 5 4 3 2 1

Special thanks to Rand Marlis.

Printed in USA.

PROLOGUE

In fourteen hundred ninety-two, Columbus sailed the ocean blue...

But in September of that year, history's most famous seaman almost ground to a halt in waters like none he had encountered before.

The properties of the Sargasso Sea are quite unlike those of the Atlantic waters around it. It's relatively still—and the weather, affected by a warm, clockwise current, is typically calm and steamy. In the days before powered boats, any crossing would have been long and arduous. No mystery there, right?

The Sargasso takes its name from the brown sargassum seaweed that floats upon it in clumped masses. The weed led Columbus's crew to believe, at first, that they had found land—but as days crawled by with little progress, this hope gave way to despair, and to fear that the weed would entangle their ships and trap them.

They might also have noticed that the Sargasso Sea was all but devoid of fish—a consequence of the fact that their most basic foodstuff, plankton, couldn't thrive there. It must have seemed like the whole area was inimical to life.

It was against a backdrop of fear and tension, then, that Columbus recorded in his log details of some other unusual events.

Firstly, his compasses began to behave erratically, veering toward the northwest and the northeast seemingly at random. It was fortunate for Columbus that the night skies were clear—for without the guiding light of the North Star, even he might have become lost.

Then, one night, weeks into his struggle with the sargassum weed, the very day before he set foot in the Americas at long last, he saw a row of greenish lights dancing on the horizon. Torches on a nearby island? Columbus thought not—not from the way the lights seemed to flit from one spot to another. He never did find their source.

Posterity may have concluded that Columbus wasn't the discoverer of America after all—but he did score one historical first. His was the very first account of strange happenings in an area of the South Atlantic Ocean that would become synonymous with such things. An area of which the Sargasso Sea forms only a small part. An area that, almost five centuries later, would be dubbed "the Bermuda Triangle."

Ten years after that first encounter, Columbus watched an armada of thirty-two Spanish caravels set sail from Santa Domingo, homeward bound. On board one of them—a ship called the *El Dorado*—was Francisco de Bobadilla, the man who had so recently had Columbus clapped in chains. Columbus knew a storm was coming—he could see it in the shapes and the movements of the clouds. It must have been tempting for him not to warn his old enemy...

And indeed, just three days later, Bobadilla was dead—along with the occupants of all thirty-two boats, torn apart by a hurricane. The Triangle had claimed its first souls—but they'd be far from its last.

In time, the list would stretch to thousands. Thousands of people aboard hundreds of ships, from one-man yachts to massive colliers—and later, aircraft from single-propeller, single-man planes to heavily crewed Navy Bombers. All last seen headed into the Triangle, destined never to leave it. In most cases, we can't even be sure what happened to them. They were missed only when they failed to arrive at their destinations. All those lives....

There's no mystery about Bobadilla's fate. Inside the Bermuda Triangle, cold air masses from the Arctic clash with tropical breezes, making the weather unpredictable. Localized squalls can flare up without warning, and in this case, there *was* a warning—if only if it had been heeded. Columbus had done his best to save those men. But what of all the others since? Those who weren't warned; those who set out on bright sunny days; the sailors and the airmen whose bodies weren't found; the ships and the planes of which not the slightest shard of wreckage was recovered?

The waters of the Triangle run thousands of feet deep—over thirty thousand at their deepest—and for all our modern-day technology, there are expanses of its floor that we have yet to explore. It is especially good at hiding its victims.

And of course, this leaves the door open to the peddlers of more outlandish theories—to the sort of person who sees intrigue in a disappearing plane or a ship found drifting empty, and who instinctively looks to a realm beyond science for an explanation. Trust me, I've heard all of them in my time. Green lights—what else could they be but alien spaceships? I've bit my tongue as I've listened to over-earnest talk of monsters and vortices and earth crystals, even of Atlantis.

I've interviewed people who claim to have seen green lights themselves, just like Columbus's—or impossible water spouts, or weird electrical phenomena from ball lighting to random discharges, even gigantic squid!

Sometimes, the truth is seized upon by those who want to believe, but distorted and exaggerated to fit their preconceptions. Case in point: A particularly persistent rumor that Columbus also saw a fireball in the Sargasso Sea. He *did* witness such a thing—a meteorite, most likely—but this was some months earlier, and in different waters altogether. Still, the incident became inextricably linked with Triangle lore, because hard facts are rarely allowed to stand in the way of a good story.

Other tales grew from pure conjecture, with no evidence

at all to back them up. Did Bobadilla really imprison Columbus because he had lost a number of ships and men to another freak Triangle hurricane? Because he was accused of summoning that storm through witchcraft? I never believed so.

I did hear one final story about Columbus and his exploits within the Triangle. I heard it from a man named Eric Benirall. At that point, I must admit, I thought I had nothing left to learn—but this was a story that surprised even me.

It was the night of the green lights. Columbus was still plowing his way through the turgid seas of the Sargasso, only hours away from land now.

He was roused from his sleep by a lookout, who had obviously been spooked by something and was jabbering incoherently. The captain's first thought was that this was a false alarm—the latest of many—and he rose from his bed in a surly mood, ready to take out his anger on his hapless crew.

He could feel his boat rocking, as if storm-tossed. This wasn't a new sensation for Columbus, of course—but coming as it had without warning, and in these unusual waters, it was cause for concern.

By the time he reached topside, where the rest of the crew were gathering, the ship was already lurching so violently that he had to grab hold of the jib line for balance. Waves slapped at the hull. Big waves. Like the wake of some larger ship—but there was nothing ahead but the open sea. Swinging to look to port, then starboard, Columbus saw his two sister ships also being assaulted by the mysterious waves. He could see lanterns swinging, hear Spanish curses carrying through the night. And everything was bathed in a greenish glow, as if one of the lights from before had descended upon them and enveloped them.

For all his experience, all his expertise, Columbus was frozen. All he could think was that his crewmen had been right, that this sea was cursed and it would claim their lives at last. And ahead of him now was a fogbank, growing thicker and faster than any fogbank he had encountered before—like a solid curtain, no more than a hundred feet away, and it seemed to Columbus that the green glow was emanating somehow from *inside* it.

Then a shape began to form within the fog, and suddenly, incredibly, another ship burst from its opaque depths. But what a ship! It was a monster, bigger than any vessel—any manmade *anything*—that Columbus had clapped eyes on before. A great iron hulk, dwarfing the three wooden boats that bobbed helplessly in its shadow. And a terrible grating, like the growl of some infernal beast, rattled Columbus's bones and made him wince. An intense, yellow light streamed from the ship's portholes, so unnatural that it seemed it couldn't have come from the world he knew at all.

The turbulence was now at its strongest, pitching men overboard. A crewman let out a wail of agony, and Columbus whirled to see that his face was being...*pulled* by some invisible force. Pulled so strongly that the skin itself was being stripped away. And then the flesh, the bone, being sucked toward the eerie fog.

Then the crewman was gone, in a spray of blood—but there was something else. A pile of bloody goo had started to form at Columbus's feet. He flinched, but was unable to tear his eyes away from it as it gained definition, as it took on—horribly, unmistakably—a shape. The shape of a man.

There was something on the man's head—the remnants of a white headset that had melted and melded into what was left of his skull. And a tattered piece of clothing clung to his chest, two words still visible: GOLD'S GYM.

Columbus stared up at the enormous ghost ship, somehow suspecting that this mockery of humanity had come from it—and as he stared, its mighty stern heaved into view, and Columbus could read its nameplate clearly.

The ship was *Winston Pride II* out of Miami, FL.

And then it was gone, back into the fog—and shortly thereafter, the fog itself dissipated so that all that remained was the sea, and Columbus's three wooden boats. And his crewmen—some of them fishing their comrades from the water, others just clutching at rosaries as they mumbled desperate prayers for their salvation.

Yes, I'd heard all the stories. Heard them, dismissed them, trashed most of them in print. Had a word for the sort of people who told them and believed in them. A few words, actually. Kook. Nutcase. Conspiracy theorist.

I never dreamed I'd become one of them.

CHAPTER 1

I first met Meeno Paloma at a community hospital in Miami.

He was twenty-nine years old. A Latino man, worked at a boatyard, family man. That was all I knew about him; all I needed to know.

To me, Meeno Paloma was just a name and a collection of statistics. He may or may not have been another nut, but it didn't really matter. I was going to portray him as one either way. That was my job. And at that point in my life, I had better things to worry about.

At the hospital's ER entrance, I was trying to hold two conversations at once. One was with my ex-wife, over the hands-free set of my mobile; the other was with the harried-looking woman who had just rushed out of the Nurse's Station. Fortunately, both were so familiar that I could have gone through the words in my sleep.

I asked the nurse if I could see Meeno. She asked if I was a relative. I told her I was a reporter, and showed her my card. Her derisive snort at this point, I knew all too well. I got that reaction from pretty much anyone with a high school diploma or better, as soon as they saw who I was working for. Hell, a couple of years earlier, I'd have reacted the same way myself.

"Immediate family only," snapped the nurse as she bustled away, "no exceptions." But what she meant was, "We don't speak to *The Observer*."

At the same time, I was arguing with Sally about the usual things: our fifteen-year-old daughter, Traci, and money. I don't remember the details—something about a vacation she wanted to take with friends—but as usual I was trying to play the big generous dad, making up for all the times I didn't get to see her, while Sally was pointing out how far behind I was on my child support payments and that we couldn't exactly afford it.

I was only half listening to her. I knew what she was saying anyway. I was scanning the Emergency Room with my eyes, until I found what I was looking for: a stethoscope unattended on the counter. I hurried over, checked that no one was watching, and threw it around my neck. Somebody's chart lay beside it, so I snatched that, too, and tucked it under my arm.

There was a half-eaten donut on a napkin near the phone, so I swiped that for good measure. I was headed for the elevators when I saw a cluster of doctors and nurses coming towards me, and took a sharp left into the stairwell.

Halfway to the second floor, Sally hit me with an oldie but goodie. "You don't exactly write for the *New York Times*, in case you haven't noticed!"

"Yes," I replied through clenched teeth, "as a matter of fact, I have noticed, thank you very much." But I hesitated, staring at the half-eaten donut in my hand as if it were a symbol of everything that had gone wrong with my life.

The conversation ended as it always did. I stopped appealing to Sally's reason—because she was right, as usual—and just pleaded. She sighed and hung up, but I knew she would give in. Traci would get her trip. Somehow, I didn't feel good about that.

I tried to put it out of my mind as a pair of nurses came toward me in the second-floor corridor. I affected an expression that said, "Don't approach me, I'm an asshole doctor," and I bit into the donut hard. They didn't spare me a second look as I shouldered my way between them.

Meeno Paloma was propped up in bed as I knocked on

his door and barged into the room without waiting to be asked. His dark, shoulder-length hair was splayed out on the pillow behind him, exposing the multiple studs and rings in his ears. His dark skin showed signs of exposure.

A sweet-looking woman—Meeno's wife, I assumed—was holding a straw for him as he drank. In her free hand, she held a Get Well card that had obviously been drawn by a kid. She looked up at me as I entered. "Are you the gastro-inter... inter...?" she asked, struggling with the word.

"Don't bother, really," I interrupted her, "cuz I'm not." I realized I was still wearing the stethoscope, and I removed it, flinging it and the chart aside.

I flashed my card at Meeno, hoping he'd be just the right side of exhausted not to take in the telltale name of my paper. "My name's Howard Thomas," I said, "and I—and my readers—would be extremely interested in hearing about what happened to you out there."

I pulled out my pad, giving Meeno no time to think.

Mrs. Paloma frowned. "I thought Doctor Makurji said—"

I fixed her with an unblinking stare—the one I always used when I was lying to someone's face, or at least misleading them. "Doctor Makurji didn't voice any objection to me about my stopping in for a few minutes." That was because I'd never even met the guy—but neither Meeno nor Mrs. Paloma were in the mood to argue.

"Rogue whaling ship," I recounted from my notes, "Greenpeace twelve-man raft... pretty damned dramatic. So, what happened?"

Meeno wasn't a big talker, but I already knew most of the story. I'd read the Coast Guard reports; all I needed was a few quotes from the man himself to round out my piece.

It had been an "intervention run," organized by a lawyer named Don Beatty. Beatty had roped in Meeno to man the tiller for him because nobody else knew that part of the Atlantic like he did. I say "roped in," but Meeno was as enthusiastic about the cause as any of the twelve men and women on that raft. Later, when I got to know him better, he would tell me that he knew and trusted the sea like his own mother, and that sometimes the thought of what human beings could do to it almost drove him to tears.

Meeno never wore a life vest. He always believed the sea would protect him. And he could have been right—for when that raft went down, by some small miracle, Meeno Paloma was the only survivor.

They'd been out for about four hours when they found it: a grungy whaling ship, pumping black diesel smoke from its stern, presenting an image about as far from Nature as you can get. Its crew had already sighted their prey. She was a magnificent gray, gliding through the water without the slightest inkling of the danger she was in. They were shouting in excitement as they rushed to their kill posts. The ugly harpoon gun was swinging around....

Meeno steered the raft expertly between ship and whale as the Greenpeacers brought video cameras to bear, taping the evidence. Don Beatty yelled through a bullhorn, reminding the whalers that they were in breach of international law.

They fired anyway.

Meeno ducked as the harpoon shot over his head, only just missing him. It grazed the whale's side, drawing blood, and she bellowed in pain and fear.

The whalers were already reloading—but they wouldn't get a second chance.

"It was like something started to... to churn the water." Meeno's eyes were blank as he swam in unpleasant memories. His wife stroked his hair, trying to comfort him. I was scribbling away, thinking about Sally and Traci. "Some..." Meeno hesitated. He hated saying this, but there were no other words. "...force."

One second, the water was perfectly calm, Meeno recalled. The next, something like a whirlpool had erupted behind the whaling ship, pulling at its stern. The men on the deck were slipping and sliding, crying out. Some jumped over the railings, but as soon as they hit the water they were sucked under.

The ship was swamped, and just like that it was gone.

And the whirlpool spread, until it was pulling at the Greenpeace raft too.

"Some force," I repeated under my breath—a reflex action to assure my interviewee that he had my full attention when he didn't. "Mysterious force... that's really good..." I glanced up, saw Meeno's devastated expression and realized how cold I must have sounded. "Oh, sorry. And you were, what, about fifty miles out, right?"

Meeno didn't answer. He looked as if he didn't want to remember.

"In the area they call the Sargasso Sea." Another short silence, then I prompted, "Also known as the Bermuda Triangle."

An expression of fear flickered across Meeno's face. Fear not of whatever had happened to him out there on the water, but of what would happen now, what people would think if they knew. "I never said anything about the Bermuda—"

I smiled. "Relax. You don't have to say it. I will."

Meeno watched me writing for a moment, my work almost done. Then, in a quiet, controlled voice, he said five words that jerked me out of myself for once.

He said: "Good people died out there."

Meeno was discharged later that day.

His wife, Helen, picked him up at the hospital entrance, but he confided in me later that all the way home he felt a distinct sense of unease.

Everything seemed out of place. The small things, such as the fact that the presets on the car radio had all changed. He rationalized, blaming his son, Ruben, for messing with them. The bigger things—like the fact that the car was a different color—well, they were a bit trickier.

Meeno knew it was the same car. It was an old SUV, just as he remembered, with dents in all the right places and the old stain on the carpet where Ruben had dropped a cherry soda. And Helen swore she hadn't had anything done to it while he was in the hospital. It had always been beige, she insisted.

But, in Meeno's memory, the car had always been blue.

Now, in my experience, people react to something like that—to something they can't explain—in one of two ways. There are those who look immediately to the supernatural, because they don't understand something, then of course it can't *be* understood. I'd come across more than my fair share of those people. It used to gall me that, even on a paper that so rarely dealt with the truth, I was only considered good for reporting on the real crackpots. Someone figures they've seen a ghost or been abducted by aliens or they can bend spoons with their thoughts? Send Thomas over. I was used to listening to their rambling theories, taking notes with a straight face, making all the right sympathetic noises. Most of them I forgot about within a few days of my story being filed.

At first, I'd taken Meeno to be one of those people. I think I tended to make that assumption, back then. But he was like me: a realist—you might even say a cynic. Faced with the impossible, he just looked all the harder for that rational explanation. And, in the case of the car, the only explanation that presented itself was that there was something wrong with *him*, with his mind.

I can testify, from my own later experience, that that is possibly the most terrifying thought in the world.

But for now, Meeno was going home, to the bright New Age colors of his own small, single-story house; to a "Welcome Home" banner stretched across the garage; to ten-year-old Ruben, racing out to meet him. To the kind of scene that can drive even the worst nightmares to the back of your mind, make you think everything will be fine after all.

Until, standing on the driveway, holding his son in a bone-crushing hug with his wife at his side and their Irish Setter, Nader, bounding around his feet, Meeno heard the screen door banging open again. Until another boy came hurtling out of his house, and made a beeline for him, arms out.

Meeno turned to Helen, bemused. "And who's this?" She gave him a look as if he was joking, and Meeno began to fear for his memory again. Was this some friend of Ruben's? Someone he had forgotten? It didn't seem likely. He was half Ruben's age.

And then the kid had hold of Meeno's leg, hugging for all he was worth—and he was crying out excitedly, but his words only brought a chill to Meeno's veins.

"Daddy! It's Daddy! Daddy's home!"

I can only imagine Meeno's expression—or Helen's, as the truth slowly sank in with her, too. The truth that Meeno had no memory of his youngest son.

I knew nothing of this at the time, of course. I was wrapped up in my own problems. Nothing new there—though this time, at least, I had the excuse that my problems had suddenly become a whole lot bigger and weirder than they usually were.

It started as I was leaving the hospital after my interview with Meeno. I'd just got into my Volvo jeep, feeling pretty crappy about my life, when there was a tap on my window. The guy standing outside I would come to know as Aron Akerman. He worked for Eric Benirall. From his appearance, though, you'd never have connected him to the third-richest man in Florida.

Akerman was a rock and roll nut. He usually wore a black T-shirt emblazoned with the logo of some band or other. He sported an untidy goatee and dressed in frayed jeans—and a wrinkled sports coat, which I guess was some kind of a concession to his boss. Benirall seemed to trust him, though, and to treat him as his right-hand man. Akerman's great talent, I would learn, was as a scrounger. Anything Benirall needed, Akerman could find a way to get it for him.

Anything or anyone.

"Mr. Thomas," he said as I rolled down the window and squinted up at him. "Howard Thomas...I've got something for you."

I stared at the yellow envelope in his hand and jumped to a conclusion born of bitter experience. "Dammit. She's serving me again? We just talked, and she doesn't even mention—"

Akerman chuckled, like a B-movie villain amused by his own secrets. "No, sir," he said. "This is nothing like that. Nothing like that at all."

I took the envelope from him. It might not have been a good idea, but curiosity got the better of me. Anyway, when you run from these things, they have a habit of catching up with you to bite you in the butt. I could at least find out what I was dealing with.

Looking back now, I can't help but wonder what I would've done if I'd known what that envelope contained; if I'd had the slightest hint of where it would lead me, how it would turn my life upside-down.

I think I might have run, after all.

CHAPTER 2

I was the first to arrive at Miami Harbor, clutching that yellow envelope in my hand.

The sun was just setting, the shadows lengthening—and it was deathly quiet. All I could hear was the lapping of the ocean and my own footsteps, ringing hollowly from the hulls of the berthed ships around me. One of those times when you can feel like there's no one else in the world. I wasn't sure what I was even doing here—though if I'd searched my conscience, I figure I'd have found a clue.

You don't turn down an invitation from the third-richest man in Florida—not when you need money as badly as I did then. I didn't let myself entertain the thought, didn't want to raise my hopes, but I'd be lying if I said it wasn't there.

I stood looking up at the cargo ship. Easily the biggest one there; it reared up from the water like some great iron golem. The nameplate identified it as the *Winston Pride* II. The name on the invitation. In the envelope.

I heard more footsteps behind me, disturbing the stillness, and I turned to meet the second member of our party. Bruce Gellar, thirty-three, Australian with a strong accent. A professor at the University of Florida, where his specialty was weather systems. I knew the name when

I heard it, but didn't place it till later. Gellar had made the local news more than once. He was a notorious thrill-seeker whose idea of an "experiment" often involved wild, dangerous, and sometimes illegal stunts. In fact, I would learn, he'd only made it here because Akerman had pulled a few strings and got him bail after an unlicensed skydive into the Everglades in the heart of a hurricane, taken in the name of research.

Stan Lathem was the next to arrive, stepping out of a taxi. He was an older man, pale-skinned, with an air of sadness about him. I didn't recognize him at all.

We were comparing names and envelopes when a black limo pulled up, carrying Akerman. He was almost hopping from foot to foot with excitement as he got out and opened the door for...well, at that moment, I thought she could have been the most beautiful woman I'd ever seen. Bruce thought the same; I could almost sense him perking up beside me.

"Welcome," he blurted out as the woman strode up to us. Almost unnoticed, Akerman got back into the limo and drove away.

What we didn't know then was that, as well as being beautiful—as well as being the youngest of us—Dr. Emily Patterson was probably, no undoubtedly, the most intelligent. She'd have been the most intelligent person in *most* company. She'd been working out on at sea until just recently—till there'd been a bust-up over a Health and Safety issue. Emily had been concerned with the health and the safety, her employers only with their profits. The upshot: She was out of a job. Akerman had swooped in at the right time with his yellow envelope. Evidently, though, he'd told her no more than he had the rest of us.

"Do any of you have an idea why we're here?" asked Emily.

And the answer came from behind us—from a man who had approached without any of us hearing him, just stepping off the cargo ship's gangplank. A suited man in his mid-fifties, who fairly radiated power and strength of will—and, though again I didn't like to admit it to myself at the time, wealth.

"You're here because I asked you," said Eric Benirall.

"Benirall Shipping Lines is the largest privately owned shipping company in the United States. Over seven hundred million cubic tons transported annually. Something you're wearing right now, something electronic you used today, came to this country aboard one of my three hundred and three cargo haulers."

Benirall was leading us—the four of us: Bruce, Stan, Emily, and me—down a passageway, deeper and deeper into the heart of his seemingly deserted ship. I wasn't sure what the point of his spiel was; it wasn't like we didn't know all this already. We were all of us looking around as if we couldn't quite believe we were here, couldn't believe he had chosen us—even Emily.

"My team. My experts," he had said, out in the harbor. We still weren't sure what he had meant by that.

He had said something else, too. Something that had made me think that, underneath all the wealth and the power, he was just another nut after all....

"Three hundred and three ships presently on the seas," said Benirall now. "But six months ago, it was three hundred and seven. A year ago, it was three-oh-nine."

I couldn't contain my derision. "The Bermuda Triangle is eating your ships?"

Benirall was unfazed. "When the first ship went missing, I took the exact same tone, Mr. Howard. My tone has changed."

But I was determined to cling on to my rationalist viewpoint. "That section of the South Atlantic is one of the busiest shipping areas in the world. Ships go down."

To my surprise, Bruce came to my support. "That region experiences two powerful sea breezes," he said, "one from the east and one from the west. The 'push' between the two forces sea surface air upward and triggers extreme weather."

Emily, too: "The Atlantic is also the deepest ocean in the world. With amazingly strong currents."

"Six ships," snapped Benirall, "in a single year. Over two hundred million dollars in cargo lost. These aren't pleasure craft with drunken day-sailors at the helm. These are very, very, very large ships, made of iron and steel, with the best professional crews in the world. No distress signals sent. No conditions—weather, currents, or otherwise—to blame. Yet they went down without a sign. Every square inch of them, every..." A slight hesitation. "... living soul aboard, gone without a trace."

"Why isn't this public knowledge?" asked Stan.

"Don't you think it's rather obvious?" replied Benirall.

"Certainly the government knows about this." I was beginning to get Stan's measure. Loopy conspiracy theorist.

"They are taking the position they always have—that there is no mystery," said Benirall. "That these disappearances all have common, everyday explanations."

"So why don't they tell us what those explanations are?" asked Stan with a scowl. "Because they don't really have any!"

"This ship," said Benirall, "had her own...encounter... two nights ago. Ninety-four miles from shore. She's the first who's managed to make it home. No explanation why she was spared—but she returned far from unscathed."

He stopped at a hatchway and turned to face us. He saw our expressions, and a slight smile tugged at his lips. "None of you believes a word I'm saying. Good. That's what I need."

Sometimes, when Bruce Gellar was excited—and that was most of the time—he spoke with rapid-fire enthusiasm, like a grown-up kid with Attention Deficit Disorder. "Look, Mr. Benirall," he gabbled now, "not that I don't believe you, you know, and I really respect all the adventurer stuff you do—the America's Cup wins, and that Arctic thing last year—I kinda do the same sorta stuff myself. And well, I really appreciate your problem with missing ships and all, but—"

"No you don't," said Benirall, cutting him off in full flow. "You don't give a rat's red ass about my problem. But I'm rich, and known to be a little crazy with my money, and that was all the magnet I needed to draw you here. To get you to stay.... I'm prepared to share some of those riches."

Now, I know I wasn't the only one whose ears pricked up at that. I didn't look at the others—I think we were all avoiding each other's eyes, trying to hide our thoughts, but...well, I *know* I wasn't the only one.

"Intrigued?" asked Benirall. "I thought so. Then let's continue. Watch your heads." And he disappeared through the hatchway.

I guess Stan must have been the least proud of us—or just the most honest—because he was the first to follow. The rest of us weren't far behind, though.

Another passageway. Deeper and darker still. Benirall was talking about Columbus, nothing I hadn't heard a hundred times before. But then came something new. A story I *hadn't* heard. A story about an encounter with an eerie green mist and a twenty-first-century cargo ship. A ship with a familiar name...

Benirall produced a printout, parts of which had been highlighted, and he began to read from it. Extracts, he claimed, from Columbus's log records; extracts in which the Bermuda Triangle was mentioned. I knew that many of Columbus's journals were missing; was it possible that one had been recently discovered? Or even kept from the public, but not from Benirall's contacts? More likely, I thought, it was a fake.

...appeared before us a behemoth...of iron...the measure of a mountain...before our eyes then not...not of this, God's known world...

"Two days ago," said Benirall, "this ship ran afoul of an unexpected fog. Sixteen members of the crew, including the captain and all five of his ranking execs, observed ships within that fog. Wooden sailing ships. Three of them. Flying Spanish flags. But flags the Spanish have not used in more than four centuries."

"You think your crew saw Columbus?" I spluttered, just getting the words out into the open to prove how ridiculous they sounded.

"We don't know what they saw."

"People build recreations of old ships all the time," Emily pointed out, "fly all sorts of flags."

"Ms. Patterson," said Benirall tartly, "I do know something about what's out on the ocean—and I trust my crew. They didn't believe them to be recreations."

We'd reached another hatchway. Ominously, this one

was sealed with that orange security tape. Benirall tore off the tape and eased the door open. It creaked a little.

"Only the requisite authorities have been allowed in here to see this. No one else," he said. "I suggest you prepare yourselves."

The stern engine room of the *Winston Pride II* was a massive space, great hulks of equipment lurking in its gloom. I didn't know where to look at first, my eyes searching the shadowy nooks and crannies for a clue.

Bruce was halfway through a question when he began to see it, his voice catching in mid-word. I wasn't too far behind.

There was more of the orange tape, cordoning off sections of bulkhead and certain pieces of equipment. And inside the taped-off areas, there was something...something red... something that appeared to have splashed and dripped and dried on hard. It looked like...

Blood. It took me a moment to see it, another moment to accept it.

Blood. Lots of blood, and the hardened remnants of— what was that? Viscera...?

Stan was having some sort of...I didn't know what. His eyes were closed and there was sweat on his brow, and he was muttering almost to himself. "Men...eleven men... working here...night...working...then..."

A long pause—and somehow, we were all watching him, waiting with breath caught in our throats although I couldn't have said why.

"Dead!" pronounced Stan, and he screwed up his face in frustration as if he couldn't quite see something. "All at the same time...something...something..."

"Actually," said Benirall, "there were nine men, Mr. Lathem. And as far as we can tell, they weren't working at the time." He indicated a playing card partially buried in a sheen of red goo. "But yes, it was at night. And they did all die, all at the same time."

Emily and Bruce were giving Stan sidelong looks, trying to understand what they'd just seen, probably wondering if he was a part of this weird theater, some stooge of

Benirall's. I didn't spare him a second thought. I'd seen his type before. I knew Stan Lathem was a fraud; I didn't have to understand how he did it.

"And it happened," said Benirall, "at the precise moment those three wooden ships were appearing on the ocean above." He handed me a sheaf of photos and continued, "The same instant that *he* appeared—in that form—on this ship's foredeck."

I blanched as I realized what I was looking at. Pictures of a human body—at least, it had been human once. Now, it was a mass of red goo, barely holding a semblance of its old form. There were remnants of clothing—old-fashioned clothing—and a small metal cross, melted around the edges, seared into its chest.

"Tissue tests reveal, whoever he was, he'd never had a single common childhood inoculation. He washed with lye soap and he was suffering from the onset of scurvy."

The others were looking at the photos, each grimacing in turn, only starting to absorb all this. "After the incident," continued Benirall, "a head count aboard this ship showed one man missing—a galley mate named Browder. Anyone not of a rational mind might begin to think that—whatever the reason or cause—this ship and the wooden ships traded a crewman." He had the same look in his eye that I'd seen in Meeno's at the hospital. This was hard for him to say, hard for him to acknowledge.

He turned and marched away quickly. As the rest of us made to follow, Bruce tried to lighten the atmosphere with a quip. "Careful. Don't step in the seaman."

Nobody laughed.

On the deck, a tent had been set up with bright lighting, a buffet with two servers standing at the ready, silver warming trays, urns of coffee—a stark contrast to the shadows below. I went straight for the wines as Bruce and Stan filled their plates. Emily didn't feel like eating.

"I appreciate the ghost ship tour," she said tiredly, "and the nifty spread and all. But I just flew in from an oil rig, I haven't been home in eleven weeks." (Bruce shot me a surprised look, and mouthed, "Oil rig?") "What exactly are you looking for from me?"

"Answers, Ms. Patterson," said Benirall. "Explanations. *The* explanation."

The rest of us wandered over with our food and drink, trying not to look too interested, too needy. "Explanation of what?" mumbled Bruce with his mouth full. He figured out the answer a second after the rest of us, and jeered, "C'mon, not the Bermud—"

Benirall interrupted him. "I want nothing less than the definitive reason for the over one thousand vessels and almost eight thousand souls who have been lost over the centuries. To every question Man can pose, there is an answer. I want this answer."

"Why...this group?" asked Emily, and I wasn't sure if I'd imagined the half-disdainful look she cast toward the rest of us.

"Why *only* us?" asked Stan, more pertinently. "You could afford—"

I already had that one figured out. "We weren't his first choices," I said. "Or tenth, probably."

Benirall couldn't deny it. "You may not have been my initial candidates, but you have each risen to that place."

"Because we showed up!" concluded Emily.

"What is important," said Benirall, "is that you each offer a very specific and distinct discipline. Scientific, as well as the more ethereal." This last part was directed toward Stan.

"And me?" I asked.

"You, Mr. Thomas, are the referee. The ultimate arbiter. You are my Triangle expert. I have examined your work for—what's the name of the publication?—*The Observer.* You have interviewed every legitimate explorer, every wild-eyed crackpot. You know every theory."

"And I don't believe any of it."

"Exactly." Benirall indicated the others. "What they propose, I expect you to vet. Hard. With every ounce of your extensive knowledge and unrelenting cynicism." His mood had shifted, as if a weight had lifted from his shoulders. Now he was filled with adventuring spirit. "This endeavor isn't about hypotheses and suppositions. It isn't about 'what if' and 'just possibly.' It is a journey—a quest—to find truth.

The truth. To uncover something that has managed to defy all others who have ventured this path before you."

It was Bruce who punctured the moment.

"You said something about money," he said. "I mean, if you're expecting me to set aside all my other projects—*all* my other projects—and start researching this, then you—"

"Not just research, Dr. Gellar," said Benirall. "This isn't some 'weekend gig' you palm off as penance on your grad students. This is field work, getting your feet wet, your hands filthy. Going wherever you need to go, doing whatever must be done, to bring me what I want. And for that—when you bring me that—I am prepared to present to each of you five million dollars."

It was several moments before any of us could speak. We were standing like statues. Then Stan squeaked, from the back of his throat, "Each?"

Out of the corner of her mouth, Emily said, "The man said each."

"Five million times four," Benirall confirmed. "The funds are already in escrow accounts bearing each of your names. In a bank in the Cayman Islands—very fitting, I thought. But it isn't payable for trying. It is yours only when you deliver."

And there it was, I thought. The catch.

"That's why the other 'candidates' before us passed," I said with a knowing grin. I doffed my empty wine glass. "Mind if I have one more drink before I go?"

"I'm very serious, Mr. Thomas."

I cocked an eyebrow. "Serious about solving the mystery of the Bermuda Triangle?"

"Which assumes as its basis that there's a mystery at all," said Bruce.

"When do you... when would you have to know if we're interested?" asked Emily.

"I have as many as a dozen ships crossing the Triangle every day," said Benirall. "I have no intention of losing even one more of them. You decide now. You start tonight."

Amid the cries of protest that greeted that pronouncement, Bruce's voice sounded the clearest. "Don't we get some part of the money up front?"

"It's an all or nothing proposition, Dr. Gellar," said Benirall. "All...or nothing." Then he added something that struck each of us like a blow to the solar plexus, not that any of us wanted to reveal it to the others. "I'm a man who does his homework," said Benirall. "I don't expect I'll be hearing no from any of you."

And, with infuriating confidence, he swaggered away from us, calling back over his shoulder, "I'll give you fifteen minutes. I suggest you try the *boeuf braisé oignous.* It's my own recipe."

CHAPTER 3

"What is the 'Triangle,' anyway?" asked Emily. "Do we even know its boundaries?"

I answered automatically. "Miami, Bermuda, San Juan." I drew the shape in the air with my fork, which just happened to have a sausage attached to it. "Fourteen thousand square miles. You didn't know that? And you're, what—our ocean person? Expert?"

"Deep Ocean Resource Recovery," said Emily defensively. "And excuse me if I'm not conversant in the current folklore—"

Stan jumped in. "You don't believe in the Bermuda Triangle? Then why did you agree to—?"

"I'm here," said Emily, "because the man has lost six ships in twelve months. That, I might be able to help him with."

She didn't mention the money. None of us had mentioned it.

As soon as we'd given Benirall our answer—and he'd been dead right about what it would be—he'd called Akerman to collect us. We'd ridden off in the black limo, Bruce on his cell phone arranging leave from his university job, Emily complaining that Akerman wouldn't take her home to pack.

"Mr. Benirall expects your complete attention to the task at hand," he had said. "You'll be provided lodging, workspace, whatever you need. Approved by me, of course." Bruce had wanted to bring some of his students along, but Akerman had nixed that idea, too. We were Benirall's team; he wanted nobody else involved.

I'd been more concerned about our expenses.

By morning, we were eating breakfast in a coffee shop at Miami International Airport—which was crammed as usual. There'd been a technical breakdown at the security check, and a long line of passengers was getting crazed as only people waiting at an airport can.

In the midst of all this activity, it felt like the four of us were in our own little bubble, offset from the rest of the world. Bruce was on his cell again, talking animatedly as he rummaged through a very cool black nylon travel bag, finding neatly folded clothes, shoes, toiletries, sunglasses, all expensive and brand-spanking new. His face was shining like a kid's at Christmas. We had a bag like that each, tucked under the table at our feet.

"Okay," I said, turning to Stan, "so how much about the Triangle do *you* know?"

"I attend my share of conventions, symposiums on the paranormal," he said. "I know some—"

"When did people start talking about disappearances in that region?"

I could tell Stan didn't care much for my good-natured teasing. Still, he couldn't resist answering. "1950. In a newspaper article."

I was impressed. Didn't stop me trying to one-up the old guy, though. "In a sidebar on an AP wire service story by E.V.W. Jones," I expounded. "He dubbed it 'The Devil's Sea.' Very good. But who came up with the name 'Bermuda Triangle'?"

"It's from a magazine article in the sixties."

"Vincent Gaddis in a 1964 *Argosy Magazine* feature. Very, very good."

Emily was just picking at her food and staring at us both, her expression saying that this was going to be a long endeavor.

Stan glanced at Bruce. "And what about him? What does he do?"

"I think he said he's weather."

Bruce heard this and briefly broke off his other conversation to boast, "The preeminent meteorological authority on the South Atlantic and environs."

"Oh, okay, I see," I sneered unfairly, "and that's why I've heard of you."

Bruce shot back, "What's the name of that newspaper you work for? Oh, that's right–*The Observer*." Into the phone, he said, "Yeah, I'm still here. No, nobody sits this one out. I want everybody on this. Grad students and undergrads– every warm body whose academic life I hold in the palm of my godlike hand... Yeah, you heard me right. The Bermuda... Very funny. Just get them started."

"Benirall was very specific," Stan reminded Bruce as he hung up. "He wanted your work, not your students'."

"Five million on the line," said Bruce, "I'm using every resource I've got."

Emily had finally had enough. She broke in: "I just want to make sure we're all absolutely clear on one immutable fact." And, emphasizing each word, she announced, "This. Is. Absolutely. Absurd. I mean, c'mon–the Bermuda Triangle?"

A guy at the next table looked up from his paper, and Emily winced at the look he shot us. "I should be out looking for a real job," she grumbled into her eggs.

And that brought us right round to the subject we'd been avoiding.

"I suspect we all need the money," said Emily, "or we would've laughed in Benirall's face last night."

"Look," said Bruce, "we're talking a lot of cash. A five with five zeroes–"

"Six zeroes," corrected Emily.

"Whatever. The pisser is what Benirall expects us to do to get it."

"People have been trying to explain the Triangle for years," said Stan. "Why Benirall thinks we, this group, will be able to uncover some new answer–"

"Definitive answer!" corrected Emily.

Bruce had pulled a new shirt out from his bag. "Hey, this is Zegna!" he cried, holding it against himself, checking the size.

Emily shot him a withering look, and continued, "Plus he said 'field investigation.' And just how does he expect us to predict when there's about to be a new Triangle incident for us to 'investigate'?"

"Easy," I said. "We rent a Cessna, load up some Kennedys and a couple of fifties rock stars, and just follow 'em."

Emily and Bruce chuckled—as much, I suspected, at the absurdity of our situation as at my line in cynicism. Stan didn't join in. I guess he didn't appreciate my smart-ass attitude. It was the sort of thing he'd had to live with all his life.

He got to his feet and went for more coffee. Bruce waited until he was out of earshot, then said, "A psychic! That's what I'm talking about." As another shot at me, he added, "But I guess having a paranormal guy around makes you feel a little more at home."

Emily waved her contract in our faces, bringing us back to the matter at hand. "We all got one of these. The offer is definitely real. The money is waiting in escrow accounts, just like Benirall said. It's all ours, just as soon as we..." She couldn't bring herself to say the words.

Bruce looked around to make sure no one was listening—and that Stan was a safe distance away. "Look," he said, "we all agree this 'quest' of Benirall's is complete and total crap!"

I nodded. "If a train disappeared between two stops, that would be convincing evidence of paranormal activity. But over the ocean, ships and planes do go down."

The "Bermuda Triangle" wasn't even a real triangle. Gaddis's name, along with the boundaries I'd outlined, had stuck because it had the right ring of mystique to it. Many of the incidents attributed to the area had actually occurred outside of those boundaries—but that didn't stop people from lumping them together, finding significance where there was probably none. As with Columbus's fireball, they would believe what they chose to believe.

"I don't even know why I'm sitting here," agreed Emily. "What do we really expect to accomplish?"

"We expect to accomplish a big chunk of Benirall's billions in our bank accounts." Bruce leaned in conspiratorially, and dropped his voice. "We all went to college, right? We've all faked a paper or two in our time."

"I never faked anything in my life!" protested Emily.

"I said 'college paper,' love," Bruce shot back.

I could see where he was going—but to my mind, it was an insane proposition. Conning someone like Benirall out of twenty million dollars? We'd probably have stood more chance of solving his damn mystery.

"We're all experts in our fields," Bruce persisted. "Well, I know I am. What's to stop us? We spend three weeks and drop six thousand pages in his lap. Lots of polysyllabic words, datum specific to our individual areas of expertise... We dazzle him."

He looked from Emily to me, back to Emily, his eyes alight with childlike enthusiasm for his idea. We both shifted uncomfortably. For my part, I couldn't deny that the prospect of a way out of all this was tempting. The last thing I wanted to do was spend weeks, months, away from my lowly but paying job in pursuit of an impossible dream—and yet I couldn't bring myself to let go of that dream either. And, hell, it wasn't like I didn't bend the truth for *The Observer* every day of my life; it was what they expected. But was I really ready to try what Bruce was suggesting? To cross that line?

And a part of me thought that Benirall wouldn't miss twenty million; if he wanted to throw it away on a fool's errand...and I realized I was trying to talk myself into it, taking that easy option. "Might be worth a try," I concluded, awkwardly. "If he doesn't buy it, what's he gonna do—fire us?"

Emily just glared at us both, like she'd stumbled into a matinee of *Dumb and Dumber*. "You guys' moral center is pretty much hollow, isn't it?" she said scathingly. "I yell down there, I'm guessing I'm gonna hear an echo."

It was at that moment that Aron Akerman chose to come bopping up to us, all grins and energy. "So...what ch'all talking about?"

The three of us froze, but he didn't seem to notice. He was busy dealing out plane tickets. "Flight leaves in ninety minutes. You're gonna love the offices we've got you—right in Cape Canaveral City, minutes from the Space Center. Oh, almost forgot..." He hefted a Cartier briefcase onto the table in between us, and popped it open to reveal an array of DVD-ROM discs in clear plastic sleeves. "This is everything Mr. Benirall has collected on the Triangle," said Akerman. "Pretty much every known scrap of information on the phenomenon. Over thirteen thousand pages here. A lot of it is bull, polysyllabic words that say nothing—" Bruce, Emily, and I exchanged looks. So much for the grand plan! "—but some of it is really great. 'Get me Art Bell on the phone' stuff."

"You believe in this?" asked Emily, indicating the discs with some disdain. She was looking for a straw, I think, just some shred of common sense to hold on to.

She didn't get it from Akerman. "Abso-freakin-lutely!" he enthused.

Emily's expression said it all.

Even later, when I got to know Stan Lathem better, when I started to think of him as a friend, I would never understand how his mind worked. How could I? He didn't understand it himself.

Contrary to my first impressions of him, though, he was no charlatan. That's not to say I can quite believe, even now, that the abilities he claimed to have been blessed—and burdened—with were genuine. But I can state with total confidence that they were real to him. Stan honestly believed he saw glimpses of past and the future. He wasn't setting out to put one over on anyone. If he had been, I think he would have given it up a long time before I met him.

He was a lonely man. Sure, he'd enjoyed some measure of fame in his younger days. He'd appeared on a few talk shows—his thing back then had been using his alleged abilities to locate missing kids—but he wasn't the sort of guy anyone really wanted to associate with. He came across as an oddball, detached from reality. His constant...well, for want of a better term, let's say "psychic visions"...were a strain on him and on everybody around him.

Stan had grown to hate the visions. It frustrated him that they were so lacking in clarity. He saw a flash here, a jumble of images there, but it was always so hard to make sense of it all. Too often, he became wise after the event, beating himself up over what he could have done. And when he did try to act, when he tried to describe what he was seeing, the words were impossible to find. He came across like one of those fake mediums, talking in the vaguest possible terms, casting the net of his predictions wide in the hope of trawling a few grains of truth.

Stan hated the visions. But they wouldn't leave him alone.

That was why, when a familiar sensation came over him at the airport, he said nothing to the rest of us. Instead, he stood alone, as usual, and sipped at his coffee and stared out of a window at the runways as he struggled to work out what he was feeling.

Later, he described to me how his gaze was drawn to a line of passengers waiting to board their plane. United Airlines Flight 28 to Zurich. And one girl in particular, maybe six years old, bright blonde hair, standing with her mother and father, a *Veggie Tales* picture book clutched to her side. The way Stan saw her, it was as if she had a special glow, as if she was lit up from the inside. He was so distracted by the image that he didn't notice he had tilted his cup, that he was pouring coffee onto the floor. The realization jerked him out of his trance as the girl disappeared through the boarding gate. But the odd sensation lingered.

Less than an hour later, the four of us were standing in line for our own flight when all hell broke loose. Security guards went racing by, joined by agitated airport execs in shirt sleeves and ties. Stan knew something had happened, and tried to say so, but my only response was a sarcastic "Wow. How'd you ever divine that?"

And then, Akerman was suddenly beside us, out of breath, literally pulling at us. "C'mon. Out of line."

Benirall had contacts at the airport, apparently. No surprise there. He'd known what was happening almost before some of the execs, and he'd got straight on the blower. Akerman already had a chopper standing by.

One of our concerns, it seemed, had just been answered. We wouldn't have to sit around waiting, trying to predict when the next 'Triangle incident' would occur. It had just happened.

United Airlines Flight 28 to Zurich had gone down.

CHAPTER 4

Of all the tales told of the Bermuda Triangle, I think the one I heard the most often was that of Flight 19: five Avenger Torpedo Bombers, which flew out from Fort Lauderdale Naval Air Station in Florida shortly after two on the afternoon of December 5, 1945. They weren't the first planes to go missing in that area—that honor went to another Avenger, three years earlier—but theirs was the first mass disappearance, and the first story to really grab the public imagination.

There were fourteen men aboard those planes—mostly students on a routine training run. It ought to have been fifteen, but a Corporal Kosnar had asked to be excused. A strange premonition had persuaded him not to fly, though conditions were described as fair to good.

At 3:45PM, a distress call was picked up from Flight 19's commander, a Lieutenant Charles Taylor. "This is an emergency," he said. "We seem to be off course. We cannot see land...repeat...we cannot see land."

When directed to head due west, Lt. Taylor is alleged to have said, "We don't know which way is west. Everything is wrong...strange... We can't be sure of any direction. Even the ocean doesn't look as it should."

THE TRIANGLE

Communication with Flight 19 became patchy after that, with the operators in the control tower unable to make out much through the static. At one point, Taylor indicated that he believed himself to be over the Florida Keys, which would have been almost impossible given his starting point and top speed.

By 4:25PM, he had apparently so lost confidence in his ability to find his way home that he'd handed his command over to another officer, a Captain Stivers. He fared no better. Stivers's last message to Fort Lauderdale was: "It looks like we are entering white water. We're completely lost."

Flight 19 was never heard from again, apart from a faint ghost message received at 7:04PM, repeating the flight's call letters, hours after the planes should have run out of fuel and gone down. Also lost that day was a Martin Mariner flying boat, dispatched to search for the other five planes. About thirty minutes out, it simply broke off radio contact and was never seen again.

The most likely explanation for what happened—the one I always preferred to believe—was that Lt. Taylor simply became confused; that this, coupled with an abrupt change in wind direction, was the cause of the tragedy. The five Avengers, hopelessly lost out over the Atlantic, would have crashed once their fuel was exhausted—and, weighing fourteen thousand pounds each, they'd have gone down fast.

As for the Mariner, it's been suggested that there is little mystery about its fate. The crew of a merchant vessel reported seeing an explosion on the water that evening—and indeed the Mariners had been dubbed "flying bombs" because of their huge fuel tanks. A rookie crew member, scrambled on board without time for a proper briefing, may have tried to light a cigarette. But the explosion was witnessed two hours after the Mariner's last radio contact.

And other questions remained unanswered. The Avengers wouldn't have run out of fuel simultaneously; why, when the first one went down, did the others not report this fact? If Flight 19 flew into freak weather, as some scientists suggested, why was there no mention of this in their communications? Why didn't the ocean "look as it should?" And how could two experienced pilots in two different aircraft have suddenly lost the ability to navigate—if not by their unreliable compasses, then by the sun? Above all, why was no debris from any of the planes ever found?

The Navy's inquiry into the tragedy absolved Charles Taylor of blame, but was unable to explain the total loss of six airplanes and twenty-seven men. One of the officers presiding stated, "They vanished as completely as if they'd flown to Mars."

And so the myth of the Triangle began to grow.

I was thinking about Flight 19 as we flew out over the clear ocean—the four of us, Akerman, and a pilot jammed into a sleek jet helicopter.

And not just Flight 19, but about the many other airplanes lost since: a C54 Douglas with a crew of seven in July 1947; a Star Tiger with twenty-nine people on board in January 1948; a Douglas DC-3 passenger airliner with thirty-one people later that same year...far too many for me to recall all their names, let alone the names of those who flew in them. A litany of tragedy, stretching right up to the present day and to planes whose onboard navigational equipment was far more sophisticated than that of those Navy Bombers.

I told myself to snap out of it. I remembered what I had said to Bruce and Emily at the airport. *Planes do go down.* And, in an area as dense with air traffic as this one, even a hundred planes in six decades only just bordered on the statistically significant. I had flown through the Triangle dozens of times without incident, without even thinking about it. I could hardly avoid it; it was right on my doorstep.

So why did it feel different this time?

Akerman was surfing the net on an uplinked PDA, picking up the latest info from the news sites and relaying the brutal statistics to the rest of us. "Full passenger list—two hundred seventy-two plus eleven flight crew." The numbers meant little to me. Just another set to add to all the others. I hadn't seen those people as Stan had seen them. I hadn't seen the little girl.

The rest of us were staring ahead, at the solid shape of a US Cost Guard ship growing in the windscreen. Only Stan thought to ask about survivors. Akerman scrolled through a couple more screens. "Reuters, CNN...nobody's saying."

"This is the crash site of a commercial airliner," Emily pointed out. "They don't need us in their way right now."

"Forget about need," I said. "That's the US Coast Guard down there. You really think they're gonna let us come traipsing around when—"

Akerman produced four gray cards, which he proceeded to dole out. They were ID cards, each sporting only a photograph, a name, and a barcode. Bruce recognized them immediately, and he was incredulous. "You cannot be serious. These are real? Tell me they're not...of course they're not real..."

"What are they?" asked Emily.

Bruce answered that they were 'DOD Indef security IDs', which left us little the wiser. "Department of Defense?" I queried.

"Indef?" Stan echoed.

"It means spook time," said Bruce. "It's 'I tell you, I have to kill you' territory. Nobody has these."

I stared at Akerman in disbelief. "You're giving us counterfeit government IDs?"

He grinned. "Counterfeit? Define your terms. Yes, counterfeit—because, well, none of you really has such clearance, obviously. But also, no—because they are one hundred percent the real thing." He gave us a moment to digest that, to wonder just how far Eric Benirall's reach extended, then he continued, "Most important point: you flash that and nobody's gonna dare question you being here."

Emily, Stan, and I were just staring at our cards like we were holding kryptonite. Bruce, however, had got over his initial surprise and was as excited as a five-year-old. "Do we get to keep these?" he asked. "I mean...after?"

We set down on the deck of the Coast Guard ship, amid a scene of frenetic activity. We could already see a security detail making a beeline for us. Big men. With guns. "This is absurd," muttered Emily. "We're going to be thrown into Levenworth for the rest of our lives."

"No we won't," I assured her, unable to take my eyes off the approaching men. "Levenworth is strictly military.

We're gonna be thrown in *someplace else* for the rest of our lives..."

The detail's senior officer was hammering on our door. There were a lot of stern faces and rifles out there. Even Bruce looked like a kid about to be caught sneaking into the movies. I held my breath as, hesitantly, he lifted his ID card and showed it through the glass. The leader guy took his eyes off Bruce to inspect it—and there was no mistaking the shift in his expression as he realized what he was looking at.

Suddenly giddy again, Bruce span round to face the rest of us. "He's probably never seen one before. Look at him! Look at his face! Look!"

He couldn't wait to get the chopper door open. The rest of us were too busy clinging onto our seats and taking deep, calming breaths.

It was probably the most surreal experience of my life to date: surrounded by uniforms, being escorted deeper into that ship by a young officer who was clearly nervous of *us*, struggling to act like I thought a government spook ought to act. This wasn't some two-bit masquerade at a community hospital, where the worst that could happen was that I'd be slung out on my ear. This was the big league. I was only just beginning to appreciate how big.

I noted wryly that Akerman had chosen not to come with us. He'd stayed with the getaway vehicle.

Bruce, of course, was loving all this. "How'd you get out here so fast?" he asked the young officer—who had introduced himself as Lieutenant Junior Grade Reilly.

"We were already in the vicinity on security patrol," said Reilly. "Navy's got some maneuvers going on, had us out here babysitting this patch."

Stan asked about survivors again. "The plane's resting on a shelf thirty meters down," said Reilly. "Not very deep—but survivors? I doubt it. We've got ROVs deployed, see what we can—"

"Why ROVs?" Emily interrupted. "Why not send divers?"

"Ma'am, we're a security contingent. I've got some divers

aboard, but none'a my boys are NTSB rescue/recovery trained. Mainland's putting together a whole cigar box full of experts from all over South Florida. When you arrived, we thought you might be part of them."

We kept our mouths shut, neither confirming nor denying that, as Reilly led us into the ROV control room. It was an impressive space, lit largely by the kick from dozens of TV and data screens. Emily and Bruce went straight for those screens, their professional curiosity piqued despite the circumstances. I hung back with Stan, trying not to look like all this was new to me.

There were three Remotely Operated Vehicles sending back pictures of the downed plane. The first was at one of the passenger windows, trying to see in; the second was at the cockpit windscreen; the third displayed a wide view of the entire plane, nestled on its undersea shelf as Reilly had described.

Emily had lost some of her anxiety, clearly caught up in the dramatic images on the screens. She hovered at the shoulder of the third ROV operator, frowned at something she'd seen, and then started to issue orders as if it was the most natural thing in the world. "Bring it around this way. This. More." Then, over her shoulder to Stan and me: "You guys might want to see this."

Bruce was thinking along the same lines—except that he'd hustled his ROV operator right out of his seat and taken over from him.

"You see what I'm seeing?" asked Emily.

"It doesn't look damaged," I breathed.

Apparently, that was the right answer. "Impact with the water alone should have cracked her in half, sheared off the tail, one of the wings...something..."

"Looks as if somebody just...set it down there..." said Stan.

"Uh, folks..." Bruce was maneuvering ROV #1 along the fuselage. We could see now, from this close-up perspective, that the whole body of the plane was covered in barnacles and plant growth. Rust flaked from decaying steel rivets.

"We *sure* this is the plane that just went down?" queried Emily. "This plane looks like it's been down there for decades."

"Last transponder transmission came from this lat and longitude," said Reilly, sounding as helpless as I felt.

I knew there was an explanation for this. A rational explanation. Somebody had to keep his feet on the ground.

Bruce reached over to jab a finger at the feed from ROV #3. "Those engines are Pratt and Whitney 4074 turbofans. Added to the line no more'n a year ago. This is a very new plane."

"And therefore it can't have been down here 'for decades,'" I reasoned.

"So where'd all that rust and the barnacles come from?" challenged Stan.

"Nothing says it came from..." My voice tailed off as I realized how many people were listening. "...where you're suggesting it came from," I concluded lamely.

Even this was enough to pique Reilly's curiosity. "Don't mind my asking," he said apologetically, "what project are you folks with?"

"You should know better'n to ask that," said Bruce quickly.

At which point, the operator of ROV #2 spared us any further awkwardness by sitting bolt upright in his seat and crying out, "Sirs! We've got other craft down there!"

On his screen, in the distance, slowly becoming clearer as his vehicle glided towards them, were five shapes. A cluster of planes, each with the US Navy emblem emblazoned upon them. "Navy planes," gasped Reilly. "But...what kind are they...?"

Much to my discomfort, I knew the answer. I'd had photographs of planes like these appear beside my byline more times than I could count. I could hardly process what I was seeing. I felt as if Fate was playing some colossal joke on me.

In a hollow voice, I said, "They're Avenger Torpedo Bombers."

ROV #3 had moved up to the cockpit of the nearest Avenger. The canopy was rolled back, open to the sea—and still strapped inside was its young pilot. His eyes were open, there were no signs of decay, but he was quite dead. Blood floated in ribbons from his nose and mouth. I winced at the sight.

"He sure hasn't been down there since the forties," remarked Bruce.

"I'd say a couple of hours at most," agreed Emily.

"Alive..." The moan came from Stan. I turned to meet his eyes, and saw that his face was a ghostly pale. I realized that, while I'd been riveted to the ROV screens, he had dropped into a chair as if weakened. He was sweating. "Inside the 747... there's someone...still alive..."

"How's he know that?" Reilly's question was aimed at me, but I didn't know how to answer it.

Bruce was still fiddling with the controls of ROV #1, and suddenly he announced, "I'm in!" He had found an emergency wing door on the 747, which must have popped open at some point. He piloted his vehicle through, and I braced myself for the sight of more death.

The inside of the plane was filled with water. A few fish had made it in before us, and they flitted across the screen as Bruce guided the ROV on. I was holding my breath, and I think the others were too. "Eerie" didn't begin to describe this.

"It's completely swamped," said Reilly. "No way anybody could have survived."

"Excuse me," I said, finding my voice. "Notice anything else, perhaps a little more unusual?"

Emily had seen it. "Where are all the other passengers?"

There were no bodies. Two hundred and eighty-three people, Akerman had said—but we were looking at row upon row of bare seats. This plane was as empty as the day it had come off the assembly line.

We were staring in silence, none of us knowing how to process that—until Stan pushed himself to his feet, his eyes fixed on some imaginary distant point, standing a little unsteady. "Listen to me," he pleaded. "Please listen. There's somebody still..." And he winced, as if a stab of pain had just gone through his head—but then his expression brightened and his voice became more confident. As if, now, he was sure of his ground. As if, now, he *knew*.

"A little girl!" exclaimed Stan. "There's a little girl still alive on that plane!"

CHAPTER 5

Half an hour later, I was starting to feel uncomfortable again.

I was still in the ROV control room, still watching images of Flight 28 on the screens. Now, though, the live feeds were supplied by the mask-cams of two divers: Emily and Bruce. Which left me alone in the lion's den with Stan—and he was even more miserable company than usual. He was on pins and needles, pacing up and down, his face wet with perspiration, trying to focus on something invisible to the rest of us.

I glanced at Reilly, who was in covert conversation with a junior officer, looking over at us every few seconds. He'd insisted to me that his own men could have done this job, but I'd assured him that Emily and Bruce were experts although I had no idea if it was true. I think Reilly was feeling put out, and I wondered how much longer this gossamer ruse of ours could sustain.

It didn't help that, suddenly, we were following the whims of a self-professed psychic. Emily had been especially dubious about that, but she'd claimed she had wanted a closer look at those planes anyway, to see what the ROVs couldn't show us—and Bruce had insisted she wasn't diving alone. Somehow, despite their surface differences, a connection had formed between Emily and Bruce. You could feel the sparks in the air when they bickered. A small part of me could almost have been jealous.

It was down in the dive dress room, Bruce confided in me later, that he and Emily had really started to deepen their relationship. Well, what he actually said was that he'd got to see her naked. Emily had just been peeling down, and Bruce had tried to control his boyish impulses but she'd caught his eyes wandering. When she couldn't take it any more, she'd just turned to face him with her arms spread wide and told him to get it over with. "Okay," Bruce had said, once he'd looked her up and down for a moment, got it out of his system. "Good. Good idea. Thanks."

Emily never admitted it, but I suspect she got in a few sly glances of her own.

Turned out they *were* both experienced divers. Bruce boasted that he'd almost lost a leg once, diving a trench off the Aleutians in search of current fluctuations. "Didn't stop me. Splash—I was right back in."

To get to the 747, now, they had to cross the field of Avengers. I swallowed dryly as the planes became clearer on the screens—as Emily and Bruce swam over them, unable to resist peering down at that creepy underwater graveyard. The movement of the water made the unnaturally preserved bodies of the pilots undulate as if they were turning in sleep. So many expeditions had searched for these very planes and found nothing. How probable was it that we'd just stumbled across them like this?

Bruce seized up and grabbed Emily, holding her back. The image on her screen blurred as she turned her head this way and that, looking for the problem. Bruce pointed, and Stan and I leaned in toward both screens.

"What are those?" asked Stan.

A flick of a tail, and suddenly the grainy images became clear to me. "Sharks!"

And quite a gathering of them. At least two dozen, of varying breeds: whites, tigers... They were just floating there, at the edge of the circle of Avengers—and, unsettlingly, all facing toward the screens. Toward us. Staring at our divers.

Reilly stepped up beside us. "Drawn by all the blood," he said in hushed tones.

I frowned. "But what's wrong with them?"

"What d'you mean?" asked Stan.

"They're not moving," I pointed out. "Sharks have to keep moving." I'd read that somewhere. I might have used the fact in an article; background for a piece about another kook with a Triangle story to tell. Sharks—at least some species of shark—have to keep moving, because it's the movement of water across their gills that allows them to breathe. But these sharks...

It looked like they were trying to swim, almost like they thought they *were* swimming. But instead, they were just...well, treading water. I wasn't even sure how that was possible. It was like they were being held back by some... some invisible wall. Good news for Emily and Bruce, though.

I caught a glimpse of Bruce's face on Emily's screen, his eyes visible through his mask, his expression clearly saying "Let's get the hell outta Dodge!"

Emily, though, was fixated on the water-treading sharks—and as we watched, something else seemed to occur to her. She ran her hand through the water in front of her. "What's she doing?" asked Stan.

I had no idea. It was as if she had seen something, or felt something—some property of the water—that we hadn't. She produced a plastic test sample bottle—and at that moment, Lt. J.G. Reilly appeared at my shoulder with a dispatch. "The NTSB teams are inbound," he reported. "Should be here any time."

I nodded firmly. "Good. That's good." But as soon as Reilly had turned away, Stan and I exchanged a look of sheer terror.

On the screen, Emily had filled her bottle with a sample of ocean water, capped it, and begun to swim for the 747. Bruce ran his hand through the water as she had, though I couldn't tell if he had seen whatever it was she'd seen. Then he threw one last uneasy look toward the sharks, and flippered fast to catch up with her.

Inwardly, I was urging them to hurry.

They found the open wing door, the ROV tether still snaking through it. Almost to prove to herself that all this was real, Emily ran a hand over the barnacles and flora that coated the 747's fuselage. Some of it came loose, clouding the water. It was real all right.

Bruce, ever the adventurer, had already pushed past her into the plane.

Stan had been pacing, concentrating again, but now he hurried back over. He was breathing fast, his nose almost touching the screens, a look in his eye that might have been fear. He operated a microphone and spoke to the divers. "I think...toward the rear of the plane..." he mumbled uncertainly. Typical "psychic," I thought—the nearer you get to his so-called predictions, the more vague they become, always shifting, squirming away from the cold light of inspection.

Emily and Bruce were moving up through the empty plane, pulling themselves along by the seatbacks, finding signs that the ROVs had missed—signs that there had indeed been life here once. Plastic trays, laptops, jewelry—nothing biodegradable—littered the seats and the floor, encrusted with decades of flora and rust. There were crabs and other bottom-dwellers crawling over everything. This man-made metal monster may not have belonged to the ocean, but the ocean was claiming it as its own.

And yet, still no sign of passengers, alive or dead.

Bruce reached down, and hooked his finger into a decaying seatbelt. It was locked tight. Same as the one beside it.

Stan was still facing the screens, but his eyes were now closed, lids fluttering. I gave him an appraising look. He was acting just like any number of fake psychics I'd come across in my career but then, these circumstances were very different, and Stan's intensity was certainly arresting.

Emily and Bruce had reached the rear galley. It was filled with water, just like the rest of the plane. Emily looked at Bruce, and we could see him shaking his head. No way was there anyone—a little girl or anyone else—down here.

But Stan wasn't letting up. He was bent almost double,

his breathing so labored that I thought the old guy was about to have a heart attack. "She's there!" he insisted into the microphone.

Emily looked around. She reached for a cupboard door and pulled at it. It stuck from apparent years of disuse. She managed to force it open, but it contained only water and packets of plastic utensils in neat stacks. Bruce, in the meantime, was muscling open another cupboard.

And suddenly, there was an explosion of trapped air, and a ghastly face came flying out at him...

Everybody in the control room leapt back from the screens. I only just managed to stop myself from crying out—some impression that would have made on the uniforms.

It looked at first like some ghoulish creature, its face shrunk over its skull. But whatever it was, it was alive, scratching and kicking, air bubbling out of its mouth.

It was an old woman—and with her air supply now gone, she was drowning.

Bruce was trying to bat her away, almost as panicked as she was, probably soiling his wetsuit from the inside. Emily, who was far enough away to get a proper perspective, acted more calmly and decisively. She took a firm hold of the crone, and pulled her off Bruce, at the same time yanking out her own mouthpiece and forcing it into the old woman's mouth.

She calmed down instantly, and sucked thirstily on the oxygen mix. Now she looked like a ghoul no longer; just a weak, terrified old lady. Bruce let her have several breaths before he wrestled the mouthpiece from her and gave it back to Emily, offering the woman his own mouthpiece in exchange.

And finally, sharing air like this, Emily and Bruce started to pull the old woman back through the plane and toward the open wing door.

In the control room, Reilly was the first to find his voice. "What about the little girl?" he asked.

Stan was standing with his nose to Emily's screen, just staring. And he touched a quaking finger to the glass, to the image of the old woman, and spoke in a tone that suggested even he didn't quite believe what he was saying.

"That's her..."

Most of the activity up on deck had ceased. Navy personnel had forsaken their posts to bear witness to our impossible discovery. Emily and Bruce were still in their wetsuits, toweling their faces and hair—but everyone's attention was focused on the old woman, who was sitting wrapped in a dozen towels, her teeth still chattering.

A seaman handed her a cup, and she sipped at it anxiously. Then her face crumpled, and she spat the drink out. "What is that?"

"Coffee, ma'am."

"Coffee?" she repeated petulantly. "I don't drink coffee!"

Stan knelt in front of her, not saying a word, staring at her intently. He took her hand gently, and she looked at him with tears in her eyes. And in a plaintive voice, like a little girl lost, she asked, "Where are my mommy and daddy?"

It was too much for me. I retreated back to Emily and Bruce, hoping for a voice of sanity, praying that one of them could make the world make sense again. All I got was a challenge. "Okay, Mr. Rational," said Emily, "explain this one."

And I realized that she was looking for the same thing from me.

"There was trapped air," I muttered vaguely. "She survived..."

"Okay," said Bruce, "but meanwhile, where's everybody else?"

I didn't have an answer for that one. Looking back, it was a watershed moment for me, although I wouldn't have admitted it then. I was searching my memory, all the stories I'd been told, and examining them afresh in the light of a new possibility. A tiny possibility, I told myself, one I could hardly believe I was even acknowledging, but what else could I do? And this was why Benirall had hired me, I realized: because I knew those stories, and because—though it ran contrary to everything I had ever believed in—there might, just might, have been a grain of truth in them.

"A few drinks," I said leadenly, "you get pilots, sailors, talking about planes, boats that disappear then show up someplace else, undamaged, passengers missing." I saw how Emily and Bruce were looking at me, and I felt I had to qualify my remarks. "Always second or third hand, though. Nobody I've ever interviewed has actually witnessed it themselves."

"Well, congratulations," said Emily dryly. "Now you have."

Stan was sitting beside the old woman now. He was talking to her as if she were six years old—because, in his mind, there was no doubt that she was. Looking at them together, I found it hard to disbelieve it myself.

"What's your name, sweetheart?" asked Stan.

"Heather," said the old woman.

"Do you know what happened, Heather?"

A tear rolled down Heather's cheek, and she asked tentatively, "A plane crash?"

"How long were you down there? Do you know?"

"H-how long is a...a movie?"

"Around two hours."

The old woman nodded, her eyes haunted. "It was getting really, really hard to breathe."

We were all watching, my team and the seamen alike, absolutely riveted. Then Stan asked the sixty-four-thousand-dollar question.

"How old are you, Heather?"

The old woman smeared the tears from her eyes, and looked at Stan.

Still trembling with the cold, she raised her hands and held up three, four, five...six fingers.

Then, breaking the utter silence with which that revelation was greeted, we all heard the pounding of helicopter blades. I looked up, shielding my eyes against the sun, and saw it: a military chopper, on approach.

With all that had happened, I'd quite forgotten we were on borrowed time.

The rotors of our own jet copter were already winding up. Akerman was in the doorway, flagging us inside. Bruce, Stan, and I scrambled aboard, but something seemed to have distracted Emily. She was just standing, staring out across the ocean, as the shadow of the incoming chopper crept across her, as its downdraft began to ruffle her hair.

Akerman shouted to her, and she met his urgent gaze for a second, her face pale. But only for a second, before she turned back to the water. She looked as if she had seen something, something that had frozen her to the spot—but the water was still calm. There was nothing out there.

It was Bruce who made her decision for her. Emily jumped as he grabbed her from behind and pulled her in after us. She didn't struggle, didn't say anything, but as we took off I saw that she was craning out of the window, staring at that same section of the ocean. And she kept staring at it until the Coast Guard ship had shrunk out of sight.

Akerman, in the meantime, was trying to reach the mainland on his headset radio, trying to get a message to Benirall. He was answered by a distant voice, but it was drowned in static. He was banging the headset, as if that would help.

"If you're reading me at all, inform Mr. Benirall that the team has had their own first real encounter!" I didn't like hearing that. Didn't like it at all.

More static. Akerman turned to face us. "We'll tell him when we touch down. He's gonna flip out!"

The rest of us didn't share his enthusiasm. Even Bruce was unusually subdued, and Emily was still staring out the window, in another place altogether. Bruce was holding the sample bottle she'd filled underwater, turning it thoughtfully in his hand.

It was Stan who brought up the matter of the Navy planes. The Avengers. The last thing I wanted was to get into that right then, before I'd got my thoughts straight. But Bruce remembered seeing something about it on the TV, and suddenly everyone was looking at me to fill in the blanks. My area of expertise, after all.

"Flight 19," breathed Akerman in awe, as I told them the story. "The Holy Grail of Triangle disappearances. You saw them down there?"

"We saw planes," I corrected him sharply.

"What do you think they're going to do with the girl?" asked Stan.

"You mean the old lady?" I said stubbornly.

He rounded on me. "After what we just experienced, you can still sit there and pretend that something extra-normal wasn't just revealed to us?"

"None of us knows what we experienced back there," I said firmly. Perhaps a little too firmly. In denial. The last two hours had seriously undermined a lifetime of blissful cynicism. Looking for support again, I gave Emily a nudge, asked her what she thought. She tore her eyes from the window, but didn't seem to have heard a word any of us had said.

"Yeah," said Bruce, "and what about the sharks?" He was holding up the sample bottle. Emily looked at it, but didn't really focus. "They smelled the blood," Bruce reminded her. "All that blood. It was a real shark's smorgasbord down there. But they wouldn't swim forward. You thought you saw what was stopping them."

He uncapped the bottle, and to the surprise of everyone present, lifted it to his lips. "You're drinking seawater!" exclaimed Stan.

Even Emily was snapped out of her funk. "Wait! We can test it—"

She was too late. Bruce had thrown back his head and tipped the water down his throat. Enjoying our stunned reactions, he made a smacking sound with his tongue as if tasting a fine wine. Then he turned back to Emily.

"You were right," he said. "It's not seawater."

CHAPTER 6

"Aren't you going to hug Dylan?"

"Dylan?"

"Dylan...our youngest..."

Meeno Paloma woke from a nightmare to find the son he didn't know pulling at his pajama sleeve. And he felt his stomach tightening.

He had been avoiding the kid as much as he could, and he knew that wasn't fair. But he'd been praying that, with time and rest, things would start to look different, that somehow everything would click back into place and make sense again.

Nothing was different. And Dylan was tired of waiting.

In a daze, Meeno allowed himself to be led into the next bedroom—the room that he remembered as Helen's office—and took the game controller that was thrust into his hands. The game, said Dylan, was Meeno's favorite, but he didn't recognize it. He sat stiffly on the unmade bed, guiding go-karts around a treacherous track, always aware of the little stranger at his side.

"No, Daddy," complained Dylan with a five-year-old's exasperation. "Like this. Watch...like this!" His fingers were a practiced blur across his controller. "Why aren't you trying?"

"I *am* trying!"

"You used to be really good. What happened?"

Meeno winced. How could he tell the kid that he'd never held a controller like this one? How could he destroy his world?

He became aware of a presence in the doorway, and he looked up to catch his wife's eye. She'd obviously been there some time, and she looked ashen-faced, worried. Meeno took the opportunity to escape to her. He laid the controller down and slid away from Dylan.

"Where're you going, Daddy?"

"I'll be back," he promised half-heartedly.

"Squishy," said Dylan. Meeno had no idea what he meant. "Squishy!" the kid repeated—more a demand this time.

Helen tapped her cheek, and Meeno got the message. He hurried back to Dylan and gave him a quick kiss, doing his duty, feeling empty.

He took refuge in his own bedroom—his and Helen's; an oasis of familiarity. Helen followed him in, closing the door so that Dylan wouldn't hear them. Her words gave Meeno no consolation. He had bought the game himself, apparently, so that he and Dylan could play it together. "I thought I was going to have to use dynamite to blast the two of you away from it. From each other." Meeno could see the pain in her expression, and it only made his own pain worse.

"Dammit, Meeno, why can't you remember him? You were there when he was born. You named him Dylan! He's your flesh and blood!"

Meeno reached for her, held her, clung on to her as if the rest of the world might go away and leave him alone. "The doctors all say there's nothing wrong with me."

"Nothing physically wrong with you." It was hard for Helen to say—harder still for Meeno to hear. "You've got to see somebody else. See another kind of doctor."

He backed away, making a vague excuse about being expected back at work. But Helen caught him with a gaze, looking so fragile that Meeno thought she might shatter, and she pleaded with him, "Do it, Meeno. For me. Us. Your family."

"Well, golly."

Dr. Brennert sat back and looked down at his notes as if hoping some ideas might magically float up from between the lines.

"Golly, golly..."

Meeno had found Brennert in the Yellow Pages. He had chosen him because he could afford his rates, and because Brennert had said he could fit him in right away. Picking up that phone had been the hardest thing he'd ever had to do—but once it was done, he had just wanted to get the rest of it over with. He needed answers.

All he got was an uneasy chuckle. "You're certainly more of a challenge than the angry fifteen-year-olds I'm used to seeing," said Brennert.

"I've never... Seeing a doctor, a doctor like you, I've never even thought about it. Not when my parents died a few months apart. Not when I returned from the Gulf. Navy offered it, but..."

Brennert nodded, finding more familiar ground here. "Well, considering what you've been through—boat sinking, stranded at sea, alone, no idea when you'd be rescued, *if* you'd be rescued..." He shifted uncomfortably. "And of course, this business with your son."

"So... what could it be?"

Brennert stared at his pad again. Tapped his pen.

Meeno prompted, "Some kind of break?"

"You'd think so, wouldn't you. But a break is usually kinda across the board. You seem pretty functional. Loaded with attendant anxiety, of course. But... you're only missing isolated memories. That's what's got me stumped."

Brennert was almost talking to himself now, letting his eyes wander across the faded seventies' décor of his poky office. "I'm thinking a selective amnesia type of deal. Of course, that is incredibly rare. I'd have to do some research to really be conversant on something like that. And even then it's a million to one shot."

Meeno had expected more. He had expected Brennert to ask the right questions, to get to the root of what was causing his problems. Because, by now, Meeno thought *he* knew their cause.

He forced himself to say it. "They all died. All of them."

Brennert just looked at him, waiting for him to continue.

"I was captaining. The boat was my responsibility. They put their lives in my hands. Seven of them died. They went down, and they were gone. I never saw them again. No sign of them." Meeno met the psychiatrist's eyes, and pleaded, "What was I supposed to do?"

Meeno went to work after all, as soon as he had left Brennert's office. It was better than going home and facing what was there.

He felt a certain measure of relief at finding the boatyard just as he had left it. The sound of grinding power sanders drew him to the shop, which was housed in a shed of hangar-like proportions. He stepped through the enormous doors to be greeted by the flashes of welding sparks and all manner of pleasure boats up on supports, each of them somebody's pride and joy.

He didn't know how to announce himself, what to say to his co-workers—his friends—so he just waited for them to notice him. They did, shutting off their tools one by one, dropping what they were doing, hurrying over to him. They surrounded him, hugged him, slapped him on the back, ruffled his hair, treated him like a hero.

Meeno had never liked being the center of attention—and this time, it was even worse than usual. He felt like a fraud.

But things became easier as the day wore on. The boatyard *was* the same as ever, and he could lose himself in his work and in the easy camaraderie of his colleagues. He even phoned Helen and told her he'd be working late, that Mr. Yarrow, his boss, had insisted, something to do with having fallen behind in his absence. She had known he was lying, but she hadn't pushed it.

In fact, Meeno was working on his own special project.

The cigar boat had seen better days—and most of them a long time ago. He had picked it up for a song from a customer who'd decided it wasn't worth the cost of repair. Yarrow had let him take over a small corner of the shop, and the boat had been a labor of love for him since. He had dreamed of being able to take Helen and Ruben out onto the wide blue sea as the captain of his own vessel.

If Dylan had featured in those dreams too, Meeno didn't remember it.

Night closed in, darkening the windows and filling the cavernous space of the hangar with shadows. He was alone now, with his boat and his dream, and that was the way he liked it. At the center of his own little pool of harsh light, he crouched on scaffolding and pressed his sander to wood. He was more comfortable now than he had been in a week... since the sea had betrayed him.

And then, something moved.

Just a shadow, in the corner of his vision. But Meeno could *feel* a presence.

He turned off the sander, flipped up his protective mask, and strained to see into the surrounding darkness.

There was something—some*one*—there. He knew it. Yarrow or one of the others, come back for some reason? His wife, come to find him? But then, why hadn't they said anything, announced their presence?

There it was. No more than a shadow again, sliding across the floor, lost to his sight before he could quite focus on it. Meeno grabbed the nearest heavy object to hand—a big, nasty wrench—and swung himself down off the scaffold. "Who's there? Who's there?!" The words only echoed eerily back at him from the high ceiling. He took a few steps, out of his protective light circle. And suddenly he could feel that presence again, making the hairs on his back stand up. Behind him.

He whirled, and saw them. They were human, but crawling like insects from a sailboat in for repairs. Heads poked through the gaping hole in its side, and Meeno gasped as, impossibly, he recognized them.

He was looking at the crew of the rogue whaling ship, still grungy, oil-slicked, their clothes soaked, their faces dripping with seawater and smeared with whale blood. He stumbled back, terrified, unable to comprehend any of this. Several of the whalers had risen to their full heights now, standing on the pitched deck, their eyes the brightest points of light in the gloom as they stared down at him.

And finally, Meeno found his motor response. He dropped the wrench with a resounding clatter, and he raced from the hangar.

He didn't stop until he had reached his car—his beige car—and put a good ten miles between him and the ghastly apparitions.

Helen found him on the living room sofa the next morning, still dressed in his work clothes, dozing fitfully.

"Oh God, Meeno!" she cried, her voice waking him. Meeno blinked up at her, his fears of the night before flooding back into him. And she rushed over to him, relieved and angry at the same time as only a wife can be. "Why didn't you tell me you were home? What happened?"

She hadn't wanted to ask the question; Meeno could read that in her face. And he didn't want to answer, didn't want to hurt her again. But she could read his face, too, and she knew it was bad. Once, she would have held him. Now, she just held back.

And Meeno kept his silence as a gulf opened between them, because he knew that Helen wasn't strong enough to cope with his latest delusion. He feared that none of them were.

CHAPTER 7

While Meeno was encountering ghosts in his boatyard, I was sitting on the edge of the biggest bed I'd ever seen, in a bedroom bigger than my entire apartment.

Akerman had brought us to a luxurious Miami townhouse, owned of course by his boss. It wasn't even Benirall's main residence, just a getaway home. It was a timely—and perhaps a deliberate—reminder of why we were doing this.

I was holding a wine glass in one hand, my cell phone in the other, and I was talking to Marty Balsam, my editor. He didn't like what he was hearing.

"Marty, calm down, will you? Marty... Shut up!" I poured myself another drink, while Marty exploded in indignation on the other end of the line. "You're the editor of a cheesy tabloid," I said when he'd quite finished, "of course I can tell you to shut up. Listen! Yes, the bad news is I won't be filing a story this week. But—"

Marty interrupted to ask why, though his language was a lot more colorful than that. "Because I'm out in the field," I told him, when I could next get a word in edgeways. "Seriously," I said in answer to his first question. "No, nothing you're paying for," was the answer to the second.

"I've just witnessed... been part of..." It was no use. I couldn't say it, couldn't get the words out. "Just trust me," I concluded lamely, "you're going to go bananas over what I—No, I'm not at the damned dog track!"

Downstairs, in the cavernous but warm space of the living room, Akerman had set up a shiny new G-4 Powerbook and was typing furiously, trying to get logged on to a Net server. Bruce was breathing down his neck, impatient to get to work. He had some research to do.

In the elaborate kitchen, Emily and Stan had a countertop TV set tuned in to MSNBC. They were covering the 747 crash, and Lt. J.G. Reilly had been collared for a statement. It was a statement that would be repeated on many news broadcasts over the next few days, delivered with conviction, authority, and faux compassion in all the right places—but not a word of truth. "We have located the downed aircraft, by sidescan sonar only. I'm afraid it's at a depth which prevents any serious attempt at recovery. The wreckage is scattered over an area estimated at nearly a mile long. And there were no survivors. Considering the physical location of the crash, recovery of victims' bodies should be considered very unlikely."

Another one in the eye for my worldview. I mean, it wasn't as if official cover-ups are exactly proof of the "extra-normal," as Stan had put it—but I'd always preferred to believe in cock-up over conspiracy.

The newscasters were saying that Flight 28 had been the victim of a pocket of extreme turbulence. Even from my room, I could hear Emily, slightly drunk by now on Benirall's hospitality, yelling at the TV. "Turbulence? No survivors? Try no bodies! Try everybody disappeared!"

Stan, of course, wanted to know what they'd done with Heather. Perhaps it was his visions that made him care so much.

I think Emily needed to talk with Stan, at that moment. There was stuff going on in her head that she didn't feel she could talk to any of us about. Stuff that the booze wasn't blocking out. Stan suspected something amiss when she asked him about his visions. When he saw them, did he know what they were? He told her that they seemed absolutely real, as real as she seemed to him at that moment. The answer didn't seem to make her any happier.

Bruce had introduced a new word into my vocabulary: halocline.

A halocline is a gradient, usually vertical, in the ocean, where layers of water with different levels of salinity meet. The more saline the water, the denser it is—and as I understand it, this prevents the different layers from mixing.

In this case, what Emily had discovered was that the 747 crash site was in an area of fresh water. Bruce assured us that such a phenomenon was extremely rare, especially in that part of the Atlantic at that time of the year. However, there was still a possibility, small as it was—and this was what I so desperately needed to hear—that it could have occurred quite naturally.

Bruce spent most of the evening on the website of N.O.A.A.—the National Oceanic and Atmospheric Administration—researching his theory. Across the room, Emily had dozed off half-cut on a sofa and was snoring a little. I sat listlessly on another sofa beside Stan, flipping channels on the TV, trying not to think too hard about what Bruce had told us.

The problem was that, okay, so haloclines might have explained the sharks, but they didn't explain the lack of passengers on the crashed plane. And they didn't explain Heather. It was the start of an explanation, though—and the kind I liked. The kind that involved long words and numbers. The kind that, if I was honest, I didn't really understand any more than I did the other kind, but it was enough for me to know that somebody, somewhere, did.

Every so often, there would be an explosion of enthusiasm from Bruce as he discovered something—and sometimes, Akerman got caught in the blast. Bruce had leapt up from the Powerbook now and was pacing excitedly, pausing only to gulp down Coke from the latest of many cans. Akerman was bent over the phone, one finger in his ear, trying to talk over the distraction. He gave Bruce a "back off" sign, but Bruce was too wired to care. "Not a simple request," he was gabbling at top speed. "I understand that, but I mean, look at this..."

"Yes," said Akerman into the phone, "I know. No, I'm not in a position to be choosy. My main criterion is, it's available."

Bruce had grabbed a sheath of printed pages, and he waved them under Akerman's nose. "Satellite thermals; we got haloclines posting through most of the Southern Atlantic! And look at this spot right here—it's halocline crazy!"

"Well, tomorrow. Actually, today—it's after midnight. I'm going to need it later today."

"You'd never see it unless you were looking. And satellite's good, I mean, wow, very valuable technology, but this phenomenon can't be examined from two hundred miles up. Not properly. No, sir. This calls for—"

Still hanging on the phone, Akerman reached up and snatched the Coke from Bruce's hand. No more sugar for him.

Meanwhile, for something to do, I was taunting Stan with another game of "Triangle Trivia." "Who was Donald Crowhurst?"

"Round-the-world yachtsman," said Stan in a tired voice, "presumed lost in the Triangle."

"Who was Mary Celeste?"

"Not a who. A what. A ship. Late 1800s. Discovered sailing very erratically in the Triangle. When she was boarded, they found the entire crew had disappeared." Stan paused for a long moment. Then, slowly, knowing exactly what he was doing, he asked me, "Who was Charles Taylor?"

I had chosen my questions carefully, anticipating an argument that Stan had forestalled. An argument I had badly needed to win.

The fate of the *Mary Celeste* was one of the most famous tales of the sea ever told. Largely, this was because it was used as the basis of an 1884 short story by Arthur Conan Doyle. His fictional *Marie Celeste* soon became hopelessly intertwined with the real thing in the public consciousness.

THE TRIANGLE

The "real thing" was found drifting off the east coast of the Azores on December 5, 1872—the same date, as I'm sure the conspiracy theorists would tell you, as that on which Flight 19 would vanish some seventy-three years later. It had evidently been abandoned in a hurry, its passengers leaving their belongings behind. But what many accounts of this "mystery"—the type that tended to speculate about time travel and dimensional vortices—neglected to mention was that the ship had taken on water and that its lifeboat had been launched. The *Mary Celeste*'s crew wouldn't have been the first to panic and abandon a ship at the first sign of danger, only for it to survive. And any number of natural causes could have led to the sinking of a lifeboat.

Another snag for those determined to link this story to the Triangle was that, assuming it had followed its planned course, the ship wouldn't even have passed through the area. But then, as I've already explained, the boundaries of the Triangle were always flexible, and some people can't let go of a good story.

Donald Crowhurst's was an even more clear-cut case. He had been engaged in a round-the-world race in his trimaran yacht but, like the *Mary Celeste*, the *Tiegnmouth Electron* was found drifting empty in the Triangle, on July 10, 1969—in a position that, given Crowhurst's last reported location eleven days earlier, it couldn't possibly have reached.

Crowhurst was a celebrity, and so his disappearance was accompanied by much fanfare and speculation in the media. Far less publicity was given to the rather mundane explanation ultimately revealed to the authorities by his own log.

Crowhurst had lied. Throughout the race, he had transmitted false coordinates, intending to claim the substantial cash prize on offer by deception. His log entries revealed an increasingly unstable mental state, particularly as his victory came within reach and guilt began to weigh heavily upon him. It's likely that he committed suicide, although his death could have been a tragic accident—and this was finally accepted by all but the most hardened conspiracy nuts. People like Stan.

Imagine, though, how different things could have been had Crowhurst taken his log into the water with him. Which theory do you think would have held sway then? Perhaps the *Tiegnmouth Electron* would have become as infamous as the *Mary Celeste.*

It was stories like this that comforted me, gave me faith that even the most baffling Triangle event was only lacking a log book or a witness statement, just that single shred of proof, to shed light upon it. I knew what Stan would have said, though. Just because something *can* be explained doesn't mean the rational explanation must be the right one. And what, I began to think with a cold chill as Lt. J.G. Reilly appeared on the TV screen again, if the "proof" we did have wasn't all it was claimed to be?

That was why Stan had mentioned Charles Taylor. Flight 19's commander. Another Triangle disappearance for which I'd thought I had an explanation. Until today. He was forcing me to think about what we'd seen on that Coast Guard ship, and below it. Because he knew that was the last thing I *wanted* to think about.

"We got it!" yelled Bruce. "We got it!"

Emily rocketed straight up, bleary but instantly awake. "Got what?"

Bruce hurried over to us, beaming all over his face. Akerman followed him at a more sedate pace. "Our sub!" cried Bruce.

I gaped. "Did he say... sub?"

Akerman nodded, proud of his latest hard-won acquisition. "Only private sub on the Florida coast rated for three hundred fathoms. It's in Fort Pierce, so we'll have to book right now to be there by sunup."

Emily was still blinking sleep out of her eyes. "A sub—as in submarine?"

"We're following up on your haloclines," said Akerman. Emily gave him a look as if to say "*My* haloclines?"

"We'll have to drive through the night," said Akerman, "to be there by morning. Anybody have trouble sleeping in a car?" He didn't wait for an answer. He was already moving toward the door.

I called after him, "Whoa. Wait one... What happened to the nice offices in Canaveral City?"

Akerman called back over his shoulder, "As field opportunities come up, Mr. B. expects you to take 'em."

And then he was gone.

"We just got back from the damn 747!" protested Emily, though the only people still there to listen were Bruce, Stan, and me. "We've got observed data we need to assimilate, research. Week's worth."

"They're *your* haloclines," Bruce teased her with a grin.

She glared back at him. "Yeah," she said, "but you're the one who ordered a submarine!"

I was back in the huge bedroom, a part of me lamenting the fact that I wouldn't get to sleep in it now. I was stuffing my neat new clothes haphazardly into my neat new bag, zipping it up, turning to leave, when...

A sound. Water. From the ensuite bathroom. I looked, and frowned.

The door was ajar. A light flickered behind it. I could hear the sloshing of water again. But I'd just left the others at the top of the stairs, and there was only one door into that room— wasn't there?

I let the bag fall out of my hand and crept tentatively up to the door. I looked through the gap, into the bathroom, and I saw:

The lights were off. The flickering I'd seen was of candlelight. I could see the flames now, reflected in the mirror. What the hell was going on here?

I called out, "Hello? Is there somebody—?"

And the answer came in a breathy female voice. A *familiar* voice.

"Howard? Finally, you're back!"

Sally's voice. My ex-wife's voice.

Startled, I pushed open the door, and saw her there. In the tub. Her hair pinned up sexily, her shoulders glistening. Candles casting a warm glow. A glass of wine in her hand, raised toward me. And she smiled.

On my Top Ten List of Things I Never Expected to See, this was definitely in the Top Three. Okay, Top Two. I was pole-axed, my mouth hanging open, my brain trying to decide which question to ask first but the words dying on my tongue.

"I thought I was going to have to send a search party for you," said Sally.

I regained control of my speech at last. "What are you doing here? How'd you know where I was? What are you doing in my tub?"

"*Our* tub," said Sally. "C'mon in." And she laid her glass down on the side of the tub and slipped playfully under the water.

I didn't know what game she was playing, but I wasn't in the mood for it. I mean, on the one hand this was something I'd dreamed of; on the other... No, it wasn't possible. I called out to Sally, but she didn't answer, wasn't moving at all. The water had settled over her, a fine layer of soap bubbles rendering it opaque.

And, reluctantly, a little alarm bell began to chime in my head.

I didn't want to, but I thought I'd best be sure. I reached in to the tub, to where I guessed Sally's shoulder would be, just to give her a nudge.

I couldn't find her.

Suddenly, my confusion gave way to concern, verging on panic. I thrust my arm all the way into the water, sloshing around. Nothing. I grabbed at the plug and pulled, watching the water drain from the tub. There was no one there. I jerked upright, upsetting Sally's wine glass. It fell, end over end, and hit the tiles at an angle. But the delicate crystal didn't shatter, at least not at first.

I was still staring at it, still wondering why, when the glass finally exploded. A full two seconds after the impact. As if, somehow, time itself had skipped a couple of beats. Instinctively, I threw my hands up to protect my face. I closed my eyes. And when I opened them again...

I had a fleeting impression of shards of glass, scattered across the floor, dissolving... The candles, too, as if I were watching some time-lapse film. I thought I saw their flames flickering unsupported in midair for a moment, but then they, too, shrank to nothing and were gone, and I was left alone in what was suddenly a very dark bathroom.

With no sign that there had ever been anyone else in there with me.

CHAPTER 8

"She's a beauty!" enthused Bruce. "I didn't know she was Russian."

"Foxtrot class," filled in Emily, wincing in the too-bright morning sun. "Probably built in the early seventies. 1870s." She was hung over, and stiff from spending most of the night in the back of a van. Bruce, in contrast, was his usual bouncy self. None of us knew how he did it.

"We're expected to go out to sea in this?" Stan was running a nervous eye over the rusting wreck of a submarine that hung suspended above us, creaking a little.

Emily rounded on him, instantly concerned. "Why? Are you seeing us at risk if we take this out?"

"Don't you?" he said dryly.

Emily took his point. "The thing's in dry dock," she pointed out. "We really think she's ready to sail?"

"We gotta find the Captain!" said Bruce excitedly.

I was only half-listening to them. I was pacing the dock with my cell phone to my ear. I'd been waiting all night to make this call. I hadn't slept at all.

Sally sounded groggy, still coming awake. "Why are you calling so early? Is it Traci? Did something happen?"

"It's not Traci," I reassured her. Then: "Isn't Traci there?"

"She stayed at Mindy Granger's house last night." A groan. "For God's sake, it's six-fifteen!"

I was about to lose her. I had to stop beating about the bush. "Something happened last night," I blurted. "I... I just wanted to make sure..." What? "To see if you were all right."

Sally treated that remark with the contempt it deserved. "You want to know if I'm all right?" She was started to get pissed.

"Where were you... Did anything... Where were you last night, well, actually this morning—around two-thirty?"

She was fully awake now, and fully indignant. "Is that what this is about? I was with Adam, is that what you want to hear? How did you—?"

I couldn't have been more surprised if she'd admitted she *had* been in my bathroom last night, and slipped away down the drain. In fact, at that moment, all thoughts of my weird experience were pushed well and truly to the back of my mind.

"Adam? Adam Leiffer? C'mon, you're kidding, right?"

"No," said Sally, "I'm not."

I took a second to absorb that. "So... it's serious?"

And Sally came down a notch, evidently realizing that she could have broken the news more gently. "It might be. Howard, why are you calling me?"

Staring out across the water, in the cold light of morning, I realized I had no idea myself. I didn't know what I had expected to hear. The memory of last night was beginning to fade like a dream, and I could almost convince myself that that was all it had been—because what other explanation was there? I was tired and stressed, and I'd been piling so much crap about psychic powers and disappearing passengers into my brain that it had rebelled for a few seconds.

I could *almost* convince myself.

"Nothing," I said gruffly. "Never mind. I'm sorry I disturbed you. Give Traci hugs." And I hung up.

Bruce, in the meantime, had found the sub's owner. Captain Jay, as he liked to be called, was a heavy, baby-faced man, maybe thirty, who looked like he'd been partying hard last night. He looked like he partied hard every night. He came stumbling out of his dockside office, popping aspirin like they were Pez, and assembled his young crew, who looked like runaways too dumb to make it to Hollywood Boulevard. Neither they nor their captain inspired much confidence in me. Nevertheless, within twenty minutes, the submarine had been refloated and Jay was striding up the gangplank, casting a critical eye over the activity on deck.

"We locked and loaded, gentlemen? We have any problems like last time, Dog, and you'll be havin' an Attica shower room flashback! Both bowlines, Weasel! We lose another cleat, you're swabbing my friggin' quarters with your friggin' tongue!"

Bruce was right at Captain Jay's heels, and Stan trailed apprehensively after them. I took a deep breath, girded myself, and made to follow—but I stopped when I realized that Emily was frozen at the foot of the gangplank. "We're actually going to let these eleventh graders take us down in this thing?"

"Can't call 'em eleventh graders," I said. "I don't think they made it that far." Emily's expression didn't lighten, and I realized this was no time for humor. She was genuinely worried. That surprised me. She was the last person I'd have expected to succumb to a panic attack. Looking back, though, maybe it was just that she knew the sea better than any of us. She knew what risks we were taking. "We're hunting those things, remember?" I said cajolingly. "What'd'ya call 'em..."

"Haloclines," said Emily. "But do we have to go? Can't somebody else take pictures, readings..."

"Can they?" I asked. It was a serious question. Emily's expression shifted, telling me that no, dammit, they couldn't. "Anyway," I sighed, "that Bruce guy is definitely going. And if it leads to something and we're not there with him, Benirall might decide we didn't do our part." I wasn't happy about this, but I had to accept it. "Either I'm doing this thing all the way or I'm going home."

I offered my hand—and, after a long, reluctant moment, Emily let out a deep breath and took it. "The three esses," she muttered as we walked slowly up the gangplank, like condemned prisoners mounting the scaffold.

"What's that?" I asked.

"There are three things in life where you don't go cheap. Sushi, surgery... submarines."

And then we were aboard, and the submarine was motoring away from the dock, toward the breakwater and the mighty Atlantic beyond.

"We ready, Ivan?"

The helmsman—at forty, probably the oldest guy on the boat bar—wiped some sweat from his upper lip, and replied to the captain in Russian.

"I wouldn't let it worry ya," said Captain Jay dismissively. "Let's dive!" But as he gave the order, he mumbled something under his breath in a language I didn't recognize. He kissed his thumb and touched it to his forehead.

The interior of the sub was as cramped and rusty and, well, just plan crappy as the outside suggested. The four of us were huddled together, and even Bruce seemed more than a little apprehensive. I was looking at a row of antiquated gauges, on which all the needles were flatlined— clearly not working. All the labeling was in Russian, so I had no idea what any of the gauges were or if they were important. I gave Stan a nudge and pointed them out to him, not making him feel any better. In return, he directed my attention to a bank of state-of-the-art plasma monitors, incongruous with the old workings of the sub, jerry-rigged over the Russian tech, loose cables still hanging. Nestled in their midst was a Bose sound system.

"What was that you just—?" Emily began to ask.

"My granddad taught it to me," said Captain Jay. "It's Lithuanian. An old Navy oath."

"I thought Lithuania was landlocked," Emily muttered.

"What's it mean?" asked Stan.

"Into the Belly of the Beast!" proclaimed the captain proudly.

"Super," Emily grumbled.

And Captain Jay hit the Bose CD player, blasting heavy metal through the confined space even as the sub angled downward and we all grabbed hold of something. Perhaps the music was meant to drown out the protesting groans from the vessel's hull. If so, it wasn't near loud enough. I could see my fear reflected in the faces of the others. But there was no turning back now.

We were knifing downward, schools of exotic fish parting before us, flitting across the monitors. Deeper and darker, leaving the last reassuring shafts of sunlight behind us. Into the abyss.

Mercifully, Jay turned off the music once we had reached cruising depth. And, from that point on, our journey became surprisingly mundane. It was easier than I'd expected to forget where we were, to forget the tons of water pressure that were bearing down upon us. The longer the hull stood up to that pressure, the more reassured I was that it wasn't about to give way.

Still, it helped to have something to take my mind off it—and off the increasing discomfort in my cramped legs. So, while Bruce was standing over the helmsman's shoulder, fascinated by the boat's workings, the rest of us decided to take a look at some of the DVD-ROMs Akerman had given us at the airport.

Emily had powered up her laptop and was scrolling through reams of information. She was impressed. "Benirall's really done one hell of an exhaustive study. Had some good people on this. Look, Paxton from MIT, Wu from Beijing, Westerfield and his crazies at Rand..."

"Notice none of them is riding a war surplus Russian sub to eighteen hundred feet," I said archly.

"He's even had some poor goofs doing serious research into UFOs," said Emily, shaking her head in derision, "and Atlantis."

"And we take up the baton," I said with a sidelong glance at Stan.

Stan sighed. "Why can't you even consider the answer lies in non-traditional science—especially after what we all witnessed yesterday?" I opened my mouth to make another snide remark, but Stan cut me off with, "We *all* witnessed yesterday."

Meaning me too. And he didn't even know the half of it.

"Look," said Emily in a conciliatory tone, "I'm willing to think outside the box here. Not all the way to Atlantis, but," she hesitated for a long moment. "I'm going to say a word. I don't want you to laugh at me. I..."

She really didn't want to say it. She couldn't look us in the eye.

"Wormholes."

Now that she had opened the floodgates, she was trying to mitigate her embarrassment by talking fast, blinding us with scientific jargon. "A non-recurring, randomly generated pathway between two distinct time/space dimensions."

I didn't know what to say. "I thought your expertise was in ocean stuff, ocean studies."

Almost defensively, she said, "I like to read. I don't know much about wormholes... well, much at all really..."

"Yeah, well," I said, "I've written about wormholes. Interviewed people who've traveled through them. One guy, named Crichton—smart, personable, wonderful interview—if you could just get past the extra-long sleeves that buckle in the back."

"I know they're only theoretical," said Emily. "I hear myself and I hate that I'm saying it, but considering what we just witnessed—the 747 that aged, plus those Navy bombers from the 1940s—"

"We don't know those were the same planes!" I stressed again.

"Oh, please," groaned Stan.

"—and the passengers. They all had to go somewhere."

"And what about that crewman from Benirall's cargo ship?" said Stan. "The one from the fifteenth century? Could the same thing have happened to the passengers on the 747? Could they all have been... liquefied...?"

"Different locations, different circumstances," said Emily. "The effects of the phenomenon may vary. Some people may just disappear, some may—"

I said it for her. "Liquefy. Terrific. So under your theory, all we have to do is prove that wormholes truly exist. Excellent. Gee, what d'we do with all the time we got left over?"

"All I'm saying is, this region is famous for its electromagnetic anomalies. For example, it's one of only two places on Earth where compasses point to true north and—"

"—and magnetic north at the same time. Yawn. Old news. That's the problem with trying to explain the Bermuda Triangle—all the theories have been studied and discussed and dismissed years ago."

Emily glared knives at me. "What the hell's your problem?" she stormed. "Ever since we left you've been..."

I broke eye contact, looked down. I didn't want to discuss it. But now Stan was staring at me, too, intently, making me feel uncomfortable.

"Something's troubling you."

Emily rolled her eyes. "Look where we are!"

But Stan wouldn't let go. "Something... at Benirall's house... last night... something..." His voice trailed off, his brow furrowing in frustration. Still, he was reaching a little too close for comfort.

I tried to cover with a caustic remark. "You really are a wonder, aren't you!"

Stan was used to such brickbats—but in his eyes at that moment, I saw for the first time how much they hurt him; just a hint of his deeply felt anguish at what he saw as a lifetime of failure. I didn't have time to regret my outburst, though.

"Hey!" Bruce called. "You're all gonna want to see this!"

We moved to join him at the plasma monitors—and I'd be lying if I said I wasn't just a bit grateful for the distraction.

Sprawled before us in the dim light from the sub was a vast undersea plain, evidently miles across. Nothing unexpected there. But cutting vertically through the water were dozens upon dozens of shafts of differing diameters—some only a few feet wide, others thirty yards or more. I wasn't sure what they were at first. They seemed to catch the light, making them stand out against the murky background. And the water within them was clear—it took me a moment to realize that that there was no sea life, no plankton, to cloud it. I could see now that schools of fish were darting away from the shafts, slaloming between them but refusing to enter them.

Bruce supplied the information I was missing. "Haloclines," he announced, "dozens of them."

"Hundreds," breathed Emily in awe.

Captain Jay's jaw was hanging open. "I was just though

this area a couple of weeks ago with some Colombians." He realized what he had said, and quickly corrected himself: "Colombian tourists."

"I've never seen anything like this," said Emily. "Never heard of this many..."

"What causes them?" asked Stan.

"Usually freshwater run-off from land sources," said Bruce. "But never at this distance from shore... this depth..."

"Something's removed the salinity from this water," concluded Emily. "Some naturally occurring process."

Stan couldn't resist saying it. "Or not naturally occurring." He looked at Emily. "Your electromagnetic anomalies?"

She pondered on that, and conjectured, "Desalinization can be accomplished by means of electrical processing."

"Somebody's zapping the ocean with electricity?" I said wryly. "Wouldn't this have perhaps a few other noticeable ramifications?"

"Not electricity like out of the wall," said Bruce, "but some electric-based power source could be causing this."

Then, suddenly, Ivan the helmsman let out an urgent cry, and jabbed at the sonar with his finger. "Whoa!" said Captain Jay. "Can't be... Absolutely not... Cannot be..."

I frowned at the display. "What are those? Ships?"

Jay didn't answer. He yelled some orders in Russian and the sub began to dive again. "What are you doing?" cried Bruce. "Where the hell are you taking us?" Then, a little worried: "What depth is this sub rated for?"

The hull was creaking.

"Listen, uh, Captain..." ventured Stan.

But Captain Jay wasn't listening. He only had eyes for the monitors—on which, now, shapes were beginning to appear as we cut down through the halocline field. Shapes that confirmed the sonar readings.

Captain Jay looked like he couldn't believe his great fortune.The rest of us were just staring at the monitors in the proverbial shock and awe.

And the creaks and groans from the beleaguered hull were growing louder, until it sounded like it was about to split...

CHAPTER 9

We were looking at the most amazing sight I had ever seen. The five Avenger bombers had been enough, but this— this was a virtual graveyard of ships and planes, sprawled across the floor of an undersea valley. All different models and sizes—commercial and private, new technology and old, in varying states of decay. From this distance, and mediated by the monitors, the scene acquired an air of unreality. It looked like a kid's toy box had been emptied out. It was eerie as hell.

"Must be two hundred, three hundred of 'em out there," breathed Jay. "I swear, none of these were out here a couple of weeks ago..." Then, abruptly, he recovered his senses and gave the nearest crewman a shove. "Get down this long and lat! Note the time! Maritime Law. Open sea salvage. As captain and owner of this vessel, anything recoverable we lay eyes on is mine." He was practically drooling. He wiped his mouth excitedly and looked at the rest of us. "I got witnesses! You're all my witnesses!"

And then, something very large began to usurp our view as we swept over the top of it. Like there was some enormous leviathan suddenly below us.

One by one, our gazes were riveted to it. It was an old ship, lying on its side, partially buried in the sand. If I'd had to make an estimate, I'd have said it had been down here for just less than a year. The processes of overgrowth and decay had begun, but they weren't too far advanced.

All the more reason, then, for my stomach to perform a somersault as we passed over the bow of the ship and we saw its name, faded but still legible.

U.S.S. Cyclops.

I stiffened. I refused to believe this. "No way," I muttered under my breath. We weren't even in the right part of the Triangle. It had been miles from here...

"Come back around!" I barked at Jay.

"What...?" Bruce asked.

I swallowed. I didn't speak. I wanted to see it again, wanted to confirm that I'd been mistaken. I told myself that, even if I hadn't, there had been more than one ship of that name. A British *Cyclops* was recorded as having been sunk by a German U-Boat during the First World War, just before... before...

"*What?*" cried Emily, Bruce, and Stan in unison.

More than one ship. But, I realized with a lump in my throat as the monstrous wreck hove slowly back into view, only one ship like this...

"I've written half a dozen articles about the *Cyclops*... the legend of the *Cyclops*." I was only telling them what I had heard. Why did I feel so awkward, like they were judging me, mocking me behind their stoic expressions? Was this how Stan felt all the time? "A nineteen-thousand-ton US Navy collier... From World War I... Went down with all hands in 1918."

There was silence as everybody absorbed this. Silence but for an ominous groan from the submarine itself.

Emily was the first to speak. "We're deep here," she said, "but not that deep. Why hasn't anyone discovered any of this before?"

"Hey, matters not, Sweetcakes," put in Captain Jay. "Bottom line: They didn't, I did!"

And at that moment, all the long-dead gauges came to life. Not only that, but they were dancing crazily. The helmsman recoiled from the yoke and jabbered in Russian, blowing on his hands as if they had just been burned. And the pressure in the sub suddenly increased.

I was clutching at my head in pain, feeling as if it were about to shatter like an eggshell. I was only distantly aware of Emily's intake of breath—until I saw what she had seen. A ragged circle of intense white light, rocketing toward us from I knew not where. Ball lightning!

And then, impossibly, it was inside the sub, in our midst, where it burst, driving us backwards against bulkheads and panels.

The power to the monitors and the other instruments was flickering and faltering. My nerves were tingling, my eyes dazzled, but I was numbed by horror as I heard everything winding down—even the engines, whining to a stop outside. And the hull was groaning like it had never groaned before, and the distant fear that it might not be able to take the strain now felt like a chilling certainty. Even the crew was frozen with fear, deaf to Captain Jay's yelled orders.

Then, as if things weren't already bad enough, the lights went out.

The darkness was complete and total, the silence almost as deep. Not a sound of anything mechanical working. Just the uneasy breaths of the people around me. I was gingerly testing my legs, seeing if I could still stand, checking that my fillings were all in place, none of them melted. Ball lightning! I'd heard of it, knew it was real, while dismissing the more outlandish theories that clung to the phenomenon: Theories that it was extra-dimensional in origin, even somehow intelligent. I never expected to encounter it myself, and certainly wouldn't have expected to come through the experience unharmed. If that was indeed what had happened.

It was only just beginning to sink in. We were dead in the water. Almost a half-mile down.

I heard Bruce's hushed voice from beside me. "Boy, I hate it when I'm this right!"

I'd read many theories about the loss of the *USS. Cyclops* and its complement of three hundred and nine men in March 1918. Mostly, it was accepted that the ship had gone down, although no one could be sure of the reason—and, in common with many other Triangle disappearances, no wreck was ever found.

The ship's captain, George W. Worley, was a reputed tyrant who made his crew's lives a misery—and some members of that crew had been heard to discuss mutiny in the waterfront bars of Bahia, Brazil, just hours before they sailed off into the history books. There were rumors that Worley had carried out an unsanctioned execution of a crewman, and that this had been the final straw.

Worley was a famously poor navigator, with a reputation for entering ports from the wrong direction, having overshot. He had recently confined his executive officer to quarters for daring to question a course change that had almost grounded them on rocks. He had also begun to drink heavily on duty—and when last seen on its way out of port, the *Cyclops* was headed south instead of north to the United States.

The *Cyclops* was carrying eleven thousand tons of manganese ore: A notoriously difficult cargo due to its tremendous mass and abrasive properties. The only person on board who had experience with the material—who knew how to secure it so that it wouldn't shift and flip the ship over—was the imprisoned executive officer. So Worley had had a young ensign supervise the loading in his stead.

The *Cyclops* had taken on too much ore. It was seen to be weighted down past the Plimsoll line.

To add to all that, the ship was transporting three men to a naval prison, after they'd been implicated in a murder on another ship. And, in its wisdom, the US Navy had transferred several crew members from that ship—old friends of the prisoners—to serve on the *Cyclops*.

Although America was at war in 1918, there was no record of enemy submarines in the *Cyclops*'s vicinity at the crucial time. However, it has been suggested that the ship itself played host to at least one spy, and that it may have been commandeered and delivered into enemy hands. A number of the crew were certainly of German descent—and a Navy investigation revealed that Lieutenant Commander Worley had falsified his records to hide the fact that he was German-born. His real name was Johann Friedrich Georg Wichman.

Similar suspicions clung to a distinguished passenger of the *Cyclops*: a Consul General Alfred Louis Moreaux Gottschalk, who had been fiercely pro-German before the outbreak of war and who, according to those who had spoken to him, had not changed his views since.

The *U.S.S. Cyclops* was headed into stormy waters, metaphorically if not literally. It would have been a miracle if it *had* arrived at its destination with all hands intact. But of all the fates that could have befallen it—from capsize to mutiny to breakout to espionage—what do you suppose became the favorite theory of the media, based on no evidence at all?

They said the *Cyclops* must have been swallowed by a giant octopus.

Go figure.

I suppose I should have been relieved to prove the octopus theory wrong. That was hardly the foremost thought in my mind, though, as I stood in the pitch-black dark, almost deafened by the multiple voices all talking and yelling over each other around me, in different languages.

Despite the situation, a part of my mind was still with that technological graveyard below us. I wondered how many other names I might recognize were we to take a closer look at its hulls and fuselages. Over a hundred planes—and the number of boats lost in the Triangle dwarfed even that. Not all of them were as "lucky" as the *Mary Celeste* or the *Tiegnmouth Electric*, to be found still floating.

A narrow beam cut the darkness. Captain Jay was wearing—wait for this—a miner's helmet, circa 1950. It was beat to hell, but it did have a light on the front. I was grateful for that, for about a second—before the light allowed me to see the very spooked look on Jay's face. "No worries," he said, unconvincingly. "Happens all the time, all the time. Have everything up and running again in no time. No time at all."

"Well, as long as the Captain's not worried!" I said dryly as Jay hurried forward to where his crew was already frantically yanking open circuit panels.

"He's wearing a miner's helmet!" commented Stan, as if the rest of us might not have noticed.

"No power means we can't surface," said Emily pragmatically, "can't maneuver, can't regulate temperature. We're just drifting."

"And there's the little matter of air," I added.

And yet, despite all this, Bruce was still stoked. "People," he crowed, "we are living our very own Triangle event here! This is what it's like! Exactly what it's like!"

Emily put him down with a withering look. "Bet the people on the 747 said the exact same thing."

"We don't know this is being caused by anything other than this sub is a joke," I reminded them.

"That was ball lightning we just experienced," said Stan, predictably. "Ball lightning is often associated with Triangle events."

A set of low amber auxiliary lights flickered on around us. They were about a third the strength of the regular lights, but still there was a collective sigh. Our relief was short-lived, however.

Suddenly, there was an awful scraping sound against the hull, and the sub was jostled wickedly. Then: a huge collision, throwing us off our feet, pinballing us around and into each other.

Captain Jay and the crew were all yelling at once. I could just make out Stan's voice, raised in panic. "Something hit us!"

"No," said Emily. "We hit something else." And there was no doubt from the tone of her voice that she considered that worse. Much worse.

Captain Jay knocked a fear-frozen crewman aside, reached deep into a circuit panel, felt around—and suddenly received one hell of an electric shock, yanking his hand out with a cry amid a shower of sparks. Whatever he'd done had worked, though. The external searchlights flickered back on, lighting up the monitors again. Jay rubbed his numb hand, and said with a certain measure of satisfaction, "Nimrod... that's how you do it."

Unfortunately, all we could see now was a wall of solid rock.

We were wedged, good and proper, beneath an outcrop.

THE TRIANGLE

Captain Jay yelled at the helmsman in Russian. Ivan yelled back. Jay gave him a shove for emphasis—and in the heat of the moment, Ivan dared to shove him back. Jay was momentarily startled by this. Then he recovered, and cold-cocked the smaller guy, dropping him like a stone. After that, he started bellowing at the other crewmen, and they scurried to obey him. Satisfied, he came up to our group and reported with a chagrined expression, "Well, looks like we're maybe a tad... stuck."

"Exactly how much is a 'tad'?" Bruce asked.

"Don't know," Jay confessed.

"When will we able to surface?" asked Emily.

"Soon as we get the engines running."

"When's that?" I asked.

"Don't know," said Jay.

"What about the radio?" asked Stan. "Can't we call for help?"

"We're a submarine at fifteen hundred feet," said Emily.

"More like eighteen," put in Captain Jay.

Emily's look at that moment said "Thanks for the encouraging update!" Unabashed, she went on, "Radio's useless. Unless..." A hopeful thought occurred to her, and she turned to Captain Jay. "You've got a comms buoy?"

"You have any idea how much those things cost?" Jay protested. He considered for a moment, then ventured that he did have a Distress Jimmy. "Don't know if it's still operational..."

"Well, why'n you at least launch it," I suggested impatiently. "If it *is* working, somebody might pick up the signal."

Captain Jay half-nodded, half-shrugged, agreeing that it was worth a shot. As he hurried away, Stan asked the one question I'd been trying not to think about. "Exactly how much oxygen do we have left?"

"It's not the oxygen we have to worry about," said Bruce dourly. "It's the—"

"—carbon dioxide," Emily took up the explanation. "Every time we exhale, we're putting a little more poison into the air."

I don't know about the others, but that certainly made me feel a whole lot better.

CHAPTER 10

There were tools and toolboxes scattered everywhere, the frantic activity of earlier having subsided into a determined, focused effort. Captain Jay was right in there with his crew, lying on the wet deck, his arms buried inside a panel. The air was hot and close, and it was beginning to taste stale, although that could have been my imagination. I didn't like to ask if anyone else could feel it, in case they could. We were all sweating, though, our nervous faces glistening.

I was sitting with Emily in a cramped alcove, just trying to stay out of the way, trying not to panic and to stay still, minimizing aerobic activity. Stan lay on his back on a bench a short distance away, practicing some breathing technique. Bruce had excused himself, and had been gone for some time.

I don't know why Emily chose that moment to confide in me. It was the last thing I needed, frankly. But maybe—I don't know—maybe she thought it might be her last chance to unburden herself, and mine just happened to be the nearest pair of ears.

"I saw something yesterday," she said.

I turned to look at her, saw the uncertainty in her eyes.

It happened on the Coast Guard ship, she told me, as the

rest of us had been piling into the helicopter. I recalled how Emily had seemed distracted, how she had spent the rest of the day troubled by private thoughts.

At first, there had just been the empty sea, a little choppy, the tips of the waves catching the sunlight. Then, a shape had popped up out of the water, about thirty yards out. Emily had thought the light was playing tricks on her, at first—but it was a person. A man in a gray business suit. A large bleeding gash running from the man's scalp to his eyebrow. He was waving frantically at the Coast Guard ship. He was drowning.

And nobody else had seen him. Emily opened her mouth to call to the rest of us, but then caught her breath as three more people erupted from beneath the surface. They were scattered—one fifty yards out, one twenty yards, one seventy yards. All with burns and gashes, all desperately treading water. And then, a little further out again, something else burst from the ocean. Something hard and metal, and gargantuan. The tail section of the crashed 747.

Emily had never thought of herself as someone given to inaction—but this had her frozen, speechless. She had just seen that plane, just searched it from end to end and found nobody on board—how could any of this be possible?

But it was happening. They were appearing now two by two, then ten by ten—the passengers of United Airlines Flight 128, injured, terrified, clawing at each other for purchase, waving frantically for help toward the Coast Guard ship. Toward Emily. It was, she told me later, without qualification the freakiest, most grisly sight she had ever witnessed. And then, Akerman had called to her from the chopper: "Dr. Patterson! Time to ride!" And she had spun to face him, stunned that he hadn't seen what she was seeing, and she'd found her voice at last, cried out to him—but Akerman had already turned away and her words were buried by the helicopter rotors. So she'd turned back, helplessly, to the water, and had found...

Nothing. No people. No tail section. Just empty ocean, as before.

"I know they had to be some sort of hallucination," said Emily now, "but... it was completely real... so real... I was looking right at them."

I could see how deeply this was affecting her. I wanted to say something, to reassure her, but I didn't know what. Normally, I would have written off such a story as a fantasy, or an outright lie. But this was Emily, for God's sake, one of the most grounded, most rational people I'd met. And then, of course, there was my own experience of the previous night. My own "hallucination"—or whatever it was—that I had been trying so unsuccessfully to forget about all day.

I was trying to reassure us both, I think, as I said slowly, "Granted, we're experiencing some very strange crap out here. One right on top of another. Which suggests that *if there was* a strange phenomenon in this region, it is, for some reason, suddenly increasing. But there's still no reason to believe it's supernatural in origin. There must still be some—"

"Everybody uses 'supernatural' like it's a dirty word!" The interjection came from Stan. He was still lying with his eyes shut, but he had had obviously been listening. "I had a friend," he said. "He had an interesting way of thinking about it. Think of a large stone that's sat for centuries in the center of an ancient township. Generation after generation of townspeople walk past it day after day, seeing only an impenetrable stone. Then, one day, a strong enough tool is created that allows that stone to be split. And inside everyone finally sees the glorious grain that runs through its insides."

Stan took a deep breath, and came to the point. "Even though no one had ever seen the grain before, that didn't mean it didn't exist. It had always existed. It was only that man hadn't devised a way to uncover it yet." He sat up, and fixed us with an intent gaze. "Everything we're experiencing has an explanation. 'Supernatural' doesn't mean impossible. It just means we haven't uncovered its secrets yet."

I was still absorbing that, still trying not to think about last night, about Sally, when Bruce came running up to us, slaloming through the sub's narrow spaces, looking excited as usual—but frightened at the same time.

"Something just happened!" he blurted out. "The weirdest thing. I was in the head. There was a mirror; I looked into it and—no reflection. I swear to Almighty God, I wasn't there!"

Emily, Stan, and I exchanged worried glances; Bruce could hardly have missed our expressions. "What?"

"Seemed completely real?" asked Emily.

"For ten seconds," swore Bruce, "I was not in that mirror."

So, that made two of us. Or rather three. I was thinking I should tell them, but I just couldn't do it. And now Emily had turned to me again. "In all your interviews," she asked, "you ever come across anybody who's experienced anything like this?"

"Hallucinations they swear were really there?" I said, slipping back into my default cynical mode. "Only about half." And that was exactly what had me so freaked. I couldn't be one of those people.

"I got it!" yelled Captain Jay, breaking a short but heavy silence. And the floor beneath us shook as the engines ground, ground, ground... coughed... and finally, fired up. The sweetest sound in the world.

"Reverse engines!" barked Jay. "Level plane! Back us the devil outta here!" And the shaking grew stronger, forcing us to hold on tight to our seats and our hopes as the engines whined with the increasing effort and the sub strained to work itself free from the jagged teeth of the rocks that held it.

The whole vehicle was shuddering now, and the dreadful grating sound of metal against rock was tearing through my nerves. The engines were screaming so loud that I thought they might explode. But suddenly, blissfully, we were free, and the rock face was spinning away from us on the monitors, my stomach lurching with the sudden violent motion.

We had taken some damage. Small jets of water came bursting through the wounded hull, and Captain Jay was still a whirlwind of activity, issuing orders. "Blow ballast! All tanks! Put us on the glass! Get me some fresh air!"

But we were *moving* again, angling upward.

Stan dropped into a chair, drained by his relief. "That was too, too close."

"Just let me see some sunshine," prayed Emily. "Then I'll breathe again."

Another eternity seemed to pass, my gaze rooted to the monitors, before I saw the glassy underside of the ocean's surface. And then we broke through, flashes of night sky lurching across the screens, and the sub was buffeted powerfully again but eventually settled, and Captain Jay gave us the news we had all been waiting for: "We're up!"

He swung onto the ladder and muscled open the hatch. Residual water rained down upon him, but he didn't seem to care. He took a deep breath of sweet, fresh air, then clambered up onto the deck. The rest of us scrambled to follow him.

The night sky had never looked so good as after I'd thought I might never see anything but metal over my head again. I just stood and drank in its infinite depths, the pinpoint lights of zillions of stars, as dark water lapped around the sub's edges. Beside me, Captain Jay, Bruce, Emily, and Stan were similarly mesmerized.

I almost didn't notice at first that the ocean had begun to churn. I thought I must be imagining the flicker of light that played across the stars. But there was no denying the evidence of my eyes, as that light grew...

I couldn't process this. After all that had happened already, just when I had thought it was all over. And I felt the distant fear that maybe I was the only one who could see this, and was somewhat relieved to see that the others were all staring upward too, in abject astonishment.

It dominated the sky, now: a ragged circle of blinding bright lights, of various colors, flashing on and off, dropping towards us from directly above. "Anybody got a theory about this one?" whispered Emily.

The water around us was going wild, and I could feel why. We were being blasted by some force, so strong that it was hard to keep our balance on the rocking submarine. Stan was almost pitched overboard, and Emily and I had to grab at him, struggling to pull him back. My spine was juddering to the sound of an unnatural but rhythmic low-end hum, which seemed to emanate from the lights themselves.

"Look!" cried Bruce. And I saw that there were more lights approaching—but normal lights, at ocean level—and suddenly, we could all hear a booming voice, commanding but swamped by so much concussive noise and distortion as to make it unintelligible.

"Does anybody understand that?" yelled Emily over the hubbub. "What are they saying?"

The voice boomed out again, even more harsh. "It's Russian!" cried Captain Jay. "He's speaking Russian! Saying—"

Suddenly, boarding nets rocketed across the sub's deck, and I could make out the vague outlines of what looked like black power boats off the port side. Sleek, muscular craft. Jay hardly needed to complete his translation, but he did anyway.

"—'Prepare to be boarded!'"

There were dark figures crawling across the nets, coming toward us. Giddily, I couldn't help but think that they looked like nothing more than giant black spiders. I didn't know what the hell was going on. I shielded my eyes, and squinted painfully at the lights overhead, almost upon us now. One of them swiveled, and I can just make out a vague outline between them. The outline of a...

...*helicopter.* It was black—so black that it was almost invisible. Ominous, certainly. But definitely a chopper. An honest-to-God, solid, real chopper. Nothing weird. Nothing supernatural. I didn't know whether to laugh or cry. Or just scream.

The dark spider figures had rolled onto the deck now, where they stood revealed as powerfully built men. They were each dressed from head to foot in black, even their faces concealed behind stretch masks—and each of them was holding some sort of hi-tech gun. Half of them made for the open hatch and disappeared into the sub; the rest surrounded us, and the man I took to be their leader barked something in Russian. Captain Jay answered haltingly, but whatever he said couldn't have been good enough, because the leader gave a signal to his men and they closed in.

Two pairs of hands closed around my arms, before I could react. It was the same for the others. "Hey, what are you—!" protested Emily.

The black-clad leader turned to her in surprise. "You speak English?" he said, in a broad Tennessee accent.

"Yes," she snapped, "I speak—" But before she could

finish, one of her captors pressed a small palm-sized device to her exposed arm, and she seemed to lose all motor response. Her eyes rolled back into her head.

The same thing was happening to Bruce, Stan, and Jay, and now I could feel something cold and metal against the back of my neck, too. I opened my mouth to protest, raised my arms to fight back, but the signals from my brain didn't seem to be getting through to my body.

I saw the deck of the submarine racing up to meet my face. Then, everything went black.

CHAPTER 11

Darkness.

The first thing I became aware of was the pain, pounding in my head, dragging me insistently toward a point of light. I could hear noises—breathing, shuffling, all oddly muffled. I gasped, and my eyelids fluttered open, but that didn't seem to help much.

I could see a gray wall. Deep shadows. For an awful moment, I feared I was still on the submarine, still submerged, that our escape had been a delusion formed by a brain starved of oxygen. But my eyes were adjusting to the gloom, and I was starting to make out:

A small, windowless room. A storeroom, it seemed, with dusty supply boxes piled onto shelves. Emily and Stan were flanking me, on the floor, as if they had just been dumped here. No sign of Captain Jay—but Bruce was here, already awake, scrabbling at the wall. Gingerly, I righted myself and crawled over to join him, my limbs feeling like sponge cake. Bruce acknowledged me with a quick, worried glance. He'd found the seam of a doorway. No doorknob, though.

I was starting to remember: the sub, the helicopter, the men in black. I looked at my watch, only managing to lift my wrist with a supreme effort.

The others were coming round now, too, and Emily clambered woozily to her feet. Too much, too soon. She teetered unsteadily. She had the same thought as me, lifting her wristwatch, but her eyes couldn't focus and her face crumpled with frustration. "A little more than two hours," I filled in for her. My voice felt odd, scratchy, against my dry throat.

"Where...?" croaked Emily. Bruce shrugged, to indicate that he had no more idea than she did.

"Can't we get out?" groaned Stan from the floor.

Bruce offered a hand and helped him to his feet. "They've locked us in," he reported.

"They who?" asked Emily. None of us could answer that. "They spoke Russian."

"But also English," said Stan. "Just before they—"

"Drugged us is what they did!" snapped Bruce. Some of his old color had returned to his cheeks, and with it his habitual impatience. He pounded on the door, every beat resonating through my tender head, and he yelled out, "Hey! Anybody out there? We're awake in here! Hey!"

"Where's the crew?" asked Stan. "The sub crew?"

"Where are *they*?" retorted Emily. "Where are *we*?"

Either our captors had heard Bruce's shouts or they had a great sense of dramatic timing—for at that moment, we all heard the click a lock being disengaged, and we froze as the door swung open. Four people entered: powerful-looking individuals in bland, unmarked civilian clothing. Their expressions were blank, their eyes not meeting ours. A security detail.

Behind them, a dark-suited woman stepped into the room carrying a hole-punched card—her key, I assumed. Her hair was short and severe, and her face wore a no-nonsense look. She was obviously in charge here. "You'll come with us please," she said coldly—and immediately, we started throwing questions at her. Questions like, "What is this?" "Where exactly are we?" "Who are you?" "What right do you have to hold us like this?"

She repeated just one word. "Please." It was a threat, this time.

We were taken down a long, gloomy passageway. We were all looking around, trying to get our bearings, trying to find a clue to where we were, but there was nothing. Nor was there any hope of veering off our assigned path: the security guys kept us tight in their midst.

"Military?" muttered Bruce out of the side of his mouth. "Government? Who else would have taken us off the sub like that?"

"They spoke Russian," stated Stan—always Mr. Conspiracy.

"We were in a Russian sub," I reminded him. "They probably thought *we* spoke Russian."

"What were they doing out in the middle of the Atlantic?" mused Emily.

Bruce had a more pressing question. "Where do they come off abducting us?" Seething with indignation, he called out to the leader woman. "Excuse me, sweetheart—you wanna tell us where we are? And who you are? And why you... Sweetheart!" he repeated, realizing that she was ignoring him.

Suddenly, there were hands seizing my arms again, and I cried out in protest as I was dragged off down a side corridor. The same was happening to the others, and their raised voices receded behind me as we were separated.

Another passageway, as dark and mysterious as the first—but there were other people here. Some were in uniform, but without any insignias I could see. Others were wearing white lab coats. Michael Crichton would have felt right at home.

We passed a trio of lab-coated men. Two were young, bearded, but the man in the middle was in his sixties, unshaven. He looked tired. Their conversation was intense, urgent. I remember that my eyes stayed on the older man as he passed me. I felt... well, Stan would have called it a premonition, but it's certainly possible that I could have seen the man's face before, in a photograph in an old newspaper.

At the time, it didn't seem important. I dismissed the sensation as *déjà vu*, and returned my mind to my own problems. If only I'd recognized Victor Osserman right then—if I'd had an inkling of what I was later to learn—

things could have turned out very differently.

My journey ended in a small, barren room with a single table and one chair. A heavy door slammed shut behind me, and I let out a sigh of resignation. I had half expected something like this. I only wondered how long they would leave me to stew before the interrogation began—because I had no doubt that interrogation was the next stage.

In any event, it didn't take as long as I'd imagined. The door flew open again, and a steely faced man in a dark suit marched into the room. I noted the hole-punched card in his hand. He was also carrying a folder, to the front of which was clipped my driver's license and bogus Indef ID card. The former, I'd already found out was missing—along with my wallet. The latter, I'd forgotten about, and the sight of it brought a sinking feeling to my stomach.

"Look..." I began, but I was interrupted by a harsh voice. I wasn't the one in control here.

"You are Howard Gregory Thomas?"

"I want to know where I—"

"You reside at 9703 Everson Terrace—divorced; one daughter, Traci. You are currently working as a reporter for *The Observer*." And then he started to ask me questions. Questions about myself. Questions like who were my parents, and where was I born. As if he needed to be convinced that I was who he thought I was.

"Look," I tried feebly, "until you identify yourself, I'm not answering—"

But my interrogator just held up the Indef ID card—my Achilles' heel. And he asked me how it had come to be in my possession.

I decided to try the bluff. I figured I had nothing to lose. "Considering what that is," I said, "maybe I should be the one asking you the questions."

"Considering that it's counterfeit," said my interrogator smoothly, "I think not."

After that, I decided to just tell him everything he wanted to know.

Shortly after, I was hauled back to in the storeroom where we'd first woken.

Emily and Stan were already there, waiting. They'd been put through pretty much the same routine as I had and Emily was pacing, beyond outraged. "Anybody have a good lawyer?" she growled. "I mean a really good one. I mean a really, really, really good one."

The door banged open, and Bruce was shoved through it, the last of us to return. Apparently, he'd given his interrogator a hard time. He showed no sign of the weariness that I, and I'm sure the others, were feeling. Instead, as the door slammed shut behind him, he turned to us and announced in a hushed but excited voice, "We're underwater."

On his way to his interrogation, Bruce had passed a sealed doorway, with red lights flashing and a sign that had proclaimed "1-1 SECURITY AREA—AUTHORIZED PERSONNEL ONLY." Naturally, his childlike curiosity had been piqued—and on his return journey, he'd got lucky. The door had been opened from inside just as he was drawing level with it. His escort had quickly muscled him on down the corridor, but Bruce had caught a glimpse.

"I saw it," he related, so wired that he couldn't get the words out fast enough. "I saw it, some sort of huge control room! Had a window—this giant window—looking out on some, some big mother of a superstructure. All underwater!"

"Superstructure?" I repeated. "What kind of—"

"I don't know what it was," said Bruce. "I saw it for a nanosecond—but it was big!"

A troubling thought struck Emily. "Maybe it was another hallucination."

But Bruce stated with wild-eyed intensity and absolutely certainty: "This was no hallucination."

And at that moment, the door burst open again, and the same dark-suited woman who had come for us before marched in, again with a cluster of security people. They split up and came for us separately. We were still getting to our feet, reacting to all this, when I caught a brief glimpse of one of the palm-sized devices that had knocked us out on Captain Jay's sub. I opened my mouth to warn the others. I tried to resist, but I felt the press of cold metal on my neck again, and it was already too late.

The last thing I felt was an overpowering resentment at having control of my muscles, my body, my life, taken from me again, without even knowing why or by whom. Then darkness fell again, and I could hear the sound of water...

Ocean waves, lapping against a beach.

Cold water slapped at my shoes and seeped into my socks. There was a chill round my shoulders and sand in my collar, scratching at my skin. My head was throbbing again, and my neck was stiff from where I'd lain awkwardly. I groaned and tried to raise my head, but decided it wasn't worth the effort.

I was the first to wake this time, but the others weren't too far behind me. I could see Bruce shifting in the corner of my vision, rolling onto his side, spitting sand out of his mouth. Emily managed to make it into a sitting position, staring out across the sea until Stan gave her a nudge and indicated that she should turn around.

The rest of us saw it at the same time.

"Miami," I said distantly. "We're back in Miami." Alone on the beach, in the middle of the night. Looking at Hotel Row.

One by one, we got to our feet, rubber-legged, still disoriented from whatever drug had been pumped into our systems—not to mention the through-the-looking-glass insanity that our lives had become.

"Y'know," said Bruce deadpan, "this really isn't so much fun any more."

It took us just a few minutes to reach the boardwalk that fronted Hotel Row. Like the beach, it was deserted—except for a homeless guy digging through the trash. He examined the four of us—dazed and bedraggled as we were—with an expression of contempt, then returned to his foraging.

"We should call what's-his-name," said Stan, "Benirall's kid."

"Akerman," said Emily. "Who's got his number?"

I reached inside my jacket, but remembered: "They took

my wallet. Money."

The others checked their own pockets. I could see from their faces that they'd been cleaned out, too. "When you come to the end of a perfect day..." I said wryly.

Bruce had spotted a payphone nearby, and he moved tiredly towards it. As we followed him, I heard a crash behind me, and realized that the homeless guy had dropped the trashcan lid and fled as if for his life. I never did find out what had spooked him, but I've no doubt it had to do with the four of us. Or rather, with whatever strange force had followed us to the shore.

Oblivious to all this, for now, Bruce had rummaged deeper and found a lone quarter. He offered it to Emily. "You got somebody to call for a ride?"

"Been working deep ocean for seven months," said Emily. "Haven't exactly kept up with anybody back here. Certainly nobody I can call at four-thirty in the morning to ask for a ride. What about you?"

"Me? Sure," said Bruce. "Got twenty people. More. Students, co-workers—any one of 'em be glad to come collect me." He turned to the phone. Then faltered.

"What?" said Emily.

"I don't know anybody's number," confessed Bruce. "Not by heart."

"Real close to them, huh?" Emily turned to Stan next, but the old guy just shook his head.

I snatched the coin, despairing of the whole sorry lot of them. I pushed it into the slot. But still, I hesitated before I dialed. Maybe this wasn't such a good idea after all.

"So," said Bruce, "what now?"

The sun was beginning to rise, spreading orange tendrils across the calm sea. The four of us were sprawled across the boardwalk, exhausted beyond sleep.

Emily was the first to say what we were all thinking. "Look, I don't know about the rest of you, but as far as I'm concerned, Benirall can keep his money. I'm taking my ball and going home. Done, zip, finito."

No one else said a word, until the sound of a car engine broke the dawn hush and Sally pulled up beside us. This was the first time I'd seen her since the bathtub incident—something I'd tried not to think about as we waited for her. If anything, though, the sight of her now made that episode—that hallucination, whatever—seem even less real. She looked tired, and resentful that I'd woken her with a phone call two mornings running. She had forced a brush through her hair, but hadn't quite untangled it all. Her cheek still sported pillow crease marks. She wasn't exactly the sexy vixen from the tub; very much the ex-wife again.

"Thanks for coming," I said winsomely through the open window.

Sally eyed my clothes, my condition, then looked at the others behind me, her expression saying that she had expected no better. "Well," she said dryly, "this's gotta be just one wholly fascinating story."

"You have any money?" I asked. I indicated the others, and explained lamely, "They need cab fare."

Sally gave me a withering look, but sighed and reached for her purse.

We drove straight into the morning commuter traffic. It seemed to be snarled worse than ever. I could feel Sally's impatience as she sat beside me, tapping at the wheel. I was gazing out of my window, my thoughts hundreds of miles away—back out at sea, to be precise—and I hardly registered the occasional glances she stole at me.

Maybe, if I hadn't been so wrapped up in myself, I'd have realized what was happening. Sally didn't want to care. She really didn't. But she couldn't help herself. When she finally asked, there was a hint of anger in her voice, but it was anger at herself. "Okay," she said, "so... why are your clothes wet? Who were those people you were with?"

I turned to her. I opened my mouth to answer.

I didn't know where to start.

"My last twenty-four hours," I said, "at least I think it's been twenty-four hours... you wouldn't believe. I..."

"Wait!" shouted Sally. "Stop. I've changed my mind, I don't want to know. I'm over wanting to know anything about whatever crazy—"

"You asked," I said defensively.

"Well, now I'm un-asking."

I could hardly blame her. It might have made me feel better to talk about it, to unburden myself—but it was hardly fair on Sally. Hardly fair to drag her into all this. Trouble was, she was the only person I could think of, the only person I knew, who I *could* talk to. And that made me feel all the more depressed.

"I didn't know who else to call," I said. "I knew you'd come."

Sally shifted in her seat, resenting the fact that I'd taken her for granted, even more pissed about the fact that I'd been right. I resolved, there and then, to treat her better in the future. To make more time for Traci, to find some way of economizing so that I could catch up on my payments. If the madness of the last few days had taught me anything, it was to appreciate what I had.

I was determined to hold on to that. Whatever it was.

CHAPTER 12

Home. My funky one-bedroom bachelor pad, half a block from the beach.

Normality. The sound of a soft breeze rattling the bamboo curtains. The feel and the rhythmic click-clack of the keyboard beneath my fingers.

The freedom to just sit around in my Dolphins T-shirt and shorts, with peanuts, pretzels, and beer laid out on my writing table: the official writer-on-deadline breakfast. Just being here, just being surrounded by—and doing—familiar things... Somehow, it made everything seem better, made the last few days seem like an adventure rather than the nightmare it had been at the time.

And not just an adventure. A story.

I was stoked, composing in frenetic bursts, simultaneously talking to my editor over the phone crooked against my shoulder. "A whale of a story," was how I described what I was writing. "A whale of a tale. That's just how great a journalist I am, Marty. It's a Triangle story." Marty didn't like the sound of that—hadn't we covered the Triangle to death? I assured him that this story was different. Very different.

This wasn't some fantasy about magnetic crystals or whatever. This wasn't about the supernatural at all. There'd be no mention of disappearing passengers or ex-wives in bathtubs or anything else that could be dismissed as the product of an overactive imagination. This was a story about something explicable, human; about an organization that had secrets and would go to any lengths to keep them.

Conspiracy theory, nagged a skeptical voice in my head. But this was not just a theory. I had proof. Three independent witnesses. Maybe four—though the phone at Captain Jay's office at the docks seemed to have been disconnected. This was the story that could make me, get my career back on the up.

The call waiting tone chirruped in my ear, and I quickly finished up with Marty. "Don't worry," I said, "I'll have it in by final bell. I've never missed a deadline." True to form, Marty reeled off a list of times when I'd done just that. "Well, since then," I conceded lamely. "Okay, and then. Look, I'll have it in, promise." Then I clicked over to the other call.

"Daddy?"

"Hey, Trace. Listen, honey..."

"Daddy... I don't know what to do."

I was still typing, trying to do two things at once as usual. I hadn't registered the urgency in my daughter's voice. "Look, I'm dying to talk to you, but how about later? I'm on this brutal deadline. What about your mom? She—"

And suddenly, my computer went dead. Just fizzled out.

Every writer's nightmare. I stared at the blank screen, the full horror of it sinking in slowly. When was the last time I'd saved my work?

"No," I groaned. "No!"

And, on the other end of the phone, Traci screeched: "DAAAAAAAAD!!!"

Kid sure knew how to get my attention.

"What is it, honey?" I asked, starting to worry. "What's the matter?"

"I'm sleeping over at Mindy Granger's house. It's Mindy's father. He's... freaking out."

"Freaking out? What do you mean, freaking out?"

"Daddy, I need you. Please."

I looked at the blank screen, thought about all the work I had to do over. But there'd been something in Traci's voice—a particular tone—that had nudged at me. She needed me.

"Okay, sweetheart. I'm coming."

The Granger house looked the same as it had when I'd last seen it—when I had lived with Traci and her mother and I'd driven my daughter over there from time to time. Perfectly normal. An old station wagon stood in the driveway, its partially peeled bumper sticker reading OUR DADDY'S A US NAVY MAN! But as I approached the front door, I heard something. Something from inside the house. Raised voices, agitated.

I quickened my pace. The front door was open, but the screen door was unlocked. I knocked and called out Traci's name.

A loud crash.

I didn't hesitate. My daughter was in there. I kicked the screen door open, and rushed in. Inside, furniture had been overturned, bric-a-brac shattered. Those voices were coming from the back bedrooms—but as I pushed my way past the debris towards them, Traci appeared in my path. She was in her pajamas, and frantically pulling her friend Mindy along after her.

I barely had time to ask them what was going on when Bill Granger exploded from the hallway behind them.

Mindy's father was approaching forty, very trim, with a military buzz cut. But I'd never seen him like this before. His skin was burned, like he'd been out in the sun way too long, his eyes were crazy, and he charged at us like a madman. We leapt out of his way, and he threw himself back against the wall. Sweat was pouring from his face. Then he caught sight of his reflection in a mirror that was hanging lopsidedly, and the image seemed to hold his attention.

Traci and Mindy were terrified. I was the adult here; I had to step forward. God help me. "Bill?" I breathed. "My God."

He turned back to face us. I thought he was reacting to my voice at first, but I'm not sure he had even heard me. He was breathing heavily. "I can't... it's in my head... please..."

"Daddy, don't!" wailed Mindy. She was trying to go to him, but Traci held her back. "Let me help him!" Mindy pleaded.

Then Bill turned as if there was somebody else in the room, and he yelled into thin air, "Stay away from me! Get out of my house!"

A moment of frozen confrontation. Then: "Who are you talking to?" I asked tentatively.

Bill Granger pointed. "Him!"

I was about to point out there was no one there, when I noticed something. Something that cast this whole situation in a worrying new light. It was tucked into the back of Bill's waistband: a blue steel .45 automatic.

"You have to leave," said Bill emphatically. "Now!" And I believed him.

"Easy, buddy," I said. "I want to help you. "I was backing off, toward the door, keeping the panicked girls behind me.

"You can't help me!" bellowed Bill. Then, in a quieter, more plaintive tone: "They exposed me to this. It's happening to me just like it happened to Kemper...and Manning!"

"Exposed you to what?"

Bill was looking past me, to the girls. "Go, dammit! Take them with you! Go!" Then he spun around, startled. "Did you hear that? He's here!"

I hadn't heard anything, but at least Bill had given me the chance I needed to get Traci and Mindy out. I half-turned to them, instructed them to wait in my jeep. But Mindi didn't want to go, despite Traci's best efforts. "I'm not leaving you!" she shouted at her father.

"You have to!" he yelled in return.

This was getting out of hand. I couldn't deal with it alone. I reached for my cell phone—but Bill saw me, and jerked the gun from his waistband.

He wasn't aiming it; I could tell he didn't want to do that. He was just holding it. For now. But it was enough to jolt Traci into taking the bull by the horns. She practically carried Mindy, who was sobbing wildly, out the front door.

I could focus solely on Bill now. I tried to talk him down, tried to persuade him that I was his friend—but with the girls safe, he seemed to have composed himself a little, found some of that steely resolve I remembered.

"Drop the phone, Howard!" he instructed. "Drop it!"

I did as I was told.

Bill was pacing fretfully—and as he passed by a table lamp, its bulb suddenly intensified and exploded. A second later, I watched in horror as a second bulb did the same in his wake. Bill didn't even seem to have noticed.

"I need to call... call them..." he decided. "They'll know what to do." He turned to me. "But I can't call them until you're gone. You have to get out!"

"Call who? Who are you going to call?"

There was venom in Bill's voice as he replied, "Weist! He's done this to us." Then suddenly he was yelling again: "Get away from me! Get the hell away!" And he had brought up the gun, and was holding it to his own head.

"Put the gun down," I cajoled him, fighting to remain calm. "Whatever this is, we'll get you through it. Please. Just..."

But the words dried up as I realized that, behind Bill Granger, in the mirror, his reflection was... turning around to face me.

I rubbed my hand over my eyes, but the image was still there—and it was growing in the glass, as if it was somehow coming closer. "They shouldn't have let this happen to us," said Bill, oblivious. "We were loyal to them. Loyal to—"

The "reflection" lunged at him, and its arms lashed out, became real, seized him by the shoulders, and *yanked* him... back into the mirror. He was thrashing wildly, screaming, "No! Let go of me!" And the gun sailed out of his grip. Instinctively, I leapt forward, tried to help Bill, but his legs were flailing and I couldn't get a hold of him—and in the chaos I wasn't sure what happened next, but one moment Bill had managed to turn his head slightly and was staring into the eyes of his "reflection," and the next it was like their heads were merging, solidifying into one head. Bill— the real Bill—his eyes were desperate, pleading. I went for his gun, not knowing what I could do with it, but I only managed to kick it further away.

And then, with a painful, tremendous exertion, Bill finally broke free and he fell to the floor, jerking in a violent seizure.

And then he was still.

"Bill?" I moved forward slowly, not wanting to accept the worst but knowing I had to brace myself for it.

Silence.

Then Bill's body jerked slightly. Just a spasm. Enough to make me flinch. Enough to bring my head up until I was looking at the mirror again, and I locked gazes with...

Bill's "reflection." Impossibly still there. Smiling at me.

And as I watched, it faded slowly away.

There was nothing normal about the Granger house any more.

The street was packed with police cars, EMT vans, a Dade County coroner's wagon. Neighbors were rubbernecking—and under the eaves of the front porch, an inconsolable Mindy was clinging to her mother, herself an emotional wreck.

I was pretty shaken myself, holding tight on to Traci as I talked with a homicide detective called Sayles. "He... he kept saying 'they' did this to him. He had to call... 'them.' 'They' could help him." I frowned as I remembered. "But he couldn't call them until I was gone."

"Maybe it was the people he worked for," said Traci with a quiver in her voice.

Half a dozen cops turned to stare at her. Sayles checked a printout in his hand. "Says here he sold computers."

Traci hesitated. I said her name out of the corner of my mouth—a warning that she didn't heed.

"He worked at some secret... some big top secret..." She drew a deep breath. "Mindy wasn't supposed to tell me. He'd be gone for months at a time. Always come home with a really bad sunburn. Mindy always suspected he'd been out on the ocean. She'd get real 24-conspiracy crazy on me when she talked about it. I didn't even really believe her, but..."

A chirp of tire skids grabbed my attention. A trio of unmarked black sedans had pulled up, and they were disgorging lines of officious-looking men and women in dark suits. I watched them with a prickly feeling as they swarmed the house, inside and outside, some of them moving in to surround Mindy and her mother. Then my gaze traveled past them to a single dark suit who was waiting by the cars at the curb. And my jaw dropped as I recognized the short-haired woman who'd been in charge at the underwater base.

She was surveying her surroundings, just starting to turn in my direction. I took hold of Traci and pulled her out of view. As the dark-suited woman marched up the walk, we slipped away around the side of the house.

"What do you mean, you're not going to run it?"

I was snaking my way through the *Observer*'s busy bullpen, dogging my editor's steps. "You're a reporter," said Marty, "you must have a vague familiarity with the English language. It's a very simple sentence. Personal pronoun, verb phrase, prepositional phrase, and punctuation. I. Am not going. To run it. Period."

He tried to escape, but I wasn't letting him go that easy. I'd worked my nerves to a frazzle getting this copy finished to deadline, images of Bill Granger going through my head every second of the process. It was important to me that the world knew what had happened to him—to all of us. The rational part of it, anyway. The part I could believe. There was no mention in my story of homicidal reflections, just an account of Bill's descent into madness and suicide, and the connection to my own experiences suggested by the presence of the dark-suited woman.

I'd left out one other piece of information, too. An important one. It had been there in my first draft, but fear had drawn my finger to the delete key.

"You've never refused to print anything I've written before," I persisted. "Why this one?"

And Marty went straight for that omission. "Your sources on these stories usually have at least some credibility. But you don't even *cite* your sources."

"That's because this story is different. My source... it... I..."

I couldn't bring myself to say it aloud: *I'm the source!*

"Look," said Marty, "it's not running. That's final!" But he seemed to take some pity on me, because—after a quick check to see that everybody's heads were down, that no one was listening—he lowered his voice and added, "Anyway, for some reason, Mr. Keoshian himself wanted it killed."

I frowned, uncomprehendingly. This came from the publisher? The guy I'd only glimpsed a few times, who had never had a word, good or bad, to say about my work before? What the hell was happening here?

"Some people came to see him," said Marty. "Ten minutes later, Keoshian is telling me to eighty-six any story of yours that has to do with the Bermuda Triangle."

"I want to see him," I said.

"Keoshian? He's gone. And by the look on his face, you're definitely not talking him out of this."

Marty took advantage of my bewilderment to get away at last. I just stood there, beneath the bullpen's flickering lights, for a minute or more, before I could accept that I was out of options. All I could do was leave quietly. I swore that Keoshian hadn't heard the last of this, though.

I strode out of the office, still steaming, just as a bus was pulling up across the street. And just getting off that bus was the last person I'd expected—or wanted—to see again. Stan Lathem spotted me, gave a wave of recognition, and hurried up to me.

"Stan? What the hell are you—"

"It's Heather," he said.

It took me a moment to register the name, to remember the girl—the old woman—in the 747. Then I rolled my eyes in exasperation, but Stan was insistent. "It's Heather!"

"Will you get off it?" I said. "With everything else that's happening, why are you obsessing on—"

The intensity in Stan's eyes was like nothing I'd seen in him before. "Because saving kids is what I do!" he insisted. Then, a flicker of uncertainty. "Did. I... Look, I know what I see isn't like it used to be. I'm wrong most of the time now. I admit it. But Heather is important. Somehow. She's important to this. To us."

I stared at Stan, at that intensity.

And I felt a sick sensation in my stomach as I realized that I believed him.

CHAPTER 13

Meeno had left the shower running.

He was standing behind the bathroom door, looking out into the hallway at his son and...

...at his *two* sons, Ruben and Dylan. They hadn't seen him. They, in turn, were watching Helen, their mother, in the master bedroom, sitting on the corner of the bed, sobbing quietly.

"It's about Daddy and me," said Dylan, looking up at Ruben tearfully. "I heard them." Ruben put his arm around his little brother's shoulders.

Meeno closed the door silently, his heart breaking. He turned to the mirror and stared at his reflection. At the face of the man who was tearing that poor kid's life apart. None of this was Dylan's fault. But Meeno didn't know what he could do to stop it. He felt like screaming, like smashing that mirror with his fists, but he knew it wouldn't do any good.

On autopilot, he moved to the shower and stepped in. He tilted his head under the steaming spray, closing his eyes and letting the water pound at his skull as if it might somehow wash his brain clean. For a few seconds, he could concentrate on that, and almost block out everything else.

But the madness found him even here.

It was just a sensation at first. Water collecting around his feet, even though the drain was open. Cold water. Meeno looked, and was momentarily frozen.

Not just cold water. It was actually belching up out of the drain, brackish, carrying bits of seaweed. *Seawater?* It was already lapping around his ankles, rising fast. Impossibly fast.

Meeno reached to crank it off, and the faucets spun in his hands but the stream of water only intensified. And, suddenly, the showerhead itself gave a great belch, and Meeno gagged as a bolt of brackish water struck him in the face. He had salt in his mouth and his eyes—and when he blinked it away, when he could see again, the water was up to his knees.

He pushed at the shower door, but it wouldn't open.

He knew this couldn't be happening. It had to be another delusion. But the small part of his mind that knew this was overwhelmed by the evidence of his senses—*all* his senses. The water was around his waist, and Meeno leaned back against the tiles and kicked at the glass door. It didn't budge.

He yelled out to Helen. She would see what was happening here—what was really happening. She would tell him what to do. And if she did find him a quivering wreck in the corner of the shower stall, screaming at nothing... well, then maybe that was for the best. Maybe she and the boys would be better off without him.

But Helen wasn't answering—and the water rose around Meeno's neck until he had to push off the floor and tread madly to keep his head above it.

Then, suddenly, another head erupted from the water beside him, and Meeno screamed.

The face was bloated, pasty white, and very, very dead. And he knew it. It belonged to Beatty. Don Beatty. His lawyer friend from the Greenpeace raft. His dead friend. Gasping for breath, Meeno tried to push himself away from it—but there was another eruption of water behind him, and another dead face surfaced.

Another of the Greenpeacers. A young woman. Meeno couldn't quite recall her name through his panic. Betsy?

Betty? Beth! She had been pretty, once. Now, her dead eyes had rolled back into their sockets and her skin was beginning to rot.

This was worse than the boatyard, worse than the whalers, because these were people that Meeno had known, had spoken with—and because, this time, there was nowhere to run. He could feel their corpses bobbing against him in the confined space, and as the water level neared the ceiling he feared that he would die alongside them. As perhaps he should have died alongside them days ago.

The idea was almost comforting. It appealed to Meeno's survivor's guilt. But his will to live was stronger, and he braced himself against the shower wall and hammered madly at the door with his feet again, letting his head sink underwater, staking everything he had on one final, panic-driven adrenaline boost.

And the door burst open, and a torrent of water gushed out into the bathroom, and brought Meeno tumbling out with it. He was rocketed hard against the sink pedestal. He blinked stars out of his vision, righted himself, and spun toward the shower, needing to know what had happened to the two bodies.

They were gone. No sign that they had ever existed.

The shower was still on, but producing a normal jet of clear water now, which gurgled away down the drain.

The bathroom floor was bone dry.

Meeno sat alone in the dark, staring at the TV, registering little more than the flicker of colors across the screen. He didn't want to sleep; he was afraid of what he might dream. But he didn't want to be awake either, because then he couldn't stop himself from thinking. The beer in his hand was a compromise, but it wasn't working either.

Mechanically, he rose, turned off the TV, left the room.

The door to Dylan's room was standing ajar, and Meeno couldn't help himself. He pushed it further open and stood in the doorway, watching. Dylan was sleeping deeply, but he had twisted around on his bed and thrown his covers.

Meeno moved over to him. He wasn't sure why. He hesitated for a long moment. Then he reached down, turned the sleeping boy around gently, and covered him again. And he lingered in the room a while longer, studying the boy's face.

Just thinking.

"Olshan's coming in today to see his gorgeous paint job. Problem is we ain't finished the paint stage on his boat yet. Can't keep the sprayers working right. Can't seem to keep anything workin' like it's supposed to."

Yarrow had been at Meeno's heels since he'd walked into the boat shed, talking incessantly. Meeno hadn't been listening, his thoughts full of Dylan. He followed his boss's pointing finger now, to a sailboat. *The* sailboat, he realized with a start, in which the ghost whalers had appeared. What had Yarrow just said about it?

But he'd already moved on, turning his attention to Meeno's own cigar boat. "Mr. Jacoby keeps asking me when I'm gonna get you to get this junk pile of yours out of here. I know you love working on her—God knows why—but you really need to think about moving her out of the shop. Meeno, are you even listenin' to me?"

"Hey, Paloma!" The shout came from a ladder, from one of the other workers. Tito. He was new, and Meeno hadn't had much to do with him, but he was talking as if they were old friends. "How's that boy a'yours? Saw him at T-ball last weekend. Got quite the arm on him for such a small fry!"

There was no getting away from it.

The only thing Meeno could do was confront it.

He made an excuse, left work early. Dylan was delighted that his father wanted to spend some time with him in the middle of the day. No computer games this time, though. Something less complicated, less frustrating. A simple game of catch in the yard, like he'd played with Ruben when he was Dylan's age.

Meeno tossed the baseball underhand, and each time Dylan fired it back with some real juice. Tito had been right; the kid did have a good arm. Nader romped around them, snapping at the ball in mid-flight; Helen watched from the kitchen—and slowly Meeno began to feel lighter, began to realize that he could get to like this.

So he'd had a shock, and parts of his memory had gone AWOL. That was something he would have to learn to live with. It wasn't as important as the present, as his family, as... this.

And maybe, if he could make this work, ease the stress he had been feeling—maybe then the ghosts would leave him alone, too.

Meeno could see a future again, and it felt good.

The baseball rocketed past him, and hit something behind him with an ominous crack. Meeno and Dylan went to look together, and found a hole in the screen door.

"I'm sorry, Daddy," said Dylan, his face crumpling. "I didn't mean to."

"It's okay," Meeno reassured him automatically. He looked down at the boy looking up at him, could see himself reflected in Dylan's eyes, and he knew that despite everything there was something, some invisible bond, between them. A long, long moment. Then, Meeno added: "...son." He put his arm around Dylan's shoulders. "No real harm done."

And he knew that something inside him had changed— that the mere act of acknowledging the truth had been a catharsis. That Meeno Paloma was now ready to accept this new world in which he found himself. This better world.

"You got what you needed?"

Meeno fumbled with his armful of shopping, and held up the roll of screening material. Helen left her simmering pan to cross the kitchen to him, to kiss him, but stopped and raised an eyebrow at the rest of his packages. "What's this?"

Meeno grinned and hefted a toy bowling set. "Think he'll like it?"

Helen looked at the gift with a curious smile. "Gosh, Meeno, I don't know. It's a little young for him, don't you think? I mean, he's almost eleven."

"No, I got *this* for Ruben," said Meeno, showing her a plastic race car. "The bowling thing's for Dylan."

And then Helen said two words that turned his life upside down again.

"Who's Dylan?" she asked.

Meeno didn't, couldn't, react to the question. He thought she was kidding at first, but the earnest look in her eyes told him otherwise—and anyway, after all they'd been through, she wouldn't kid him about something like that. Would she?

Something twisted in Meeno's gut. He dropped the toys, and the screening material, and raced from the room. To the bedrooms. To one particular bedroom.

He threw open the door. And froze.

He was looking at an office. Helen's office. Stacks of papers, magazines, files. Everything just the way he remembered. From before. Before Dylan.

"What were you expecting to see in here?" Helen, at his shoulder, beginning to worry. "Meeno?"

Meeno sat on the kitchen stoop, at his emotional nadir. Another beer beside him. His hand was on the kitchen door, and he was absently squeaking it open a few inches, then closed. Open. Closed.

There were tears on Helen's cheeks. She didn't understand. She kept asking him what was wrong. "There's no hole in the screen door," said Meeno distantly.

"Hole? What? Meeno..."

"It's like he never existed."

"Like *who* never existed?"

Meeno looked up at her, lost. How could he explain? How could he communicate the fact that his life made no sense any more; that nothing had any meaning; that, from minute to minute, he had no idea what was real and what might be taken away from him? "Why did God let me live?" he pleaded hoarsely. "Why is he making me live through this?"

Helen looked as if she was about to shatter. "Meeno," she said. "I know you don't want to think about... I know how you feel about... about the Bermuda—"

"Dammit, Helen!" he snapped.

They had had this argument before. She must have been

at her wit's end even to have raised the subject. But, now that she had, she was determined to press it. "Others claim to have had experiences out there."

"Crazy people!" Meeno retorted.

"Maybe they aren't crazy!" The words came through a renewed flood of tears. "If the psychiatrist can't help you, then... then help yourself. But I..."

A pause. Just long enough for Meeno to know what was coming. Not long enough for him to know how he felt about it. Did it matter any more?

"I can't live with you like this," said Helen, "and I won't have you doing this to Ruben. Do whatever you have to, Meeno, but... I want you back. I want *us* back. Find an answer to this. Or I... "Another pause. Longer, this time. "I'm leaving you."

She wasn't saying it to be cruel. She simply didn't know what else she could do. And Meeno just sat in silence and played with the kitchen door.

CHAPTER 14

I was back in the bullpen, hunched over a computer. Stan stood anxiously at my shoulder. "First name Heather," he prompted me unnecessarily—then, probably for want of something else to think about, he asked how it was that I could access airline passenger lists.

"We're a newspaper," I said.

"You're *The Observer*!" Stan shot back.

I gave him a look, and continued my search. As I was waiting for a response, I asked Stan, "What was the *S.S. Marine Sulphur Queen*?"

"Just find the girl," he said tiredly.

No surprise that he wasn't in the mood for Triangle Trivia. Stan had spent the past two days trying to track down Heather by phone, being stonewalled at every turn. No survivors; that was the official word. Stan had reasoned with the authorities, pleaded with them, even threatened them—I'd have liked to have heard that—but that was all they would say. No survivors.

He just wanted to know she was okay.

I told myself I was taking his mind off it. "Do you know?" I teased. "I bet you don't know."

"The first liquid sulfur tanker in the world," said Stan.

"Lost in the Triangle. Last radio transmission was sent when she was two hundred miles off Key West." After which the ship was almost certainly ripped apart by an explosion caused by contact between cold seawater and hot liquid sulfur, giving its crew no time to send a distress call nor to reach the lifeboats. Not that I'd expected Stan to acknowledge that.

The S.S. *Marine Sulphur Queen* certainly wouldn't have been the only sulfur ship to have suffered such a tragedy. It was only because of its location, because the deep waters of the Triangle stole its corpse as usual, that the Coast Guard were forced to record an open verdict on its fate.

"Year?"

"Howard..." moaned Stan.

"Year?"

"The early sixties. I remember reading about it in the paper."

"1963," I clarified. "February fourth. Thirty-nine men lost. And here..." The computer had come up with the information we wanted, and I started to scroll through it. "...is Flight 128. Wednesday morning. First name Heather. Got her."

She'd been sitting in Seat 31-B. Last name Sheedy. Stan nodded and repeated the name to himself, as if it was familiar. "Take a look," I said. "Heather Sheedy—senior discount fare. Senior. As in: She's old. Just like when we last saw her on that Coast Guard ship."

I expected this to faze Stan, but he took it in his stride. "She was traveling with her parents. Check the seat assignments on either side of her."

I wasn't sure why I was going along with this, but I scrolled through the data again. "31-A: James Sheedy," I reported. Then, to my surprise: "31-C: Allison Sheedy."

"They put their six-year-old daughter between them," said Stan. "Like parents do. And tell me—exactly how many sixty-eight-year-olds do you know named Heather?"

He had a point.

"No matter how old she is now," said Stan, "she was a child—right up to the minute her plane went down in the Triangle!"

We looked up Emily's number before we left, and I called her from the car on my hands-free set. I expected some resistance. I thought she'd be the hardest to talk around. I was surprised.

"She's back in," I told Stan, who was riding shotgun.

"I thought she was quitting."

"Something's happened."

"What?"

I shrugged. Emily had said only a few words.

"What about Bruce? We should call—"

"He's coming, too," I said. "He was with her."

We exchanged a look. What was the dish on that, then?

The offices of Benirall Shipping filled a large, impressive building near the harbor. Emily, Bruce, Stan, and I met at the doors, and announced ourselves at reception. We explained that, no, we didn't have an appointment, and were told that Aron Akerman would be down to see us as soon as he was able.

We waited near the elevators, and exchanged stories—or rather, the others did. I just listened, with that now-familiar sense that everything I knew, everything I believed in, was shifting beneath my feet.

Bruce went first. After we'd parted on the beach, he hadn't slept. He'd just showered, changed his clothes, and gone back to work. He had found his department at the University of Florida empty; at that time of the morning, that had been no surprise. The first shock had come when he had opened his office door.

Everything had been packed up. His shelves were empty, his desk bare. There were cardboard boxes overflowing with his belongings. At first Bruce had taken this to be administration crap, something to do with his unscheduled absence. He'd grabbed his phone, found it still working, and punched in a number, preparing a verbal blast for whoever picked up. But then, his eyes had alighted upon a newspaper, folded back to the obituary page—to an all-too-familiar name.

"It was right there," he said, "in black and white. 'Bruce Gellar,' it said. 'Professor of Meteorological Studies at the

University of Florida.' Photo and everything."

According to the obit, Bruce had died during a meteorology experiment that had found him attempting to skydive into the heart of a Stage Four hurricane. The very dive he had taken on the day Akerman had approached him.

Under the circumstances, I could hardly blame him for wondering—just for a second—if the paper was right. If his luck *had* run out that day, and if everything—all the freaky stuff—that had happened to him since then had been... what? A dying dream? Or something more disturbing?

And then, a grad student had arrived, and called to Bruce across the department, showing no sign that she was freaked out to find a walking corpse there. And when he had looked back at the paper, the paper that had never left his hands, he had found it was different. The obit—like Emily's survivors, like Sally in my bathtub—had just disappeared.

The boxes had gone, too, and the shelves were full again. Bruce's office was restored to the disaster area of clutter it had been when he'd left it. Everything back to normal. Whatever passed for normal these days.

Emily's experience had been similar, in some ways, and just as personal. Her account, though, was less emotive. She was determined to retain her detachment.

She had found a stranger in her kitchen. A woman, in her late fifties or early sixties, just calmly washing Emily's dishes. When challenged, she had reacted as if she had every right to be there, had even chided Emily for leaving so much of the housework for her to do. Even as she had backed away from her, trying to work out what was going on, Emily had seen something in the woman's face—a resemblance to somebody she thought she knew. "Do I know you?" she had asked.

The older woman had chuckled and shook her head. "Only since birth," she had said. "That's kinda the way it works with mothers and daughters."

Emily shifted uncomfortably as she explained to us that she'd never met her birth mother. She had been brought up by adoptive parents, both of whom were now dead—and even they hadn't known who her birth parents were. In accordance with the laws of her home state of Montana, those records had been sealed. Emily wasn't allowed to see her own birth certificate.

She found it even harder, I think, to admit to what happened next—to what her reaction had been upon realizing just who it was she was facing. She had fainted dead away.

She had woken on her bed, as if somebody had carried here there. Or as if the whole thing had been a dream—although Emily was sure that it hadn't been. By now, none of us were surprised to hear that she had found her kitchen—her whole condo—empty of mothers and other strangers. And that the dishes by the sink were still dirty.

When Bruce had called her, just looking for a friend to talk to, somebody who might understand, she had agreed to meet him without hesitation.

"Your mother?" Stan said now, his eyes dripping with sympathy.

"My birth mother, yes," said Emily, trying and failing to hide just how much this had affected her.

"Hey, remember me?" interjected Bruce, holding up a hand. "I saw myself dead!"

Stan indicated himself and me. "We have proof that the survivor of the 747 crash *was* a six-year-old."

"Not exactly proof," I corrected him awkwardly.

The elevator door opened, sparing us another predictable war of words. I turned to the arriving Akerman, and told him curtly that we had to see Benirall.

"Really?" he said. "Okay, well... Why?"

"Because what's happening," said Emily crisply, "is now happening to us."

"I'll see if Mr. Benirall has a few minutes for you," said Akerman. He was leading us down a top-floor hallway, looking out of place in his customary T-shirt and jeans against the richly appointed décor.

"He has to see us!" Emily insisted.

Something about Akerman's demeanor triggered my reporter's radar, and I asked suspiciously, "Why wouldn't he? Two days ago he wanted everything we could bring him as fast as possible."

With some reluctance, Akerman explained, "He's been in some sort of... he's been acting... Another of our boats has gone missing. Just a repair barge, sent out to tend a stalled tanker. But still... fourteen crew aboard... Maybe that's it."

He seemed far from certain.

Eric Benirall stood with his hands behind him, his back to a large framed mirror that dominated one wall of his office. As Akerman had said, he looked disturbed—even more so than when we had last seen him—and his eyes were red-rimmed as if he hadn't slept since then.

Emily and Bruce took the lead in recounting our experiences, but Benirall didn't give them the chance to finish. He seized upon one particular detail as soon as it was mentioned. "Hallucinations?"

"Yes, sir," confirmed Emily, "but... they aren't only hallucinations. Not in the classic sense."

I was watching Benirall as his eyes burned into her. For some reason, her statement had touched a nerve. "What do you mean by that? Tell me—exactly!" he demanded.

"They seem to be..." began Emily, but the words wouldn't come.

"...glimpses," Bruce continued for her. "Of..." But now, he faltered, too.

Emily and Bruce had discussed this when they met this afternoon. Neither of them had liked the sci-fi implications of what they were saying, but they hadn't been able to think of another explanation.

Bruce had suggested that, as Emily had never actually met her birth mother, then the woman in her kitchen may not have been her. She could have been a product of Emily's subconscious—just an image of how she imagined her mother might look. Emily had dismissed this. She was more used to thinking with her head than her heart, but in this case she had a gut feeling, stronger than any she had ever known. She *knew* what she had experienced, who she had seen. "We're not even out there anymore," she had said, frustrated. "Why is this still happening to us?"

"Maybe..." Bruce had conjectured, "...maybe we were exposed to something. At sea. Some sort of pollution.

People dump all kinds of crap out there."

"So your theory," Emily had recapped, "which is supposed to make me feel better, is that we've been exposed to some sort of brain-affecting toxins out at sea?"

"At least I'm trying," Bruce had protested. He hadn't known what to say. He had never been good with the personal stuff.

Emily had been the first to say it—though Bruce had had to finish her sentence then, too. "It's like we're... we're seeing alternate... alternate..."

"Realities?"

"But why?"

Bruce had considered. "It all comes back to electro-magnetic disruption. Our thoughts, our perceptions, are entirely electrochemical. Maybe our proximity to the 747 so soon after its experience with the Triangle has somehow... opened our minds... changed our perceptions... These other realities may always exist outside our usual ability to perceive them. Only now, because of our experience in the Triangle, we're getting these momentary glimpses..."

"Alternate realities." murmured Benirall now. Bruce had finally got the words out—and much to the surprise of all of us, our employer seemed to be taking them seriously. Very seriously indeed.

"Sir," ventured Emily, "there *is* something wrong with us. We went out into the Tr— into that region, and now we're—"

Benirall interrupted, "When did these hallucinations of yours begin?"

"When we dove on that 747."

"It's like," Bruce tried to explain, "something affected us out there. Maybe something... some discharge... the plane was throwing off."

"We don't know what it could be, or how it could be doing this to us, but—"

Benirall's face suddenly twisted into a scowl, and he bellowed, "I sent you out there for answers!"

We were all frozen by the sudden outburst. Emily was the first to recover. "It's only been two days."

"But it's all escalating," cried Benirall, now sounding more desperate than angry. "Even faster than before."

I'd been hanging back, trying to remain detached from this crazy talk—but whatever was troubling Benirall, it sure had him by the balls. I was going to have to be the adult again. I stepped forward and said reasonably, "Look, Mr. Benirall, we've observed things, events, in the last sixty hours that we can't explain. Not yet anyway. Whether it's related to the so-called Triangle or not—"

Stan spluttered, "How can you possibly think it isn't?"

"*Whether or not* it's related," I pressed on, "I think..." I glanced at the others. "I think it's time you expanded our team. Bring in others, from other sciences."

"There are no others!" snapped Benirall. "I've tried. You four have to do this."

Akerman had been standing in the doorway, listening in silence. Now he eased himself a step forward. "Plus," he said, "there was the Navy."

"Navy?" echoed Bruce.

Akerman grimaced almost apologetically. "They sent people here this morning. They wanted Mr. B. to call the four of you off."

Benirall's thoughts were clearly someplace else as he expounded, "They prefaced it all by saying how they think exploration into something as ridiculous as the Bermuda Triangle is a fool's endeavor. And yet, they came to me, door closed, and threatened me."

"Directly threatened our company's government contracts," said Akerman, "indirectly threatened much more, if Mr. B. didn't pull the plug."

"The United States Navy?" asked Emily in disbelief.

Something occurred to me—a thought I didn't much like—and, almost inadvertently, I spilled out a name: "Granger."

"Who's Granger?" asked Bruce.

"Guy I saw die in front of me earlier today," I answered distractedly, turning the events over in my mind again. "He could've been Navy, too."

"Why would the Navy want to stop us?" asked Stan, pragmatically.

"That place out at sea!" realized Bruce. "With the big underwater... whatever... that I saw! Easily could've been Navy!"

Emily caught Benirall's uncomprehending look, and

filled in the part of the story that he'd missed. She sounded uncomfortable saying the words "hi-tech facility" out loud, but Bruce leapt back in eagerly: "It was in the Atlantic! Beneath the surface!"

I was studying Benirall, trying to read him. Did he believe us or not? What was he not telling us? "So, what happens now?" I asked.

"*I need you to find me my answer,*" said Benirall intensely, and he leaned against the corner of his desk as if physically drained by whatever emotions he was feeling.

Ever protective of his employer, Akerman bounded forward. "Thank you, Mr. B.," he said brusquely. "Come on, everybody. Please, let's... Time to go."

I was nowhere near satisfied with the outcome of our meeting. I still had questions—but it was clear that we'd get no more out of Benirall now. The others must have agreed because, reluctantly, we allowed Akerman to herd us out of the office.

None of us spoke as we rode back down in the elevator. Emily was the first to break the silence as we left the building, none of us quite sure what to do next. "What just happened in there?" she wanted to know.

It was Stan who answered. "The government's trying to shut us down, that's what's happening!"

"He looked worse off than we do," said Emily, meaning Benirall.

"What the hell does the Navy have to do with all of this?" I stormed.

"They probably went to him because we crashed some restricted area of theirs," considered Bruce. "That's why they drugged us, captured us, questioned us..."

"Uh, people..."

I realized that Emily had a pronounced frown on her face. She was staring at something, and I followed her eyes.

The evening was drawing in but, through the haze of dusk, we could see men in uniforms patrolling the docks, the ships, the gangplanks. Sentries. *Armed* sentries. They were carrying machine guns, slung over their shoulders.

And they hadn't been there when we'd arrived, I could have sworn to it.

"Has Benirall gone completely round the bend?" exclaimed Bruce.

"I don't think it's Benirall," I murmured. I pointed to the nearest cargo ship to us. To the name on its side. An hour ago, it had read BENIRALL SHIPPING—another thing of which I was certain. It didn't say that now. It said: KRUPP TRANSPORT CO.

Emily gasped something under her breath. It sounded like, "My God!" And we all turned, to see what she had seen.

A pair of armed sentries were marching past us, eyeing us with cold suspicion. In return, our eyes roved over their brown shirts and uniform jackets. And their red armbands. Each of which was emblazoned the American flag...

CHAPTER 15

Alternate realities...

A favorite theory of the supernatural brigade—at least, of those who want to believe, or want you to believe, that they're interested in scientific explanations after all. It's pseudo-science at best, of course, but the important thing is that we can't *dis*prove it. We can't say for sure that there *aren't* other worlds existing alongside the one we know—worlds in which history took a wrong turn somewhere. Worlds that might occasionally break through into our own, causing sightings of ghosts or monsters... or Triangle disappearances.

We'd taken refuge in a Starbucks, a couple of blocks from the harbor looking for signs of normality. But the more we looked, the more *ab*normality we found. Some of the differences were minute: The décor of the place was normal Starbucks, but with a slightly more muted color scheme than usual. And the chairs and the tables were a little less designed, more functional, almost industrial.

The place was crowded, but everywhere I turned I saw dour expressions and defeatist body language. And brown shirts, of course, scattered across the room. Brown shirts and red flag armbands. I couldn't deny it, much as I tried.

This was not the America I knew.

"My visions," said Stan quietly, "are nothing like this."

"How is it possible," I asked, also in hushed tones, "we're all having the same hallucination at the same—"

"Because they're not hallucinations," said Emily flatly.

And I think it was in that place, sitting uncomfortably, stiffly, trying not to draw attention, that I finally began to accept the truth of what she was saying. Of what everybody had been saying to me. I remembered all the people who had told me their ghost stories in the past, for the paper—and I think my greatest worry was that, when I told *my* story, everyone would look at me as I'd looked at them.

Or I could keep it locked within me, never able to talk about it.

Bruce eyed a pair of Brown Shirts at the next table, their machine guns lying prominently on the surface between them. "We better order something," he said, but none of us stirred. "I'll go," he volunteered.

"Why the hell Nazis?" Emily whispered, as Bruce moved off.

"Trust me," said Stan, "there are plenty of theories out there about points in history where, given the right extreme circumstances, America could have taken a radical political turn. Fascism, Communism... all those sorts of 'What if the British had won the war' kinds of speculations... It's not that outlandish really. We like to think it isn't possible, but—"

"Great, it's possible," snapped Emily. "But what the hell are we doing here, and how do we get out?"

Bruce was already returning with four cups of coffee. "That was fast," I commented as he sat down and handed them out.

"They're very efficient," he said wryly. Then he leaned forward and confided, "Everybody speaks English. And they accepted the money I had in my pocket. It's still twenty-first century America." None of us were especially encouraged by this.

Emily sipped her coffee, and practically spat it out. "It sure ain't Starbucks," she said ruefully. "It's actually stronger!"

Her gaze flickered to the next table, and I realized that one of the Brown Shirts had noticed her. He was eyeing her up and down, smiling—and there was no mistaking the lascivious edge to his expression. Emily shuddered, and in a low, intense voice, suggested we get out of here.

Bruce wasn't sure where we could go. "If this is an alternate reality, a zillion other things could've changed, too. We may not live in the same places, might have different jobs..."

"Some of the people who've had experiences in the Triangle," I said, "they talk about extreme disorientation. Including hallucinations." It was a last-ditch attempt to deny what I already knew, and Bruce put his finger on the biggest flaw in my theory.

"But that was *while* they were in the Triangle. You get lost in a thick fog, lose your orientation, sure. But this..."

I persisted, "I interviewed a neurologist about it who said our perception of reality is dependent, moment to moment, on trillions of minute chemical and electrical fluctuations in our brains. The fact that our perceptions maintain any semblance of order at all is the real miracle."

"And I'll bet you used that to malign those Triangle survivors," Stan grumbled.

"Uh, guys," murmured Emily, throwing a covert glance at her admiring Brown Shirt, "stay on topic. I'm sitting next to Hermann Goering's grandson here."

"What we're seeing doesn't matter," said Bruce. "We're seeing it. Experiencing it. Why?"

Emily suddenly froze. The two Brown Shirts were getting up from their table—and Emily's admirer made eye contact with her, and began to step toward us. She tried to disappear into her chair, but the Brown Shirt was beside her, his blue eyes staring with an unsettling confidence. "I don't think I've seen you in this neighborhood before," he said. "I would've remembered you."

Emily forced herself to look up at him. "I'm... just visiting."

Sounded like a reasonable response to me—but the Brown Shirt frowned. Somehow, it was a bad answer.

"Are you registered?"

"Yes," said Emily, trying to sound confident. "Of course."

But the Brown Shirt had noticed something, and he looked now from Emily to the rest of us, he shifted his weight. "Where are your identifiers?"

None of us dared move. The Brown Shirt indicated a bar code patch on the chest of his shirt—and as the other patrons began to shoot nervous glances toward our table, I realized they were all wearing similar patches.

Bruce turned on his Aussie charm. "Listen, mate, I don't think we need to make a Federal case outta—"

But as soon as he opened his mouth, the Brown Shirt stiffened—and a few of the people around us were gasping, stiffening, edging away.

"You're Australian?"

And the Brown Shirt had whipped his machine gun from over his shoulder.

Suddenly, there was pandemonium. I rocketed to my feet—didn't have time to think about what I was doing, just did it—as the gun came around to cover all four of us. People were throwing back their chairs and stumbling away, and the Brown Shirt yelled, "Don't move!" Then his free hand moved to his lapel, to a small clip-on mic, and he began to report, "Tango Base, this is Edward One. I've got a—"

I stared in shock. The Brown Shirt's mouth was still moving, but the sound of his voice had just cut out. I thought I must have wax in my ears or something, but the ambient noise in the room went on as before, the voices around me becoming calmer. And the gun in the Brown Shirt's hands began to... I don't know how else to describe it... to *crystallize*. Like an intense white light was streaming from between its very molecules. Then the gun disappeared, but the Brown Shirt didn't seem to notice, just kept talking, even as his ID patch crystallized, too, and vanished in the same way.

Then, another outburst of light, and he was no longer a Brown Shirt at all. His uniform was replaced by a grubby pair of jeans and a construction worker's flannel shirt. His hair had changed, too, his military cut growing out into a shaggy mop. His blue eyes were the same, though. We were looking at the same man.

And he'd had the same thought about Emily. His voice

was audible again now, less self-assured than before, more casual. "I know this smokin' little bar not far from here. Great music, even better company."

Emily didn't answer. Like the rest of us, she was whipsawed by what had just happened before our eyes. We were looking around, seeing the tiny signs that everything had changed again, that the Starbucks was now just a regular Starbucks.

"Well, darlin', what d'you say?"

Right at that moment, Emily couldn't say much of anything. I was just about together enough to put my arm around her and to guide her away with a mumbled "Excuse me." Bruce and Stan came with us, still staring around.

At the door, I glanced back over my shoulder and felt a shiver. Emily's admirer was watching us go, and boy, did he not like being snubbed like that. I caught the malevolent gleam in his eye, and I knew that, on a different world, in a different time, that guy could definitely get his rocks off by wearing a brown shirt...

"Everything *looks* normal again," said Bruce tentatively, as if afraid that once the words were said, one of us would see something to disprove them.

We were hurrying down the street, still shaken, trying to put some distance between us and the scene of... of whatever had happened... as if it might help.

Then Bruce put our greatest fear into words. "How do we know we're back to the exact same reality we've always known?"

None of us wanted to visit that thought, least of all me. Alternate realities. If they truly existed, if they were the cause of so many disappearances—the *Cyclops*, the *Marine Sulphur Queen*, those enormous ships—then why should we be the lucky ones? Why should we make it home?

"I say we go back to Benirall," said Emily, "and make him get us help."

"He looked worse off than we do," Bruce reminded her.

"It's not just about his missing ships," said Stan. All turned to look at him and saw the frustration in the old guy's eyes. He was reaching for something, but he couldn't quite put his finger on it.

It was the last straw for Bruce. "Look, mate," he exploded, "I'm getting sick and tired of these stinking little hints you keep dropping on us!"

But Stan couldn't help himself. "It's something... I just can't..."

"Enough!" cried Bruce. "Dammit. New Stan Rule: Unless you've got something concrete to say, just keep it to yourself."

"You're such a jerk," grumbled Stan.

"At least that was concrete," said Bruce, glaring back at him.

"Look," I said, stepping between the two of them before they could come to blows, "we're not entirely without a direction to go. The Navy. There's got to be some reason—some *concrete* reason—why they've been going around trying to stop us. There's that whatever-it-is out in the Atlantic, and there's what happened to my friend Granger."

"The Navy's never going to tell us anything," said Bruce dismissively.

I gave him a look as if it to say "Just watch me." Prying information out of reticent officials—that was my specialty. Something nice and normal.

"I'm with you," said Stan determinedly. "The last people to have Heather was the Coast Guard. That's close enough."

"I say we work with science," said Bruce. "Our world has very inviolate laws. Everything we're experiencing, all the events out there, have to have some empirical explanation." He threw a hopeful look at Emily.

She was still in a rough emotional place, but she took a deep breath and said, "Eliminate all wrong answers, and whatever's left, no matter how implausible, has got to be the right one."

Bruce grinned. "We can work at my lab. At the university."

We all looked at each other as if we might not meet like this again. Bracing ourselves for what would come next—not necessarily for the work but for what it might reveal. Then, I said, "Let's do this."

And Bruce muttered, "Yeah, before the dinosaurs decide to come back."

Back at the Granger house again, dark and quiet. I stood on the front porch and knocked for a third time. Still no answer. Mindy and her mother must have decided to stay with friends or family. I couldn't blame them. It was hard enough for me to return here. I glanced at Stan, who was looking apprehensive. I asked him what was the matter, and he said something about oppressive vibrations.

"Yeah, a guy died here today," I said, unable to restrain the cynic inside me.

I stepped off the porch, onto the path, and started around the house. "Where are you going?" Stan called after me, but I didn't answer. He would see soon enough.

He caught up with me as I was trying the sliding door at the back of the building. "What if they've got the house under surveillance?"

"I didn't see anybody out there," I said, "did you?" I was already looking for a rock. I found one, and hurled it through a small basement window, to Stan's obvious alarm. I squeezed myself through the gap, and left it up to him whether he followed or not.

Stan hesitated, glancing around nervously. But in the end, he decided he would rather be inside with me than left outside on his own.

"What exactly are we looking for?" asked Stan, as we moved through the shadows of the living room. The room in which I had watched Bill Granger die. This time, I didn't answer because I didn't *have* an answer.

The carpet was crisscrossed with a very distinctive, very precise grid of thin green fluorescent tape, which also reached up the wall to the mirror. Somebody had been taking measurements. We moved through into a small den, where the windows faced the moon so that everything was bathed in a silver glow. Saved me having to put on a giveaway light, given that I hadn't taken time to pick up a torch.

I hurried to the desk and started opening drawers, while Stan watched with a disapproving frown. "So this is a common, acceptable means of gathering information for you? Going through a dead man's desk?"

"In my line of work," I said, setting aside a file folder that might have held something of interest, "you do what you have to do."

"And write what you want to write," said Stan under his breath.

"What's that supposed to mean?"

"I mean the kind of stories you write."

"You know my stuff?" I asked, surprised.

"You wrote about me once," said Stan.

I stared at him.

"You don't remember," said Stan. "I didn't think you did."

I narrowed my eyes, trying to roll back the years, trying to appraise this face I had come to know in a different light. Stan was right. I didn't remember. But if I had written anything about him, back then, I knew it wouldn't have been complimentary.

I was still plucking up the nerve to ask, thinking it might be better if I didn't, when a new light played across the room. A flashlight beam. And another. They were coming from the windows.

I ducked behind the desk. Stan was just standing, frozen, until I yanked him down beside me. There were dark figures behind the glass, peering in. And I heard the sound of the front door opening...

Stan's face was an almost pure white—even paler than usual. I dared another look and saw that the figures at the window had gone. I hurried over, Stan at my heels, and took a cautious glance outside.

There were two cars at the curb. Black sedans, unmarked, possibly two of the same vehicles I'd seen here earlier today. "That doesn't look like the police," murmured Stan.

"It's not," I said grimly. "It's much worse."

Through the open door of the den, we could see more flashlight beams playing along the hallway. They were coming our way.

CHAPTER 16

On December 4 1970, Bruce Gernon, Jr. lifted off from Andros Town Airport in the Bahamas in a brand new Beechcraft Bonanza A36 airplane co-piloted by his father. Both were experienced fliers—but nothing in their experience could have prepared them for what was about to happen to them.

Gernon's first hint of something amiss came with the sighting of a cigar-shaped cloud ahead. Nothing strange about that except that this cloud was unusually low, hovering about five hundred feet above the ocean.

Reassured by good weather reports, he made to climb above it—at least, that was the plan. But the cloud itself seemed to build up, expanding at a phenomenal rate, until the plane could no longer out race its growth. Within minutes, it had formed itself into a doughnut shape, an incredible thirty miles wide, reaching from the ocean all the way up to a height of at least sixty thousand feet. And Gernon was trapped at its center.

He did the only thing he could. Spotting a U-shaped opening in the cloud, he dived into it, praying it would lead to clear skies. He found himself in a tunnel, with glowing white walls that had already shrunk to a diameter of two hundred feet and were still constricting around him. Gernon had estimated the length of the tunnel at something over ten miles—but, only twenty seconds later, his plane erupted from its far end, both pilots experiencing a momentary weightlessness as their escape tunnel collapsed behind them.

The Triangle hadn't finished with them yet.

Gernon found himself flying through a gray-white mist, in which his navigational equipment went haywire, his compass rotating madly. Like me, he was lucky; he made it home. The mist cleared, and Gernon was amazed to see Miami Beach below him. A journey that would normally have taken at least seventy-five minutes had, on this occasion, even with the diversions he had been forced to take, lasted only forty-seven.

Gernon's gray-white mist—described by him as an "electronic fog"—has been a feature of many Triangle stories, often seen sitting out over the ocean in otherwise clear weather, sometimes swooping in to envelop another unlucky traveler. Often, it has been associated with equipment malfunctions of the sort reported by Gernon and by Columbus before him. And perhaps a clue to its nature can be found in the work of a Canadian scientist, John Hutchison.

Hutchison's experiments with electromagnetism have produced some apparently extraordinary results, from spontaneous changes in the structure of metals to the combustion of non-flammable material to the fusing of metal and wood to the levitation of heavy objects. Also observed during these experiments have been swirling clouds, green lights, and a thin, gray fog.

The so-called "Hutchison effect" suggests that conventional science still has much to learn. If electromagnetic forces are indeed at work within the Bermuda Triangle, then we have no way of predicting what they might do. Could some of the missing ships and planes have disintegrated? Could time itself have become warped?

Many scientists have dismissed Hutchison's claims as a clever hoax. It might be instructive, however, to note that his lab has been raided several times by his own government, and all his equipment confiscated. Hutchison himself was present for one such raid, and told of the presence of dark-suited men who identified neither themselves nor their department.

I was yet to catch more than a glimpse of the strangers in Bill Granger's house, but I didn't doubt they would be wearing dark suits.

Their flashlights were flickering closer, down the hallway, and I heard an instruction barked in a harsh voice: "Check every room!" No escape that way. I was trying to open the window, but it was either locked or stuck. The latter, I hoped. I pleaded with Stan to help, but he was frozen, staring at the open door. I grabbed him and pulled him to where I wanted him to be—and somehow, he got the message and got it together enough to push with me.

I didn't think we could make it. There was bound to be somebody outside, maybe guards at the front door, though I couldn't see them from this angle. But I didn't see another option.

The window creaked open, the sound seeming unbearably loud, although it was probably no more than a squeak. I helped Stan through the gap—actually, it would be more accurate to say I shoved him. I was about to follow when I remembered the file folder on the desk and made a grab for it.

Then I was stumbling over the window frame, out into the open, hunkering down beside Stan as footsteps entered Bill Granger's den and flashlight beams played through the windows over our heads.

We waited for long, tense moments before the beams moved away. Then, for the second time that day, I slipped around the side of the Granger house with my companion and we made a run for it.

"I thought you'd grabbed something, I don't know, some top secret papers or something."

It was morning, the light of day banishing the cold shadows of the previous night and reaffirming my commitment to my mission. If nothing else, I'd yet more

STEVE LYONS

evidence that we were onto something. At least, somebody thought so.

So, here I was with Stan, standing at the corner of a nondescript commercial street, holding the contents of Granger's file: stacks of credit card receipts, which I'd gathered into bunches and paper-clipped together. "If he kept any of those at his house," I pointed out, "the Men in Black would've cleaned them out when they were there yesterday morning. These, they didn't care about."

"And we do?" asked Stan—his turn to be the cynic, for once.

I indicated a bunch of receipts. "These are all from Reilly's Sandwich Shop." And I pointed up the street, to where the sign for that establishment was visible. Another bunch: "Beijin's Dry Cleaning" And there it was, just a few doors away.

"So this Granger guy visited these places," said Stan. "Often."

"According to the receipts, almost every day for the past five weeks." Then, tongue-in-cheek, I asked: "You think maybe he worked around here?"

And we turned, slowly, to look across the street to where a high wall fronted what I already knew to be an enormous facility. The Hichen Naval Command Center.

"But you said you thought he worked out at sea."

I shrugged, watching a queue of cars crawling by a sentry kiosk. "Maybe he was reassigned here. Maybe something happened to him out there, and they were trying to help him here. Fix him." We fell silent for a moment as the implications of that idea sank in.

We both knew what we had to do next—even though it felt like walking into the lion's den. Again.

It was easy enough to get past the gate. Surprisingly easy, in fact. A flash of my reporter's credentials, a brief explanation that I was working on a story about a naval officer's death The guard didn't even sneer at the name of my paper. He just called for a security officer to escort us across the extensive grounds of the facility, past glass-walled buildings and hangars. I could see carriers and destroyers docked in the distance—and the Atlantic beyond them. The sight of it brought a shiver to my spine.

There was plenty of activity around us, people running from place to place with a real sense of urgency. At one point, we passed a row of unmarked dark blue vans and SUVs, among them a Hummer H-2 of the same color. A contingent of young intern-types were fussing around the vehicles, all in their twenties, wearing crisp, non-military clothing. I let my eyes rove over them, trying to work out what was going on—until I met the stern gaze of the Hummer driver, who was standing beside his vehicle, and then I looked away quickly.

We were taken into one of the glass buildings, up one floor, and left in a large, comfortable waiting room while a young ensign checked out our bona fides. He returned, apparently satisfied, to announce that one of the base's information officers would be out to see us shortly. Stan paid him no heed. He was standing at the window, watching the activity in the grounds, apparently troubled by his thoughts.

"I took the liberty of checking Navy personnel records for an individual named Granger," the ensign added. "Granger, William. Common enough name. We've actually got two of them on active duty: a CPO presently serving aboard a Destroyer escort in the North Pacific, and a dental tech stationed in the Azores."

I studied him, unsure whether to believe him or not. The ensign maintained a completely neutral expression. "This guy could be designated as retired," I suggested.

"That's all our records showed," said the ensign with a small, apologetic shrug. "Anyway, as I said, if you're still interested, an information officer will be happy to speak with you."

"I'm still interested," I said flatly.

The ensign held my gaze a moment longer, then turned and exited. I watched him go, certain now that I had just been lied to. I turned to Stan at the window, and was startled to find that he was no longer there.

I scanned the room, but it was empty.

I was used to being kept waiting in places like this, by people who knew they would have to talk to me eventually but could at least punish me for it in the meantime. Just my luck, then, that this was the one time they decided not to play those games.

The ensign returned too soon, leading me down a passageway to a door marked with a single "D." He held it open for me, and ushered me into a small, empty room, furnished like an office with a desk and a small sofa. "Mr. Thomas, wait in here please," he said. Perhaps they *were* playing those games, after all. I didn't have time to think about it, though—because the ensign had just come out with the question I had been dreading: "What happened to your friend?"

"Bathroom," I offered. "He's old."

"I'll send him in when he returns," said the ensign, but I couldn't shake the feeling that my lie had been as transparent to him as his had been to me.

About ten minutes later, the door to Room D opened. I had been pacing fretfully, and had my back to the new arrival. There was something about her voice, though, as she apologized for keeping me waiting—her words and tone perfectly polite, and yet somehow cold. Something familiar.

I turned to find a woman in a naval uniform, identified by her badge as a Lt. Commander Landon. The name meant nothing—but the face was burned into my memory. It was the woman from the underwater facility—the one who had been giving the orders.

"It's Mr. Thomas, is that correct?" she said. "A pleasure to meet you, sir." And she approached me, holding out her hand to shake, smiling as if we were meeting for the first time. But as I stood there, frozen, I was certain I could see the slightest twinkle in her eyes.

She remembered me, all right.

It must have been about this time that Stan was making his own discovery.

As I could have guessed, the old guy had wandered off in pursuit of his visions. I'm not sure he had even meant to skip out on me, he had just been oblivious to everything but the wordless tug in his head.

He had stepped out into sunlight and moved away from the admin building, keeping just enough presence of mind to avoid any uniformed personnel and military vehicles. The square block of the infirmary had drawn him to its doors, and he had stepped into the foyer.

There had been no hiding, then. Navy medical personnel had swept past Stan, but none of them had glanced his way. Most likely, that was because he was too focused inwards to feel nervous. He must have looked the way I always tried to look when I was somewhere I shouldn't be—like I'd every right to be there.

Stan had found a stairwell, and emerged into a third-floor corridor. He was clearly out of bounds, because the walls here needed a paint job. Badly. None of the false cheer and comfort that greeted legitimate visitors. Stan had wondered if this was the mental ward. It certainly had that creepy, *Silence of the Lambs*-feel.

The corridor was lined with unmarked doors, their inset glass panes reinforced by wire mesh. Stan had started as he'd heard a wail from behind one of those doors. Apprehensively, he had moved up to it and peered into a small hospital room, where a man was lying, strapped to a bed, wearing only gray briefs. The man had been writhing in torment—and Stan had noticed that all the skin on his body, his arms, his legs, had been covered in red blotches.

Like Bill Granger, I thought, when he described the symptoms to me.

Disturbed, Stan had walked on, hearing more wailing from the other rooms, not daring to look this time. The room he had wanted was at the end of the corridor.

His hand had touched the door grip—and he had felt something like an electric shock. Definitely here. He had pushed the door open.

The occupant of this room had been hidden behind a thin curtain, but Stan had seen the diffused silhouette of her body on the lone bed. His hand had reached out, gripped the curtain, pulled it back.

And she was there, as Stan had known she must be. Sixty-eight-year-old Heather Sheedy. Looking like she must have been drugged, her eyes dancing under half-open lids.

He had eased himself toward the bed and looked down sorrowfully at her lined face. Sensing his presence, she had opened her eyes a tad wider, struggling to find focus. She had looked at Stan with a little girl's innocence and fear, and he had reached out a trembling hand to stroke her hair.

And it was in that position, just staring down at Heather, that he was found by an indignant nurse some minutes later.

CHAPTER 17

While Stan and I were breaking into Bill Granger's house and being stalked by Dark Suits, Bruce and Emily were playing with a toy ship.

More precisely, they were standing in Bruce's research lab at the university, surrounded by the best and brightest of his students, watching as a toy ship floated in a Plexiglas tank—until suddenly, a stream of bubbles erupted beneath it, causing it to bob violently and then sink.

"We got on this right after you called us a few days ago, Dr. Gellar," said one of the onlookers—a pretty young grad student named Marie. "At first the idea of seeking an explanation for the Bermuda Triangle seemed a little... odd." With a shy smile, she added, "Even for you."

I remember Emily telling me how enthusiastic the students seemed, how excited, like being asked to work on a project—any project—with Bruce Gellar was a great honor. Like they would do anything for him. She had been grudgingly impressed.

Bruce eyed the tank. "And this is your explanation for hundreds of ships sinking?"

A younger, Brillo-haired student spoke up proudly. "It's widely known, sir, that there are methane gas hydrates—gas pockets—trapped beneath the ocean floor. If a big enough undersea pocket were to escape, any ship unlucky enough to be above it would—"

"What about all the planes that have disappeared?" asked Emily.

"Methane released into the atmosphere in concentrated enough form could—"

Bruce held up his hand, stopping Brillo-Hair in full flow. He turned to another student, who was waiting anxiously beside his own Rube Goldberg-esque demo. "Zones of Compression," he explained earnestly. "Areas where continental masses abut and compress against each other, leading to—"

"Okay, okay," Bruce cut in impatiently, "great work, kudos, terrific, fantastic, thank you all, but we've got a new direction. Whole new direction." He looked at Emily, not sure exactly how to say it. "We want to look into... well, we're thinking..."

This time, it was Emily's turn to finish his sentence. She had gotten over the shock of all she had been through—seeing her birth mother; Nazis—and now she just wanted answers. She had no time for coyness.

"Listen up, people," she announced. "Your new research directive is in the area of time/space displacement. Wormholes. Don't panic—we're not looking for hard lab work, we are after pure data collection. Research. But we want everything. All you can bring us. And we want it fast."

The students just stared at her. But then they looked at Bruce, and saw that this was serious. And they did it for him.

By sunrise, Emily felt like she was drowning in a sea of numbers. They swam across her computer screen, her eyes too tired to focus, but she refused to give up. There was something out there, something in those numbers, that would explain everything, make everything she had seen make sense—and she was close to it, she could feel it.

She had been able to feel it for the past eight hours—but it wasn't getting any closer.

She yawned and stretched, took off her glasses, and moved to the coffee machine. It hadn't been cleaned in months, but that fact seemed to disturb her less with each fresh visit to it.

Dully, she became aware of Bruce's presence beside her, holding his cup, waiting his turn. "You should sleep," he said.

"You're not," Emily pointed out.

"I don't sleep. Not much, anyway."

Emily indicated the students working about the lab. "What about them?"

"They're all new. The bunch from last night all went home around four. Didn't you notice?"

"I was concentrating."

"Obviously."

Bruce got his coffee and invited Emily over to his computer. She slid in behind it, and blinked at rows of arcane data, scrolling, constantly updating, numbers changing before she could fix her bleary gaze upon them. Bruce looked over her shoulder, and Emily felt the brush of his cheek, wondered if he was leaning this close on purpose. Another distraction she didn't need.

"And I'm looking at?"

"This is geo-electromagnetic data," said Bruce, "streaming off an old CANSTAR satellite out over the Atlantic. Same general area you just showed me, using my own proprietary program. These numbers are indicative of a major, major weather event. Massive. A Category Five hurricane."

"Out in the Atlantic?" asked Emily, concerned. "Now?"

"That's what it says."

Bruce flipped screens to a simpler weather map. "This is the nautical weather broadcast out of San Juan. Based on area radar, Skybird photos, ships' radio traffic. Look."

"Look at what? I don't know what I'm supposed to be—"

"It's blue skies and calm seas in every direction. A beautiful day out there."

"Your satellite data must be wrong."

Bruce shook his head. "I've checked it five times."

"Other people—US Weather Bureau, whoever—have got to be seeing this, too."

"Not if they're not looking for it."

Emily mulled this. Then, her brow furrowing into a frown, she said: "An invisible storm...?"

Later, Emily pored over her computer, her concentration sharpened as much by the adrenaline of Bruce's discovery as by the pints of caffeine in her system. Her eyes still needed a moment, though, just every now and then.

Surfacing from her calculations, she glanced over at Bruce. He was at his work table, feet up, playing with one of those toys with the eyes that bug out when you squeeze them. "Hey," she called over to him, "don't work too hard!"

"I'm thinking," he said defensively. "This is how I think."

"I'll remember that," said Emily. "Squeezing silly toy: brain on. Not squeezing silly toy: brain off."

"Why out in the ocean?" asked Bruce, as if to prove he had had his mind on the job.

"What?" said Emily.

"Why build this big honking behemoth of a facility out in the middle of the Atlantic?"

"We don't know it's in the middle."

"We know generally where we were when our sub got stuck. The only reason they'd bother to capture and question us was if we'd come too close to their place out there." Bruce was still squeezing the toy, still thinking. "So why the ocean?"

Emily was pissed because now he'd got her thinking about this, too. "Secrecy," she suggested but she answered herself right away. "No. That's too extreme. Who'd go to the expense and difficulty to build out there just for privacy?"

"There's got to be a good reason," muttered Bruce.

"Look, don't throw something at me, but..." Emily took a deep breath. "Maybe they're out there *because* it's in the middle of the Triangle."

Bruce looked at her. And he threw the squeeze toy at her.

"So why build in the ocean?" asked Emily. "What's in the ocean?"

"Water," said Bruce.

Emily picked up the toy and threw it back at him—but, slowly, his flippant answer began to sink in. "Not just any water," she realized. "Seawater." And, as a new idea began to take root: "What's the foundation of everything we've been talking about? Electromagnetism. All water has resistance. But salt water has a lower resistance than fresh. That resistance is cumulative per unit of volume of water."

"You're losing me," complained Bruce. "I don't do ocean, I just do the weather."

"If you were trying to generate an enormous amount of electromagnetic power," said Emily, "you'd want to do that sitting in some really big puddle of seawater."

"You think the Navy is out there doing something to the ocean?"

Emily just gave Bruce a look as if to say "Well, what do *you* think?"

And then they were both up and pacing, practically bumping into each other, their minds racing at top speed, longing thoughts of sleep all but forgotten.

"It has to be manmade," said Emily. "It can't be a natural phenomenon."

"Entropy," said Bruce. "The Second Law of Thermodynamics. The natural tendency of energy is to decrease, not increase. Systems unacted upon will only run down. What has that got to do with—"

"This energy out in the Atlantic—it isn't dissipating. It's building. You can only overcome entropy by the introduction of energy from some external source. So there has to be something out there creating this. We're talking an enormous amount of energy. Wait, let me correct that. An *en-oooooor-mous* amount of energy. Problem is: there's nothing mankind could build even, in theory, that could generate that kind of—"

Bruce cocked an eyebrow. "The government keep you in the loop about everything they're working on? Must be very cool!"

"I'm telling you," Emily shot back, "it's not possible!"

"That's what you just said about your whole entropy thing! Meanwhile, I've got hurricane-level electromagnetic readings centered three hundred and twenty miles off shore, except, oops—*there's no damned storm!*"

There was silence, then, for a long, tense moment, as they both absorbed all this. But Bruce could never hold still for too long.

"I'm going out there," he decided.

Emily stared at him. "What, where? Are you nuts? You're gonna go back out there? Out *there*?"

"That's what I just said."

"What, in a boat?"

"A plane."

"Oh, better. Because it's better to be *flying* out over the Atlantic when all of this is going on."

"Come with me."

"*What?*"

Bruce was serious. "We're never going to solve this thing sitting here scanning data."

"But the Navy doesn't want us out there," said Emily.

"This phenomenon is huge," said Bruce. "We can check it out and still stay close enough to approved flight lanes."

Emily narrowed her eyes skeptically. "Close enough?"

"We have an opportunity," said Bruce, "to observe a manifestation of what's going on out there while it's happening." And then he said the words that Emily, to her own frustration, just could not resist:

"We're looking for an answer. The answer's out there."

The *Weather Seeker* was Bruce's pride and joy—even though it didn't actually belong to him. He had pushed his department hard for the funding to acquire it and the equipment it carried. He had made do where possible, buying secondhand and carrying out reconditioning work himself and it showed. The plane's rear compartment was cluttered with near-obsolete components, jerry-rigged together, wires everywhere. What they lacked in neatness, they made up for in an almost comical complexity. Emily said later that she was reminded of nothing more than Captain Jay's sub—not a comforting thought in the circumstances.

But here was an even less comforting one: She had expected, at least, to be met at the airfield by a professional pilot—the sort with whom Bruce usually flew, leaving him free to monitor his students and his readings in the back. Not this time. This time, Bruce had the bit between his teeth, and he was flying this baby himself.

"You definitely know how to fly a plane?" asked Emily nervously, as they taxied out onto the tarmac.

"You've asked me, what, four, five times already?" said Bruce. "Ask me again. C'mon, no really, I want to hear you ask me again."

"You just seem like the kind of guy who takes a couple of lessons at something, loses interest, but still thinks he can do whatever–"

"I've been flying since I was sixteen." Bruce caught Emily's look, and protested, "Look at me, I'm flying!"

"You're taxiing," Emily corrected him. "And we're about to fly *waaaay* out over the ocean."

Bruce just grinned, and put on his headset–backwards. "Tower, this is WS Eleven Alpha, requesting... Oops, not good." Realizing his mistake, he turned the headset around and spoke into its microphone. He requested clearance for take-off, then turned to meet Emily's speechless glare. "It was a joke," he said. "You know, a joke?"

"WS Eleven Alpha," crackled a voice from the radio, *"you're cleared to Runway Two-Niner South."*

"How's the weather look out there today?" Bruce spoke into the microphone.

"Visibility fifty plus. Clear as spring water."

Bruce's expression darkened. He looked over at Emily again and shook his head soberly. And that was when she realized something.

She'd felt a hell of a lot more comfortable when he was being a jerk.

The weather report had been accurate–at least, to judge by the sky. It was crystal clear, blue. But for a couple of minutes now, the *Weather Seeker* had been shaking–just slightly at first, nothing out of the ordinary–but more and more strongly until, now, Emily and Bruce were being rattled in their seats.

"I assume this isn't regular turbulence," Emily ventured.

"You assume correctly," said Bruce. "We're being buffeted by weather."

To Emily's alarm, he leapt up from his seat and started

toward the rear of the plane. "Where are you going?!" she spluttered.

"Don't worry, autopilot's got it."

Emily watched the yoke moving on its own. She was not happy. Not happy at all. She hurried after Bruce, hoping that if she couldn't *see* the controls, she could forget they were unmanned. She found him at his weather stations, frantically typing and mousing new instructions into a lashed-up control panel. When she had come back here earlier, to fetch a couple of bottled waters from the cold locker, the readouts had seemed pretty even, lines keeping steady flows across the screens of battered old monitors. Now, they were fluctuating wildly.

She didn't want to be the hysterical non-professional but it was a hard instinct to suppress. She swallowed and said with as much detachment as she could muster, "Why hasn't anybody else reported this phenomenon? Other people have to have flown through this, or sailed."

"Not necessarily," said Bruce. "Right now it's a relatively small cell in a very, very big ocean."

Emily watched him working with his funky equipment until she couldn't take it any more. "What *is* this crap?" she burst out.

Bruce didn't seem to take offense. "Some of it's standard, off-the-shelf weather monitoring stuff. But these... and over there..." he waved a hand vaguely, "...those are my own creation."

Emily boggled. "You built these? You?"

"Just part of my genius," murmured Bruce, focused on his work, not really paying attention to her. She stared at his back. Was it possible that, beneath the immature exterior she had come to know and tolerate, he really was some kinda smart?

And then, all of Bruce's readings gave a violent jump—and he let out one word that didn't exactly inspire confidence:

"Uh-oh."

"Uh-oh what?" demanded Emily.

She got her answer sooner than she'd expected. The plane was slammed, hard. Her stomach became weightless as they dropped twenty feet in a fraction of a second.

"We're still forty miles from the center of the cell!" yelled Bruce as they leveled off, as Emily held on to the nearest panel for dear life. "How powerful is this thing?"

She pointed into the cockpit, through the windscreen, to the blue sky. "You keep saying 'cell.' Except there *is* no weather cell. Look out there!"

"Look in here!"

Bruce's readings were dancing crazily. The *Weather Seeker* was really getting banged about now, tossed and slammed from side to side. It was like riding in a paint shaker. Bruce seemed more excited than afraid—he'd flown through hurricanes before, if none quite like this—and Emily tried her best to trust him. But as a particularly violent lurch almost sent her spinning back into the cockpit, she felt her breakfast straining to leave her.

She made a grab for the closest thing to hand—a manila envelope, which fortunately proved to be empty—and barfed into it, wrapping her arm around a stanchion for balance. Bruce didn't take his eyes off his screens. "You should be about done," he commented after a few empty retches. "We didn't stop for lunch today."

"...think... it's time... we head back...?" said Emily queasily.

"We gotta do this."

"Do what?"

"Collect full data. We'll need it."

Emily looked at his console and blinked, as it swam out of focus. There was something. A *ripple*, across the weather stations, forward into the cockpit, making the windscreen shimmer for a moment before it was gone. Another trick of her tired eyes? She didn't think so—for when the ripple had passed, her vision was perfectly clear again.

"Did you see...?" she began tentatively.

And at that moment, the *Weather Seeker* took one humongous drop.

Even Bruce was caught unawares, and flung from his seat. He collided with Emily, and they went tumbling violently to the back of the plane.

Nobody at the weather stations. Nobody in the cockpit. Nobody at the controls.

They were tangled together awkwardly in a ball against the bulkhead—and Emily caught her breath as she realized that Bruce wasn't moving.

And that they were still falling.

CHAPTER 18

My stomach sank as Stan was bustled into Room D by a pair of grim-faced naval security guys. My first thought was that, whatever he'd been up to, he had well and truly blown it for us both, giving Landon all the reason she needed to clap us in irons for the rest of our naturals. My second thought was that she didn't need a reason.

It came as a surprise, then, when the Lieutenant Commander greeted Stan with a smile as if he'd just dropped in for a coffee, and told the guards to remove his plastic zip restraints. Stan gaped at the sight of her, and quickly turned to me for confirmation that he wasn't seeing things. I nodded ruefully: *It's her.*

"We'll be fine," said Landon, waving the security officers away. Then, once the door had closed behind them, she rounded on Stan and said mildly, "You should know better than to go wandering unescorted on a US military installation, Mr. Lathem. Especially in today's climate."

He didn't answer her. He was watching her nervously, his mind racing behind his eyes, as he said to me, "Heather's here. I saw her. They've got her hidden away in—"

"You're talking about our elderly guest in the infirmary?" Landon interrupted.

"Heather Sheedy," I said.

"She survived that plane crash," said Stan.

"The sole survivor," I added. And a flicker of an expression crossed Landon's face. I think she was disconcerted that we knew so much. I felt a surge of triumph, like we had the upper hand now—but it passed as I reminded myself that we were on Landon's turf.

Still, Stan was determined to press our advantage, however slight. "Why do you have her hidden away here?" he demanded to know.

"She's not hidden away," said Landon coolly. "You made your way in to see her without any difficulty, didn't you?"

"What about her family? Why aren't they here?"

"I'm afraid she has no family—other than her parents, and they died in the crash. So unfortunate."

"She has a grandfather!" stated Stan baldly. It was a challenge—and Landon hesitated for a moment as she considered it, studying the old guy's determined face.

"At her age," she said at last, "I doubt that very much."

"I saw him," said Stan.

It had happened at Heather's bedside, he told me later. Another Stan vision, almost subliminal. A cabin: simple, comfortable, with homemade furniture—and books, thousands of books. And a man: sixties, gray beard, longish hair, smoking a pipe. Where the "grandfather" part came from, I never did quite understand—but I could see from Landon's eyes that it was dead on the money.

"What about your guy?" Stan asked me. "Granger?"

Landon answered, "I've been trying to help Mr. Thomas understand that we have no record of any Mr. Granger such as he describes in our records."

Yeah, that was what she had been saying—and I hadn't tried to contradict her, hadn't wanted to show my hand. It was time now, though. Stan had Landon on the back foot—time to tip the bucket. "That's funny," I said, "because you were at his house yesterday."

Got her again. Another good one.

In for a penny... "You—or somebody you work with—also paid a visit to my publisher, and Eric Benirall of Benirall Shipping. You were very, very busy yesterday, Commander. Covering up... something."

And the polite façade vanished. Lt. Commander Landon was all icy business now, closing her file with a snap and shaking her head. "I think we're finished here," she said.

I blocked her path to the door. "I will find out what the Navy is doing," I promised, "at this base and out in the Atlantic. I will write about it."

Landon looked me squarely in the eye, no pretense between us now. "Writing it and getting it published where anyone will read it—those are two very different propositions," she growled. "I recommend you go back to writing about ghosts and UFO abductions—*those* stories will get published. Leave the US Navy—and our business—alone."

Then the mask was back. "Gentlemen," said Landon with a polite nod—and this time I let her pass; there seemed no point in obstructing her.

She paused in the doorway. She turned back to us, and in a quieter, less strident voice, she said, "Understand The Navy *is* a very positive force. It's just that we can't always do what we need to do in the bright glare of world scrutiny."

Then she was gone, leaving Stan and me to stare after her blankly, and to wonder what the hell she had meant by that.

We were escorted off the base politely but firmly. I watched the security officers as they disappeared back through the gate, and I simmered with resentment and frustration.

I was still glaring back at the facility when another gate opened and those unmarked dark blue vans and SUVs came sweeping out in tight formation. Stan was daydreaming, and I had to practically pull him out of the way to keep him from getting hit as the vehicles whooshed past us. In their midst was the Hummer, and I got a glimpse through its open rear window. An older man sat in the back seat, phone to his ear. Even from this distance, my reporter's senses got a definite vibe of power from him. He was some sort of extreme VIP.

THE TRIANGLE

Not that that did me any good. A moment later, and the vehicles were gone, disappearing down the street.

"We need to find her grandfather," said Stan, jerking me out of my thoughts.

"We already looked for relatives," I reminded him. "Phone books, school records. There was nobody. If there *is* a grandfather, the Navy has already gotten to him! He's not—"

"I don't think they have."

"If she has a grandfather out there, why can't anybody find—"

"I can," said Stan.

And something about the way he said it—so... not confidently, exactly, but just matter-of-factly—somehow, those two words worried me more than anything else I had experienced thus far.

I never did find the article I'd written about Stan—and I'm glad about that, in a way.

I do remember some of it, now. I know I hadn't met the guy. He'd been called in by the Miami PD to consult on a missing persons case. That was my story. He'd been getting all the credit for finding two lost kids—a brother and sister, I think. Of course, I'd taken the opposing view, decrying this waste of police resources, poking holes in Stan's evidence, describing how any of us could have done what he'd done with a little bit of luck and a whole lot of misdirection.

I was writing for a more influential paper than *The Observer* in those days.

There was still a part of me that thought I had been right. That part was shrinking, almost gone, but it remained fiercely defensive. And it didn't matter a bean—because as we pulled up outside Stan's place, I still felt a stab of guilt in my heart.

Stan lived in one of the less salubrious areas of town, in a 1950s stucco apartment building, cheaply constructed, pink walls with gold flecks. His living room was poky, sharing space with a modest dinette, and his furniture had seen better days. As I waited in there—Stan had gone through to the bedroom without saying a word, and was up to I-knew-not-what in there—my eyes fell upon a cabinet strewn with mementos of his brief "career." Newspaper clippings with, stories of kids found, photos of Stan in crazy seventies' lapels with old talk show hosts—I recognized Merv Griffin and Mike Douglas from my childhood.

It didn't seem much to show for a life. Little more than a hint of what might have been—and immediately, I regretted any part I may have played in that. By the time I'd written about Stan, of course, his heyday, such as it was, had already passed; still, I'd given him a kick just when he'd been trying to pick himself back up. Maybe, if I'd taken the trouble to talk to him then, and to listen, to get to know the man behind the story...

I heard soft footsteps, turned—and did a double take at the sight of Stan in the bedroom doorway, stripped down, wearing only a pair of crisp, new, white boxer shorts. He looked at me with a mournful expression, then turned and disappeared again. I wasn't sure if I was meant to follow. I wasn't sure I wanted to.

I found the old guy standing beside his single bed. He had just pulled down the window shades, plunging the room into gloom and casting a strange pastel pall upon his alabaster skin. I noticed that the sheets, the blankets, the pillow had all been stripped off his bed, leaving only the white bottom sheet.

Stan perched on the edge of the mattress, looking small and weak. "The images I see," he said, "they come to me randomly, always unclear."

"Gee, I hadn't noticed," I said—wishing I hadn't spoken at all when Stan looked up at me, no reproach in his eyes, just an apprehension bordering on dread.

"There's only one way I know to actively bid the images to me," he said.

I looked at the bare bed, and the almost bare Stan. I wasn't seeing it. "You want to give me a clue here?"

Stan reached into the nightstand drawer, and I saw that his hand was trembling. He rummaged out something black and tubular, about six inches long, but I didn't get a good look at it. Then he lay back on the bed, and stared up at the ceiling. He took the tubular thing and curled his hands around each end of it, then rested them lightly on his abdomen.

"Wait outside," said Stan. "Keep the door closed. Give me twenty-five minutes. No more than twenty-five minutes. Then, come in and... wake me. Any way you can."

All this weird talk was starting to freak me out. "Stan, c'mon," I said, "this is—"

"Go!" he barked with surprising intensity.

I retreated, taking one last look through the crack of the door as I closed it behind me. I saw Stan taking a long, deep breath, then closing his eyes.

And then he just lay there, stone still, his chest and his clasped hands rising and falling in a slow, steady rhythm.

Twenty-five minutes seemed to crawl by. I tried pacing, but Stan's living room was too small, forcing me to turn round so often that I started to get dizzy. I looked at my watch a hundred times, and always less time had passed than I had imagined.

At last, though, the deadline approached, and I stood and counted down the last minute and a half. I concentrated on the flickering numbers on my watch, and tried not to think about what I would find in the bedroom.

There was no reply to my first tentative knock, so I called out Stan's name and knocked louder. Still nothing.

I eased open the door, my heart pounding in anticipation.

Stan was still on the bed, lying on his back. He didn't seem to have moved at all. But he was wearing something now... wasn't he? In the muted light, I couldn't tell for sure, but there was something different about him.

"Stan?"

The old guy's breath caught in a deep, long rasp. It sounded as if his respiratory system was restarting after being shut down—and, come to think of it, I couldn't be sure I'd heard him breathing before. I hurried over to the bed—and as I did so, my eyes widened at the realization of what I was seeing.

Stan's body was no longer bare—but it wasn't clothed either. It was covered with... writing. Black script—letters, numbers symbols, spaced haphazardly, all different sizes and orientations. It blanketed every inch of him, like a madman's tattoos. Angling down his skin, across his pale torso across his boxer shorts even onto the bed sheet. Covering it all. His face was bathed in sweat, and he was as pale as... well, as paper.

Stan's eyes were open, but glassy, unfocused. It took him several moments to regain control of his motor response—then, with great effort, he began to sit up. I helped him, exposing a perfect, blank outline on the sheet where his body had lain.

He dropped his legs over the edge of the bed, looked down at his right hand. He was still holding that black tubular thing, and I saw what it was now. A pen, of course. A black marker pen. In the heat of Stan's trance, it had been cracked in two, the black ink pooling onto the bed sheet beside his thigh.

Beyond spent, Stan stared at the sea of words that swirled over him. Then he looked up, meeting my eyes with an apprehensive gaze as if he had just revealed to me the deepest secret of his soul.

CHAPTER 19

Stan was sitting on his bed, a pad and a ballpoint pen in his hand. Whatever he had been through, it had left him utterly exhausted, but he wasn't about to quit. He was straining to make out the words on his body, on the bed sheet, to transcribe them. As for me...

In the old days, I would have looked for an excuse. I'd have told myself I hadn't actually witnessed this alleged trance of Stan's, that twenty-five minutes was long enough for him to have faked all this. I didn't do that. My typical stoicism had gone right out the window. I accepted, without question, that all this was real, that this was the weirdest thing I'd ever seen anybody do.

"This is the only way you could have..." I ventured.

"It's called auto-writing," said Stan.

"I know what auto-writing is. But this—"

"I can't be conscious when I do it. I've tried holding paper, but my hand just immediately writes off the page. This is the only way I've found to... to..."

He was having a hard time seeing the words on his side. I hesitated for a moment, then I beckoned to him to hand me the pad and I took over copying duty.

"It all looks like nonsense," I commented. "None of it makes any sense."

"I can't control what comes through," said Stan. "It just flows. And I have no idea where it comes from. But if I enter into the state with some specific information I want... need... then..."

"Uh, Stan..."

I indicated a spot on the old guy's side, where I had just seen something impossible, where his scrawled letters, numbers, and arcane hieroglyphs had combined into something that actually made sense to me. "I've got a name here."

And not just any name; not a few letters thrown together by chance into a word as was likely to happen in the midst of even the most impenetrable gibberish. This was a name— a surname, at least—that I knew.

"Okay," I said, "so we found the name 'Karl.'"

"And the last name 'Sheedy'", Stan reminded me—as if I could have forgotten.

"What *looks* like the name Sheedy," I corrected him. Couldn't resist it. My cynicism, making a belated effort to reassert itself. "Looked more like 'she pig' to me."

Stan flicked through the pages of his pad. "And someplace else, it says 'Highway 1.'" And this, I couldn't refute.

That was why we were in my Volvo again, sweeping south along the seven-mile Overseas Highway that snakes out over the ocean between the tip of Florida and Key West. The weather, and the view, were breathtaking.

"And 'Mile Marker 47,'" I muttered. Turning to Stan: "What, you couldn't have come up with an actual address? Or a phone number maybe?"

Stan took the ribbing in good humor, the way it was meant. Still, I had a sick feeling in the pit of my stomach at the thought that, just a few days earlier, I would never, ever have done something like this, never have given the slightest credence to information obtained in this way. Auto-writing, for God's sake. Right at that moment, I didn't know which would make me feel worse: if this lead panned out, or if it didn't.

There was a turnoff just past the mile marker. A travesty of a road, thick with mud, the Everglades crowding us from each side. And finally, even this, too, came to an end, and we were forced to get out of the car and plow onward by foot.

"There's no road," I complained, after what seemed like an adequate length of time to show willing. "What the hell can be out—"

And with perfect timing, we pushed our way through into a clearing, and we found it.

Karl Sheedy lived in a small cabin home, surrounded on all sides by the thick green. An elaborate natural water capture system was attached to the cabin's side, and there were stacks of wood and washtubs and smoke trailing from a pair of chimneys. "If this is him," I breathed, "no wonder the Navy couldn't find him."

The front door was ajar, so I eased it open and called in, "Hello?"

Inside, there was homemade furniture and thousands of books, just as Stan had described—and chopping sounds coming from the kitchen. We crossed to it, and saw a woman standing with her back to us. A woman in her sixties, dressed in simple country clothes. "Ma'am..." I said—and at the sound of my voice, she spun around, startled.

"Who are you?" she demanded in a shriek. "What do you want?" Obviously, she wasn't used to receiving visitors.

"We're not here to harm you," I said quickly.

Stan was just staring at her, his jaw open. "Heather?"

At first, I wondered what he was talking about. Then I looked back at the woman, and I saw it, too. It was *her*. Her hair was different, but, it was the woman from the plane. "My God—"

"Who are you men? What do you want here?"

"It's all right, Heather," said Stan, "I—"

"What is this about Heather?" cried the woman. Then, instantly concerned: "Has something happened to her? Is she all right?"

And it started to dawn on me. "Ma'am," I said. "We're sorry to disturb you. We came looking for... a man. A man with a granddaughter named Heather. Heather is *your* granddaughter, isn't she?"

The woman was still wary of us. She didn't know whether to acknowledge her identity or not. I gave her what I hoped was a comforting smile, and said, "She looks... just like you."

"Like I did when I was six," said the woman, nervously. "How do you know Heather? Please, for God's sake, tell me what–"

"We've seen her," said Stan, "been with her. She's all right" But the woman could see it in his eyes. She knew there was something more–that something was wrong.

The back door opened, and a man entered carrying a fishing pole and a string of fish. A man with a gray beard and longish hair, smoking a pipe–like the main room of the cabin, instantly familiar. Karl Sheedy had the look of an academic gone native. And he froze at the sight of Stan and me, his fish falling to the kitchen floor, hitting it with a wet slap.

"Alice?"

"They say they're here about Heather!" said the woman.

"What about Heather? Who are you?" Sheedy's eyes narrowed in suspicion, his body language defensive. "Are you with the Project?"

It took me a moment to make the connection. Then: "You mean the project out in the Atlantic? The Navy Project?" I could see it in Karl Sheedy's eyes: I had hit pay dirt.

But there was something else: He considered the two of us a real threat.

We sat around the kitchen table. Alice Sheedy's eyes were glistening with tears and her husband was squeezing her hand tightly. "Oh, God..." she sobbed, "Jimmy..."

Karl Sheedy looked up at Stan and me, and said in a hollow voice, "Jimmy... our son... Heather's father. His wife, Allison..."

In the excitement of the search, I hadn't thought ahead to this part. I hadn't considered the fact that, when we found Heather's family, we would be bringing them news that would be unbearable for any parents. I hadn't thought about how we would break it to them, hadn't practiced the words. I remembered the passenger list for the 747: Heather's mother and father, sitting to each side of her.

And there was worse to come.

Karl Sheedy took a quaking breath. "I tried to warn them," he whispered. "Tried to get them to join us out here." Then, hopefully: "You said Heather is where?"

"There's something you need to know about Heather," said Stan softly. "She survived the plane crash. But she... *aged.* She's no longer a six-year-old girl."

I flinched, afraid that this absurd statement was going to blow it for us. But Karl Sheedy seemed neither shocked nor confused. His eyes flickered across to meet his wife's, and she had the same look. Dread.

Emboldened by this, scenting a trail once more, I spoke up: "Sir... before you mentioned 'the Project.' Did you... are you somehow involved in what's going on out in the Atlantic?"

Karl Sheedy didn't reply. But in his haunted eyes, I could see the heavy burden he was carrying.

It was still an eye-achingly beautiful day. We walked along the shoreline, a narrow strip of sand—just Sheedy, Stan, and me, leaving Alice in the cabin, to her grief.

Sheedy was in a contemplative mood, staring out across the ocean. Finally, I prompted, "Did you work out there?"

He took a few more moments before he replied, "Not only worked out there. I, sir, am responsible for it."

As Stan and I absorbed this revelation, Sheedy picked up a seashell and studied it absently. I knew that expression. He was retreating into the past. So often, it's easier to wallow in memories than it is to confront the present.

"There were two of us," he said quietly, almost to himself. "My partner's name was Osserman. Victor. We were members of the Physics Department at Florida State. Undistinguished. Neither of us tenured. Just... teaching. Victor's brother-in-law worked laying deep ocean cable. South Atlantic. He called Victor one day. Seems whenever they'd hit a particular stretch of ocean, the cable would suddenly be sheared in two. But each time they recoiled the cable, it was somehow several hundred feet shorter. So, as a favor, Victor and I went out there. Never been so seasick in my life. Anyway, we discovered what was shearing the cable. Boy, did we discover it..."

Another few moments, then he delivered the punch line: "Exotic matter."

"You discovered exotic matter?" I sneered, my cynical

reflex kicking right in before I could stop it.

Sheedy gave an almost dismissive shrug, as if it didn't matter to him in the slightest if I believed him or not. "A 'window' onto it, yes. Centered out in the Atlantic."

"What's exotic—" Stan began.

"Some sort of super matter," I explained. "It's one of the things UFO wackos theorize little green men use to make their ships." With properties ranging from negative mass to negation of gravity, depending on which wackos you believed.

"It's a highly stressed matter with enormous tensile strength," said Sheedy. "The tension of exotic matter exceeds its energy density. Up until our discovery, science had only hypothesized its existence as a result of solutions to Einstein's equations for General Relativity."

Not that I quite followed all that—but two words stood out for me. "Einstein's Relativity? As in... the bending of time? Wormholes?"

"That is one of the more controversial subsets of Einstein's work," said Sheedy. "But, yes. Proximity to an occurrence of exotic matter could theoretically distort time." He was turning the seashell in his hand, allowing his memories to transport him to the past again.

"Victor and I went back to the school, spent sixteen months worrying the data, fought like cats and dogs." He was shaking his head reflectively. Clearly, whatever he and his colleague had fought about, it seemed so trivial to him now. "Victor could be such an asshole," Sheedy recalled, "and I was worse. We were just about to publish when the Navy showed up. Someone there had gotten wind of what we were about to reveal to the world. They prevailed upon us not to publish. Instead Victor went to work for them."

"You didn't?" I queried.

Sheedy shook his head.

Stan spread an arm wide to indicate the strip of beach, the jungle behind it, Sheedy's own private island. "How did you end up being out here? Why are you—"

"Because of what I suspect is coming," said Sheedy. "And..." He turned, and fixed us with a sorrowful gaze. "I'm a coward."

CHAPTER 20

Early morning.

I was still asleep, dreaming of being pursued through empty houses by Dark Suits, my visit to the Hichen Naval Command Center still looming on the horizon. Bruce and Emily were still crunching numbers in the university lab. And Meeno Paloma's old, beige SUV was parked at the curb outside a well-tended house.

Meeno stood beside it, watching as a paperboy did his rounds. He had always known he had to come here. He'd put it off as long as he could—but last night, lying awake on the sofa, afraid to close his eyes in case the world changed again when he wasn't looking, he had come to a decision. It was time to face it. Maybe then he could lay his waking nightmares to rest.

A light came on in a downstairs window, and Meeno took a steadying breath and moved up the walk. He rang the bell, and waited.

The door was opened by a middle-aged woman in a bathrobe. She looked pale, haggard, as she had every reason to. The woman's name was Cathy, and she had been married to Don Beatty—the lawyer who had organized the Greenpeace intervention run that had ended in tragedy.

The man whose corpse Meeno had seen—had *thought* he'd seen—in his shower.

"Meeno," said Cathy, surprised to see him.

This was so very hard for him—for both of them. He stumbled through an apology for not having come before, but Cathy just gave him a hard look. "I'd like to come in," he said, and she considered for a moment. Then she stepped away from the door, leaving it open. Evidently, this was as close to an invitation as she was prepared to offer right now. Meeno had to take it.

He entered the house.

The living room was in some disarray. Paper plates and cups were scattered around, and a display of framed photos and albums had been set out on a table. "Excuse the place," said Cathy, with an accusing edge to her voice. "We had Don's wake last night."

Meeno looked at some of the photos: Don Beatty as a younger man, a vital man, smiling at him from the past. "We had almost everybody from the local Greenpeace chapter," said Cathy. "And of course, families of the survivors." A painful moment of eye contact. "You understand why you weren't invited."

Meeno felt as if he had been punched in the stomach. He had come here for some measure of absolution, for closure. Much as he blamed himself for what had happened, he hadn't really expected Cathy to blame him, too. He had hoped she would understand. He had hoped she would help him to understand.

"Cathy... I wish I knew what to..." He swallowed, steeling himself. "I did everything I could out there. Everything I knew how. I've been on the sea all my life and what happened out there, it wasn't... there was no logic to it."

"No logic? Including the fact that you were the only one to live?" She was obviously hurting bad. Meeno didn't know what he could say.

Then, the piercing whistle of a kettle came from the kitchen. "I was fixing tea," said Cathy. "Don always liked tea in the morning instead of coffee. Twelve years of marriage, it's become my routine as well. Would you like a cup?"

It wasn't much of an offer, more a challenge. Meeno knew Cathy was angry with him—but he also thought that if he could stay a while longer, maybe she could get over it. Maybe he could help her—and, in the process, somehow help himself. He nodded, and she turned and shuffled away through a swinging door. A moment later, the shriek of the kettle ceased.

Meeno's eyes were drawn to the displayed photos again, and he was disconcerted to find his own face looking back at him. A younger face, from more carefree times. In the photo, Meeno was standing beside an apron-wearing Beatty at a fundraiser barbecue, a big Greenpeace banner partially visible behind them. Meeno remembered that day; he remembered the photograph being taken. And, floating for a moment on a current of bittersweet recollection, he didn't notice that somebody else had entered the room from the bedrooms.

"Oh, hey, Meeno!"

Meeno's head shot up. His stomach sank into his shoes. There had been no warning, no clue that his world was about to go mad again. But...

"Gee, brother, you're the last person I was expecting to see here this morning."

Don Beatty had just bustled into his own living room, knotting his tie, getting ready for work. It had to be a hallucination, but it felt completely real. As real as when Meeno had last seen his friend alive, on the Greenpeace raft. Or as real as when he had last seen him, in the shower.

"What's the matter?" asked Beatty. "What are you doing here so early anyway?"

Meeno looked at the table. The photos were gone. Somehow, he found the strength—and the presence of mind—to call out a hoarse plea. "Cathy!"

"She in the kitchen?" asked Don. "I gotta tell her I don't have time for breakfast this morning. Give me one sec, I'll be right back to you."

And he headed for the swing door—but Meeno couldn't let him go, couldn't let him out of his sight. Not until Cathy saw this, proved to Meeno that it wasn't just him, that he wasn't delusional. He reached out and grabbed Beatty's shirt. It felt soft, cool, *real*, and Meeno froze. It felt as if he was really touching his friend—his friend whom he had thought was dead. He didn't know whether to be relieved or terrified.

Beatty looked at him askance. "I'm only going to the kitchen."

And then, like an angel sent to save him, Cathy reappeared holding two cups of tea. Meeno caught his breath, waiting for her reaction, waiting to see if she could see what he could see. He thought she might scream or faint, probably drop the cups; worst case scenario, look right through Beatty as if he wasn't there.

She did none of those things. Cathy greeted her husband with a casual "Morning, honey," and a light peck on the cheek. She handed him a cup, and offered the other to Meeno. He didn't take it.

She was still in her bathrobe, but her demeanor had completely changed. She was back to her old, buoyant self, the Cathy that Meeno remembered. The Cathy that hadn't just been widowed, hadn't just had to bury her husband.

Don Beatty put his arm around his wife, and regarded their visitor with curiosity. "So, tell me," he said, "what can I do for you this morning?"

Meeno took refuge in his unchanged bedroom, sitting at the small table that he and Helen used to do bills. He had closed the door and drawn the shades, working in the harsh glow of the table light. He had rescued the last few days' papers from recycling, spread them out in front of him. All the newspaper accounts of the Greenpeace incident. He was frantically scanning each of them, finding lists of the deceased, finding that one name was no longer among them.

"Don was there," he muttered repeatedly under his breath, clinging on to what he knew was true even as everything told him it couldn't be. "Don was there. He died with the others. I saw him drown."

He was looking at a memorial page. Headshots of the deceased. Just a few days ago, Don Beatty's headshot had been among them. It wasn't now. The other photos had shifted around, the layout of the page changing to close up the gap.

His eyes red-rimmed, Meeno stared at the pictures as if he expected them to shift again beneath his gaze.

THE TRIANGLE

That was when he spotted another article. *My* article, based on our brief interview, rattled off in an hour before I went to answer Benirall's summons. My face, pictured beside a boxed sidebar with the headline BERMUDA TRIANGLE 'FACTS' AND FALLACIES—YOUR TRI EXPERT EXPLAINS IT ALL. And although he never said as much, I'm sure Meeno must have grimaced in disgust.

He stared at the article, then raggedly tore the sidebar from the paper. He continued to stare at it for several minutes longer. Maybe, if he had made a different decision, if he had chosen to call me then at the very least, I could have assured him that he wasn't alone.

But then, why *would* he have called me? It was the last thing Meeno was prepared to believe: That the Triangle was, in some way, connected to all that had happened to him. I know how that must have felt. And he would have been telling that story to me, to the one person he thought was most likely to laugh in his face. Maybe a part of him wanted that—wanted that final confirmation that he was insane. And maybe another part of Meeno knew it wasn't necessary, was sure that nothing I could say could make a difference to him.

He had made his decision.

He crumpled up the newspaper cutting and thrust it into his pocket. He opened a dresser drawer and rummaged under a pile of shirts for the gun he kept hidden there in case of need. He turned it over in his hands as he contemplated the release it would bring him.

Meeno drove his car onto an ocean breakwater, skidding to a halt a little too close to the edge. He had already drunk four cans of beer as he'd driven around in search of a suitably deserted spot. There were two cans left, piled up with the empties on the passenger seat. He cracked them open, one after another, drained them, and tossed them aside. Then he turned and looked at the handgun, nestled in the cans' midst. But it didn't seem right.

He climbed out of the car, unsteadily, leaving the gun behind. He stood on the edge of the breakwater, and he looked out across the intransigent sea, the source of all his agony. The sea that had saved his life, then made that life hell. All he had to do was step over the edge, and the sea would take him as maybe it should have taken him the first time, sweep him away as if he'd never been. His life in exchange for Don Beatty's—and then everyone else could be happy. It seemed fitting.

He had left a note for Helen and Ruben—for Dylan too, if the sea would only grant him one final request and make the boy real. It was a long, meandering account of all he had seen, an outpouring of his feelings, of all he had been unable to say to their faces. It was an apology for abandoning them. An assurance that it was for the best, because *he* was the problem—his continued existence, anyway.

And then, he saw something that changed everything.

Out over the sea, a storm had appeared. Black, laden clouds, shot through by forks of lightning. It was growing out there. Like a malignancy, thought Meeno—because whatever this storm was, it was certainly not natural. It had sprung up too quickly, without warning. And somehow it was connected to him—and to the Triangle.

He wasn't insane. This was real.

And it was coming this way.

The storm had built with impossible speed, and Meeno could feel the first traces of wind stirring his hair. He heard the crashing of thunder, and he could see, in the shapes of the churning clouds, the suggestions of other shapes—manmade shapes. Airplanes. Of various types, from all eras.

If Meeno had known all the stories of the Triangle, if he'd studied them as I had, then he might have recognized some of those planes: Five Avenger Torpedo Bombers like those of Flight 19, and a Martin Mariner flying boat of the type that went in search of them in 1945; a Phantom fighter jet like the one that dropped off the radar in 1971, a search party reporting a rectangular "area of disturbance" in the ocean over which it was last seen; two KC-135 Stratotankers, similar to the ones lost in 1963, presumed the victims of an in-flight collision—until the two wrecks were discovered one hundred and sixty miles apart...

...a modern-day 747 that could only have been United

THE TRIANGLE

Airlines Flight 28 to Zurich.

But one thing Meeno *did* know—one thing he felt with every fiber of his being as he looked out across the sea that had become a stranger to him, as he gaped slack-jawed at this amazing phenomena...

He knew that something was coming.

Something bad.

CHAPTER 21

"You know what," said Bruce in a muffled voice, his face buried in Emily's back, "I think it's time we headed back in."

"If you insist," said Emily, trying to match his forced casual tone although she was screaming inside. She was just relieved that her pilot was still conscious after all, and that the *Weather Seeker* had come out of its drop. For now. She couldn't bear to think about what might have happened if he'd left her alone up here. She couldn't tear her eyes away from the unattended controls, the yoke jerking around as if shaken by a spectral hand. They had to be well off their flight path by now. What if they encountered another plane? Was the autopilot sophisticated enough to avoid a collision, even in these conditions?

But then, who else was crazy enough to be flying in this sort of weather?

They disentangled themselves from each other, helped each other to their feet, straining their muscles to counter the plane's violent lurching. Bruce labored towards the cockpit. He was thrown off-course several times, but finally made it to the pilot's seat and took the yoke. But they were far from out of the woods.

THE TRIANGLE

The sky around them was still clear, still blue—but that seemed to count for nothing. They were still taking one hell of a beating.

It was still a fine day where I was, a light ocean breeze cooling my face and ruffling my hair as I stood on the shore behind Karl Sheedy's cabin.

Sheedy had become quite talkative. Perhaps he appreciated the chance to unburden himself after all these years. Perhaps he was thinking about his granddaughter, and knew he had already waited too long.

"Victor and I started out just trying to discover something," he said, "prove something that the world only knew as a theory. But the Navy, they wanted it to have a function. They wanted something they could use."

Suddenly angry at the memory, he threw his seashell into the water. "It was all just a theory," he said bitterly. "Theories can't hurt anybody, right? Can't end anything."

"What do you mean," I asked, "'something they could use'? Use it for what?"

"They're the Navy," said Sheedy, witheringly. "The military. What do you think they'd want to use it for?" The waves were beginning to lap against his shoes, but he didn't move his feet.

And suddenly, I remembered something I had heard once: That Albert Einstein regretted giving the world the atomic bomb.

"What do you think is going to happen, Doctor?" asked Stan, quietly.

But Sheedy had returned to his own private world. "Little Heather used to love to visit me at my lab," he murmured, staring down at his wet feet. "She was there one day when one of our tabletop experiments got out of control. She was in my office, drawing but she still might've been exposed to something a force that was sloughed off..." He shrugged, and I realized that for all his expertise Sheedy was still uncertain, fumbling in the dark.

"Maybe it somehow affected her," he conjectured. "Maybe that's why she didn't disappear from that plane, but all the others did."

"Exposed to what?" I pressed him. "Dr. Sheedy?"

Sheedy just shrugged again—but I needed answers. "Doctor," I said, "what are you and your wife hiding from?"

"I'm not certain," he confessed. "Maybe nothing. Maybe..." He took a deep breath. "If it comes, I expect it will be electromagnetic in nature. At least to begin. But it won't stop there."

Sheedy paused again, as if hoping he could leave it at that. But then he caught my stubborn gaze, and seemed to decide that he'd said enough already, that he may as well continue, tell us the rest.

"Why isn't it getting any better? It seems to be getting worse."

Bruce had managed to turn the *Weather Seeker* around. It was headed back west now, but it was like the invisible storm was following it, reluctant to relax its grip. He was fully focused on the controls, more nervous than Emily had seen him. He answered her question without sparing her a glance. "The farther we get from the cell, the more the energy should dissipate."

"Should," she said, "but entropy doesn't want to apply out here, remember?" She clung on to her seat as the plane rocked madly. "We can outrun this thing, right?" she asked, desperate for reassurance. When it didn't come, she repeated, in a higher-pitched voice, "*Right?*"

Bruce was staring out the windscreen at something. Emily followed his eyes, and gasped. The storm was starting to appear, and it was one big mother. Dark, ugly, roiling clouds formed out of nowhere, filling the sky—like reality was just catching up with the weather station readings. Emily and Bruce just gaped, pole axed by the power of what they were seeing. It dwarfed the *Weather Seeker*, spitting out stabs of lightning at it. And, illuminated in those flashes, they could see other airplanes—rippling as if they had no right to exist on this material plane.

The ghosts of those machines that had flown this cursed route before them.

"Electromagnetism isn't just the electricity that comes out of the wall. It's the force underlying all matter, all space, all time. We, humanity, exist only by a quite remarkable courtesy. Even the slightest change in any number of basic laws or fundamental constants and we never would have been here in the first place. Upset any one of those laws or constants now, and all of this..." Sheedy indicated the world around us.

All of it could just... it could all just cease to be."

I laughed. Really, that's what I did. Just a nervous chuckle—because what he was saying, the magnitude of it all, it was just too big. "You're overstating," I said. "Exaggerating. C'mon, you've got to be. " But Sheedy's expression stopped me in my tracks. He wasn't overstating anything.

"What is that game that children..." Sheedy began vaguely, before answering his own question. "Chicken. Victor and those with him are playing chicken with all creation. They could win. Or—"

It took me a few seconds to find my voice. "If what you're saying were to happen," I said, "you realize, you and your wife won't be safe even here."

"Nobody will be safe anywhere," murmured Stan.

But I could tell from Sheedy's eyes that he knew this already. He knew it far better than anyone. It was the very thing he had been trying to avoid facing, the one thing he didn't want to face now—though I didn't know which he had been running from the hardest: the threat itself, or his own part in its creation.

We had to stop him from running. Bring him back.

"Your granddaughter is alive, Doctor," said Stan. "She's scared beyond words—and surrounded only by strangers. Don't you want to be there for her? With her?"

"Come back with us," I said. "Please. If you speak up, people will listen. I swear to you they will. I'll see that they do." And I pleaded with him: "You can try to stop this, sir. Somebody has to. Let us help you do it."

Alice Sheedy waved goodbye to us from the doorway of her cabin, left behind for the illusion of security it might give her, her face nevertheless taut with concern for her husband. A few minutes later, we were back on the Overseas Highway, racing north, the ocean blurring past to each side of us. I was on my cell, trying to get hold of Bruce at the university—but my gaze kept straying to the rearview mirror, to Stan and Sheedy. I think a part of me couldn't quite believe we'd done it, that we'd solved the mystery, that I had the proof in my backseat. I half expected Sheedy to up and vanish, like Sally in the bathtub or Bill Granger's reflection.

Bruce wasn't around; Emily neither. I left them a message. "This is Howard Thomas. Tell them I'm coming in, and I'm..." I lowered my voice, as if it would keep Sheedy from hearing "...bringing a guy with me. Somebody who's gonna bust this whole thing wide—"

I broke off. The guy at the other end of the line was saying something—asking me to repeat myself, I think—but his words were drowned in static. "Can you hear me?" I called, frustrated. "You're breaking up. Howard Thomas. I should be there in about three hours. Three—"

"My God!" cried Sheedy. "What is that? What's happening?"

And Stan screamed my name.

I almost leapt out of my seat. I forgot the phone. I focused on the road ahead, my foot going to the brake pedal. But there was nothing.

My eyes flicked to the mirror again. Stan and Sheedy were still there, present and correct—but they were staring out of their windows in horror. Not wanting to take my attention off the road, I stole a quick look to my left.

Nothing unusual, at first glance. Just a few cars, whizzing along beside us. But, on a second glance...

They were disappearing. Randomly. One, then another... another... And the cars in front of us, too. Just... just popping out of existence.

And there was something else up there. SomethingGiant cranes. Just materializing at the sides of the road, two hundred yards ahead, lifting huge girders. As if, somehow, time had gone backwards, and the highway was suddenly under construction again.

All the other cars were gone now. We were alone on the

road—and I was only just beginning to register what this might mean, beginning to fear that we might blink out of existence before we even knew it. Before we could tell anyone what we knew.

But then, I had a more pressing problem—because the highway was beginning to dissolve behind us like a fast-burning fuse, its end speeding toward my bumper. And I was about to step on the gas when I saw that it was happening in front, too. From where the cranes were, about a hundred yards away now—where construction workers were beginning to appear, laboring on the highway's jagged edge.

My foot was on the brake again—but I *couldn't* brake.

And then the end of the road caught up with us, reached the underside of my car, and there was nothing at all beneath us.

Nothing but the open sea, and that was two hundred feet down...

...and closing...

"*Get us out of this!*"
"*I'm trying!*"
Emily was hyperventilating like she was in a Lamaze class. Bruce was wrestling with the controls, giving it everything he'd got. But still, the storm was gaining on them. The *Weather Seeker* was dwarfed by a ceiling of raging clouds. Lightning, thunder, and rain exploded from within its black mass. It was almost as if the storm itself were a living entity, pursuing them.

And then the clouds blotted out the sun altogether, and the cockpit of the plane darkened. Rain pounded down on the fuselage; lightning stabbed at it, bolts worthy of Zeus himself. The light and the sound and the sheer force was unbearable.

Instruments began to spin haywire. The yoke flew from Bruce's grip.

And just that quickly, they were going down again.

The ocean was growing larger through my windshield,

racing up to meet us like we were on a Six Flags Ride From Hell.

When we hit, it was like being smashed into a concrete wall. I was thrown forward, arrested by my seatbelt, dazed. Glass shattered; airbags erupted. I didn't know where I was for a moment. Seawater was already gushing in, pooling around my feet.

I fumbled with my seatbelt, tried to push the airbag aside, tried to blink away the stars in my eyes. I turned to the backseat. We were sinking fast from the rear, upending. The water was already churning at Stan and Sheedy's chin level. Sheedy was working at his seatbelt, but Stan...

Stan was unconscious. His head bobbed on the water.

"Help him!" yelled Sheedy.

I clambered over my seat, hampered by the airbag, catching my foot, plunging under, feeling for Stan's seatbelt release. I'd just found it when Stan began to struggle, loosing my grip. The water had hit his face, waking him, and he was panicking. I had to fight to get my hands on the release again, to hit it.

I pulled Stan from his seat and tried to surface, but the water had reached the roofline. I wrestled the old guy through to the front of the car, where there was still some air, and I shoved him out through the smashed driver's side window, watched him flailing as he tried to stay afloat.

Sheedy was still struggling, submerged now. His belt was stuck. My lungs were aching, and the car was almost completely swamped. I took a last gulp of air and tried to pull myself back down to the backseat. But the car lurched into a full upright position, and I was thrown back, jammed up against the windshield.

I kept pushing off the glass, trying desperately to get down to my trapped passenger. I couldn't make it. The car was sinking further, and I was almost out of air again. I stared helplessly at Sheedy, and saw the acceptance in his eyes, the absolution from guilt. He knew there was nothing I could do.

I tried not to look back. It was enough of a trial to pull myself out of the broken window, to strike out for the surface, before the black shapes that were crowding my vision could close in and steal my consciousness. I felt myself kicking madly, my legs feeling like rubber—and, just when I thought I couldn't kick again, I exploded into fresh air, gasping and spluttering.

The highway had gone altogether, now. Stan and I were alone, adrift, and I knew that neither of us had the strength to swim the three or four miles back to the shore. It was all I could do to tread water and keep the old guy afloat.

The sky was still bright and blue. I didn't notice that at the time—didn't have any reason to. It was only later, when I got to compare notes with Meeno Paloma, that I learned about the storm, learned that—from his perspective out on the breakwater—it had already engulfed the whole of Highway 1.

The *Weather Seeker* was diving, screaming, assaulted all the way down by whip cracks of lightning. Emily and Bruce were plastered back in their seats by the G-forces. Bruce had managed to get his hands on the yoke, and he was pulling back on it with everything he had. Emily could only watch, with saucer eyes, as the gray, choppy, storm-tossed ocean became visible through the front windscreen. They were heading right down into it.

Bruce braced his feet against the control panel, and used every ounce of his strength on the yoke—arms, legs, back—and slowly, painfully slowly, their perspective on the fast-approaching water changed.

Too slowly.

Emily looked at Bruce's face: red, veins protruding, a determined look like she had never seen on anybody in her life, like he was *going* to make this *damned plane* do *as it was told!*

And he began to do it. Emily caught her breath as she felt the *Weather Seeker* pulling out of its nosedive, praying that Bruce could level it off in time. Before they hit. And then they were flying straight and level again, still being rattled mercilessly by the elements, but *not plunging to their deaths*, and Emily looked at Bruce with relief—and surprise, because she realized now that she hadn't really believed he could do it. Maybe she was even a little impressed. If so, she kept it to herself.

"Are you going to be able to get us home?" she yelled over the din of the storm.

Bruce yelled back, "That's my definite plan!"

CHAPTER 22

Darkness sliced across Miami like someone had pulled a curtain.

It was followed, a few seconds later, by a torrent of freezing rain. People ran for cover, while those already inside moved to their windows and doorways to see this odd, instant downpour.

They were only curious, though, not afraid. I doubt a single one of them truly thought there was anything unnatural about the sudden storm. They couldn't have guessed what had caused it, nor what it presaged—and it was probably best that way.

By the time Stan and I arrived at the University of Florida, the storm had reached here, too. The rain lashed down, and students were running with books over their heads—while some tossed Frisbees, reveling in the surprise break from Miami's hot climate.

Our taxi splashed up to the science building, and we paid the driver with damp bills. The rain didn't bother us too much; we were still soaked from our unplanned swim, still thanking our lucky stars to be on dry land at all.

Stan had been running out of strength. It had taken all I had to keep both our heads above water. The waves had slapped at our faces, filling my mouth with the taste of salt, and I'd known we didn't have long. Then, suddenly, something enormous had begun to form in the water right next to us—so close that I thought we would be crushed. It was concrete. A concrete stanchion.

The highway had been returning. I could see construction cranes and workers again, in the distance—but as suddenly as they'd reappeared, they were fading again, and the road was stretched out over our heads as if it had always been there. I was clinging to Stan, and to a rusty rebar handgrip in the stanchion's side—a ladder to safety.

And it was as I was craning my neck to look to the top of that ladder that I realized the sky was suddenly cloudy.

In Bruce's research lab, we pulled on dry clothes bought on the fly from the Student Union: denim shirts over university golf shirts, chinos. Bruce had locked out his students—for their own sake, he'd said—and I could see their faces crowding the little window in the door, trying to see what was happening in here, as we exchanged stories.

Bruce's near-disaster in the *Weather Seeker* had become an exciting adventure in the retelling, of course—though I could tell from Emily's frown and from the odd, haunted look in Bruce's eyes, that even he had been more worried than he was prepared to admit.

He was more comfortable talking about what had happened to Stan and me—and both he and Emily were fascinated to hear about Karl Sheedy, albeit a little suspicious when Stan brought up his pet subject of Heather. I had to confirm to them that, yes, Stan was right—that he'd been right all along—and that Sheedy had been Heather's grandfather. "It was his discovery out in the Atlantic that started what the Navy is doing out there," I summarized. "He and his partner."

"But now he's dead?" asked Bruce, making sure he was understanding all this. "Fell off the Overseas Highway?"

"Somewhere between Mile Marker 94 and 95," I confirmed, "in about a hundred feet of water. In my car. Nobody knows about it." A horrible thought occurred to me, and I looked at Stan. "His wife doesn't know." As if we hadn't given that poor woman enough bad news already today.

Stan seemed out of breath, but he insisted when asked that he was all right. I resolved to keep an eye on the old guy.

"Okay," said Emily, skeptically, "so he's not here any more. But if he *were* here, what he would be saying is..."

"The Navy is definitely conducting some sort of experiment out there," I said. "Some kind of test."

"That's not exactly a fast-breaking bulletin," Bruce cut in.

I continued, "Using exotic matter."

And that stopped Bruce cold. He and Emily stared at me, and I shrugged. "That's what the man said."

"You can *say* anything," said Emily, uncertainly.

"I've interviewed hundreds of nut jobs," I reminded her. "This guy—"

"You can *say* anything!" she repeated—and I couldn't disagree with her.

But...

"*What if it's true?*"

"Exotic matter only exists in theory," said Bruce.

"So did radio waves," I said, "until Heinrich Hertz. Same with X-rays, and atoms, and a round earth. If exotic matter does exist—and this Sheedy guy said he and his partner discovered an instance of it out in the Atlantic—then this could be why the Navy is doing whatever they're doing at that precise location."

Emily and Bruce shared a look, as if each was looking for the other's reassurance that it was okay to even consider this. Bruce was the first to take the plunge, speaking in a thoughtful tone. "It could account for the energy extremes and all the unstable electromagnetic—"

"Great, fine," cried Emily, flinging up her arms in exasperation, "exotic matter, why not? So the Navy's just out there screwing around with space-time, hoping to do what exactly?" I gave her the same look that Karl Sheedy had given me when I'd asked that question. She got the message. "A weapon? They're trying to use something like this as a *weapon*?"

"It's not without precedent," I said.

And Bruce began to get jazzed again. "You realize—this could be it! The answer! Benirall's recent ship disappearances, everything we've been experiencing... all of it!"

He was subdued by Emily's cold glare. "*They're developing it as a weapon!*"

"Well, yeah, okay, that part's not real good."

"So what are we going to do about it?" asked Stan. Then he added two words that sent a chill down my spine—down all our spines—as the implications of them slowly sank in with the rest of us.

"We *know*."

Akerman was waiting for us at Eric Benirall's yacht berth, standing under an umbrella, his face etched with lines of concern. He explained, as we climbed out of Bruce's new-model SUV, that Benirall had left the office yesterday—in the middle of the day—and come straight to his luxury private yacht. "He's refused to see anyone. Until I told him *you* wanted to see him."

The yacht was a huge, dark shape cut out of a sheet of rain, and I felt a shiver of foreboding as I looked up at it. Its interior, too, was heavy with shadows, and eerily silent. As Akerman led the rest of us aboard, he called out tentatively to his employer but got no reply.

Stan suddenly flinched, and put a hand to his head. I asked him what was up, but he didn't know. "I've never felt..." he gasped. "It's like a vice..."

"You want to wait outside?" I asked. Stan shook his head, but winced at the effort.

"Mr. Benirall?" Akerman called again. Still nothing.

We eased our way into the main stateroom. I'd expected light in here, but the expansive window had been firmly shuttered, so the dark still held sway. I strained to make out what seemed to be a beautifully appointed living area: 52-inch TV, fully stocked bar, oak bookshelves... Then I blinked, and looked at the window again.

It wasn't shuttered at all—it was painted black. *Spray*-painted; uneven strokes straying onto the wall, like whoever had done it was in a damned big hurry. And the TV... its screen had been spray-painted, too. Emily had seen it; she nudged Bruce, and they shared an uncomprehending look. I turned to tell Stan, but he had his eyes closed, his hand pressed to his head, his teeth gritted.

I looked around the room again, and saw something I'd missed. A shape, low against the wall. A figure—sleepless, distraught, his hair mussed. Spent cans of spray-paint lay on the floor in front of him, another can held absently in his hands.

I frowned. "Benirall?"

And Eric Benirall turned his head to look up at us but his eyes were staring, vacant.

With Akerman's help, Benirall had been moved to a chair in the adjacent galley, and we'd turned on a few lights. Emily and Bruce, again, took the lead in explaining our findings, although most of them were *my* findings. I was just trying not to stare at the paint can that Benirall was turning absently in his hands.

"But you already suspected the Navy was doing something out in the Atlantic," he said, leaning tiredly against the dining table. He broke off to throw a quick aside at Akerman as he came fussing around with a glass of water. "Put some Glenfiddich in that and I might drink it." Then back to us: "How is anything the Navy might be doing out there capable of—"

Emily glanced at the rest of us, and decided to just go for it. "Because—we *think*—they may be exploring some radical new energy source."

"New energy source?"

"We believe the Navy may be out there," said Stan, evidently feeling a little better, "developing some sort of a new weapon."

I eyed the wet bar through the stateroom door. The mirror above it, the crystal decanters, even the glasses, had been wantonly spray-painted black. Akerman was gamely sniffing at the opaque containers, trying to find the scotch.

"Look, sir," said Bruce, "this storm. Normally, storms build. This one isn't doing that. It is spontaneously generating out over the Atlantic."

Benirall grimaced. "The Navy is controlling the weather? To develop a new weapon?"

"The weather could only be a symptom of–" I began, but my voice tailed off as Benirall got up and began to pace, ignoring me totally.

I suppose this was what you call irony. Now, I was the one with a fantastic story, wanting–*needing*–to convince everybody of the truth of it, knowing full well I would have dismissed it myself only a week before. I can't say I was comfortable with that thought.

Akerman delivered Benirall's drink; he sniffed at it and proclaimed it to be bourbon. Akerman made to take back the glass, but Benirall kept it. "What has any of this got to do with the Triangle?" he demanded. "With my ships disappearing? With the damn visions... the visions you were all having?" His hasty, mid-stream correction didn't go unnoticed by me; nor did the fact that Stan chose this moment to wince again as his headache spiked.

"What the Navy is doing," said Emily, "could be affecting the electromagnetic balance of that section of ocean."

"Electromagnetic balance?" repeated Benirall, dully.

"The Navy could be out there in the Atlantic right now," said Bruce, "sticking their big fat finger into a dark hole and stirring it around–and causing this weather, and ships to disappear, and time to come unstuck, and–" He was getting worked up at the possibilities, and Emily put a restraining hand on his arm. *Enough–let's try not to appear too crazy.*

"Maybe they think it all won't go too far out of control," I said. "Maybe they're too focused on their hoped-for results to care."

"You can't be sure of any of this," said Benirall.

"No, sir, we can't," admitted Emily. "But if even only a portion of it is true..."

"There are ships and planes still crossing the Atlantic," Stan pointed out. "And the weather hitting the state. The Navy hasn't warned anybody!"

"We need to do that!" I stated grimly.

Akerman stepped out of the background at this point. "What–you mean like go on TV, hold a press conference."

"If we bring it to light," I insisted, "the Navy will have to—"

"We go on TV," said Benirall, "and say the Navy is making it rain and causing ships to disappear?"

This stopped me in my tracks, making me feel that discomfort again. It was bad enough saying all this to one man but to say it on TV, in front of millions? If I'm honest, I'd been hoping Benirall would deal with that side of things—be the voice of authority—and we could just be the anonymous "experts" who had dug up the proof he needed. Fat chance of that.

But what choice did we have?

"You asked us to bring you an answer," I said. "We believe—the four of us believe—this may be your answer." I let that sink in for a moment, before I added, "At least, all that we can uncover. Only the Navy knows the rest."

Benirall carried on pacing, running his hand through his hair, deep in thought. There was a long, long silence. At last, he said, "Then we ask them."

"Them who?" frowned Emily. "The Navy?!"

"We've talked to the Navy," I said. "They've tried everything they can to keep us from finding out—"

"They'll lie!" said Emily, more succinctly.

"Sometimes," said Benirall, "you learn the most by what someone chooses to lie about." And in that moment, despite his current mental state, I got a glimpse of the impressive, take-charge businessman I'd always known Eric Benirall to be. "Is Douglas still in town?" he asked Akerman.

"I spoke with his adjutant at the Four Seasons just this morning."

"Douglas?" queried Stan.

"Douglas Weist," said Benirall.

Emily gaped. "The Secretary-of-the-Navy Douglas Weist?"

And I made a connection I'd been missing before. The old man in the back of the Hummer outside the naval base. The big VIP. Weist. The name on Granger's lips before he died...

I narrowed my eyes suspiciously. "He's here? In Florida? Now?"

We pulled up outside the glass tower of the Four Seasons Hotel in Benirall's limo. Valets were going nuts trying to bring up cars in the storm—and I wasn't surprised to recognize the unmarked vans and SUVs from Hichen parked in front of the entrance. Those government intern types were here, too, rolling wheeled metal suitcases and chests from the hotel to the vans.

I got another dirty look from the Hummer driver as we were escorted inside by a female lieutenant, leaving Akerman with the car. She was all very cordial—and even deferential towards Benirall—but I couldn't help feeling more than a little apprehensive.

The Navy had taken over a whole floor of the hotel. We stepped out of the elevator to find SPs posted to each side of it, with slung assault rifles. The hallway was full of interns, intermingled with uniformed naval officers, everybody moving quickly and purposefully. It looked like they were evacuating.

We slalomed past personnel and ultra-hi-tech equipment, and were led to the double doors of a suite at the end of the hallway—the only doors that were closed. Two more armed SPs stood guard beside them. The lieutenant knocked and entered, and the five of us followed.

There was as much activity inside the suite as there had been outside. It looked like it had been a temporary office-cum-command center, but now all the equipment was being broken down and packed up. The lieutenant stepped up and muttered something to a male captain, who glanced over at our group, poker-faced, then disappeared into one of the bedrooms.

I felt a nudge in my ribs, and Stan pointed to a large mirror on the wall. I examined it for a few seconds, seeing nothing unusual.

"What am I looking at?"

"Look at Benirall," hissed Stan.

"What about him?"

Stan was massaging his temple again, clearly in some pain. "Right beside Benirall," he grunted, "behind him... there's another man..." I turned to look at Benirall, but Stan squealed, "*In the mirror!*"

I looked at the mirror again, focused on the reflection of

Benirall's back. Nothing. I turned back to Stan with a helpless shrug. His face fell, but it wasn't like I didn't believe him. I believed him only too readily. Stan could see something in that mirror, just like I'd seen something in the mirror at Bill Granger's house.

And, I realized with a start, looking at Eric Benirall's troubled expression... he *had seen it, too!* That was why he had turned away from it—and why, it struck me like a lightning bolt, he had painted out all the reflective surfaces in the stateroom, on his yacht.

Stan was staring at the mirror—and suddenly, a word escaped his lips. "*Winston...*"

"Eric!"

Douglas Weist had just entered from the bedroom, a big, warm smile on his face—and I got the same powerful vibe from him that I'd had when I had seen him in the back of his car. He must have been in his eighties, but he was still slim, healthy, almost athletic. We should all look so good. His only concession to his advanced age was the cane with which he walked: a handsome shillelagh. He was wearing half-glasses, and carrying a sheaf of EYES ONLY papers—and his steps were dogged by numerous aides, holding yet more documents. He looked like somebody's grandfather. Instant likeable, and with an air of sincerity.

"Eric," he beamed, moving up to Benirall, "you look..." Then his voice faltered, as he took in his friend's disheveled condition.

"Hello, Douglas," said Benirall with a grimace. "I know how I look."

Weist glanced over at the rest of us—pleasantly, but sizing us up nonetheless. He may have been a decent guy, but he was also a smart man in a position of responsibility. To Benirall, he said, "I'm so sorry about those people of mine showing up at your office yesterday. I didn't know until you told me. If I'd known, I surely would have called you personally. As you can see—" he took in the room with a sweep of his hand, "—we've got a little something cooking around here. But then, I believe that's why you're all here. I'm grateful you came to me."

And he beckoned us to follow him as he headed back into the bedroom.

CHAPTER 23

The bedroom was crowded, too. Computers, satellite comms stations, TV sets playing local news broadcasts about the weather and on the table, one of those access keys, the hole-punched cards, like Landon had at the underwater facility. Just lying there, as if Weist didn't care whether we saw it or not—because somehow I didn't get the feeling he'd have overlooked something like that.

Weist called out, gently but firmly, "Everybody. Everybody, please. I need you all to step out, please. I need the room. Just a few minutes. Captain..." And the Captain we'd seen before started to herd everybody out, until only Weist, Benirall, and our team of four were left. Then, Weist turned to face us, leaning on his cane with both hands. "Okay, so tell me: What exactly do you think we're doing out in the Atlantic?"

Benirall answered. "They think you're performing some sort of test." (Note the careful use of the word "they.") "Very likely a weapons test. That is—"

Emily leapt in. "We believe, sir, you're screwing with the molecular stability of that entire region." She spoke with intensity and passion, trying to short-circuit her own uncertainty as much as she was Weist's.

"Wow," he said.

I was watching him. We all were. All ready for the denial, ready to go ballistic on him. When it came, it was in the form of a challenge. A quiet challenge, and polite—but a challenge nonetheless. "Are any of you physicists?" asked Weist. And he looked at each of us in turn. "You, miss?" he said to Emily.

"Deep Ocean Resource Recovery," she said defensively.

Weist shook his head. "Not a physicist among you." He raised an eyebrow in Benirall's direction. "Why the dickens didn't you include a physicist?"

"None would take my offer to investigate this," said Benirall with painful honesty. "These did."

It was a body blow to our credibility, no denying it—and Weist was shaking his head again. "You've come all this way—everything you've laid out for me, including the leap to 'molecular stability,' all based on what? A little field observation and a lot of conjecture?"

"Look," I said hotly, "we may not have the expertise—"

Bruce took up the baton "—but we damn well know what we saw. What we're experiencing. And we can—"

"Relax, please!" To my surprise, Weist was smiling his warm smile again. "You had me at 'hello.'"

And we all just stared at him, because this was totally unexpected.

"Douglas," growled Benirall. "What the hell are you people up to?"

Weist looked at us, took a long, long moment. Shifted his weight on his cane. Drew a deep breath. "Understand," he said, "what I'm about to tell you is of the highest, highest security classification. It has been, bar none, the most closely guarded military secret of the last five decades."

He meant it. We were all just standing there, hardly daring to breathe. I felt as if all the air had been sucked out of the room.

"Have any of you heard," asked Weist, "of the Philadelphia Experiment?"

I filled in the information automatically. "An experiment, pretty universally considered apocryphal, purported to have been conducted back in the 1940s. Story is the Navy took one of their battleships, rigged it with giant electromagnets, and tried to screw with the ship's..." I broke off as I realized what I was saying.

"With the ship's molecular fidelity," Weist continued for me. "Go on."

"They were trying to make the ship invisible," I said, hearing the words but hardly believing I was saying them. The Philadelphia Experiment—another favorite of the nutcases, tied up with wild rumors not just of invisibility but of teleportation, and of travel through time. They even made a film of it. And all this triggered by one letter, written in multi colored crayon by a merchant marine to a noted UFOlogist, claiming he had seen a ship disappearing and reappearing. Now, they were telling me that this, too?

I couldn't think about it. I just recited the words. "Everything went horribly wrong. Sailors started disappearing, independent of the ship. It was even reported that some of them... Some of them melted into walls of the ship... into the deck..."

I should have made the connection earlier—but Philadelphia is a thousand miles north of the Triangle. I just hadn't thought about it. About those poor sailors aboard the *Winston Pride II*. "But the Navy's always denied it," I said firmly. "Always!"

"The battleship," said Weist, "was the *USS. Eldridge*." And he said it with such authority—such conviction—that we all froze on the spot. So much for apocryphal. "Year was 1943. Height of World War II. The concept would, indeed, render the massive ship invisible. Not just to radar and the like, but to all manner of perception."

"Are you saying," asked Bruce tentatively, "the Navy's out there trying the same thing again?"

Weist lowered himself to sit on the bed.

"But if it didn't work the first time..." said Stan.

"Oh, it worked," said Weist. "Just didn't work the way the eggheads of the time expected it to. And there was one other repercussion. A rather significant one, as it turns out. That's the secret we've been so desperately guarding all these years." And the pause he left, then, seemed to stretch into infinity.

"A tear," he said.

"Tear?" said Benirall. "What do you mean, a tear?"

Weist looked up at Emily. "Your specialty may not be physics, my dear—but you do look scary-smart. What do I mean by a tear?"

In a small voice, she hazarded, "As in... space-time?"

Weist nodded in approval. Then, with an effort, he reached down and pulled the lace on the shoe of his bad leg, like he was releasing the pressure on it. "You've heard it referred to as the 'fabric' of space," he said, "the 'fabric' of time? Well, the 1943 experiment didn't just affect one ship and a couple of hundred sad-sack sailors. It started a tear in the fabric of space-time itself. For some reason, it centered itself out in the South Atlantic. That area has always been a nexus for unexplained phenomena."

"Columbus," murmured Benirall.

"Going back to Columbus, yes. But the greatest number of disappearances have been reported in the last fifty years—ever since this new phenomenon, this tear, has parked itself out there."

"Dammit, Doug," flared Benirall, "if the Navy has known this, *you've* known it, why haven't you warned anyone? I've lost ships!"

"How many innocent people have been lost?" asked Stan.

"Think about what you're asking," insisted Weist. "Placing a quarantine on over fourteen thousand square miles of ocean. Eric, you know how many billions of dollars in cargo traverses that region every few days, how many commercial carriers count on flying through that area on key routes. The hard reality is, the number of vessels taken over the years pales in the light of the devastating economic impact such a quarantine would have had."

It was Bruce who asked the $64,000 question: "Taken where?"

Weist just looked at him.

"You said 'all the vessels taken over the years.' *Where* were they taken?"

I could tell this affected Weist greatly—because he didn't know. "Another dimension," he said vaguely. "Another time."

"You're saying," I chipped in, "for decades, the Navy has actually known the Bermuda Triangle exists? And the reason they've known about it is because they *caused* it?"

"Why is it taking more of my ships now?" demanded Benirall. "Why is it causing visions? What—"

"Because," said Weist, "the tear has continued to expand. Exponentially. In size and intensity. Since 1943." He sighed. "Y'know, *we* first coined the phrase 'the Bermuda Triangle.' Everybody's always thought it came from some magazine writer in the sixties, but...

"To us, the 'triangle' in 'Bermuda Triangle' has always referred to the ever-widening tear. The increase in disappearances you've been experiencing, the distortions of space/time in the region, the aberrant weather—it's all because we're approaching something my people call 'the Crux Event.' A moment in time when the tear has widened so much that the stability of our existence can no longer resist its forces."

We all just stood and tried to absorb this. I was trying to find a reason why Weist might be lying; I almost hoped he would turn round and laugh and admit that he was just playing "wind up the conspiracy freaks." Instead, he continued:

"We've known it was coming since 1971. Back then, our scientists were able to extrapolate the precise date and time in the distant future when the Event would arrive." And he left another significant pause before he told us.

"They determined it would occur at twenty-three-oh-six and nineteen seconds Eastern Standard Time. Today..."

"Eleven o'clock tonight?" I boggled.

Weist nodded. I couldn't help but think he seemed incredibly calm about all this.

"What's going to happen?" asked Stan.

"We have no real consensus," said Weist, "but every opinion from every expert has generally started with a colorful variation of 'Holy crap!'"

"You seem pretty damn cavalier!" said Emily, accusingly.

"Because we're going to stop it," said Weist. But he said it with the force of one who was willing something to be true rather than just knowing it.

"I've been part of the Navy Secretary's office for forty-six years," he said. "Been the actual Secretary for the last seventeen of those. Through nine different administrations. All because I took point on this project. *The* Project."

And then, Secretary Douglas Weist showed us something truly shocking: He grabbed hold of his untied shoe, and he pulled it off—and, with it, his entire foot.

I felt my jaw dropping as he tossed the shoe aside—but I could see now the prosthetic foot that was built inside it. And now, Weist was peeling down his sock, hiking up his pant leg—to reveal that the lower part of his leg, from knee to ankle, was tapered. As if it had been sliced cleanly on a diagonal. And I could see that the roping of scar tissue was decades old.

"I was an ensign on the *Eldridge*," said Weist quietly. Still, none of us spoke. We were just... overwhelmed was the best word. "My entire career, everything I've done since that day aboard that ship has been aimed at one thing. Finding a way to close Pandora's Box."

Silence for a moment. Then, Emily asked, "What can you do to stop it?"

"A backblast," said Weist.

"You're going to do the same thing again?" exclaimed Bruce, horrified.

Weist nodded. "The tear will close. Permanently. The Crux Event will be prevented. And everything we're experiencing right now—it ends. Ships and planes disappearing, done. The Triangle, gone. Forever."

More silence.

"The people working out there," I said, "at your... facility. Some of them have been injured, affected by what you're doing."

Weist acknowledged this. "We've suffered more than our fair share of casualties... most unusual casualties."

"A man named Granger," I prompted.

"I'm sorry," said Weist. "I don't know the name, didn't know him personally, but..." And I was in no doubt that he meant this: "We're in a war here. A war with the forces of Nature herself. There have been many, many sacrifices—men have been affected by the forces at work out there—losing phase with time, hallucinations..."

"Why tell us?" asked Stan. "Why now?"

"Because you've come as far as you have. You know as

much as you do. And in less than six hours, it will all be over. Even if you were insane enough to want to interfere—at this point, what could you do? Who could you tell that matters?"

And Weist made firm, sincere eye contact with each of us in turn as he concluded wearily, "All we want to do is finally put an end to the nightmare that we ourselves began. That's all we're trying to do..."

And, just like that, it was all over. Finally. The four of us stood, sheltering from the rain, under the eaves of the Four Seasons, watching as Benirall's limo pulled away. Stunned? Dazed? Sure—and that was just for starters.

Without communicating with each other, we found ourselves drifting back into the hotel lobby. It was busy—guests walking, talking, laughing, blissfully unaware of what was going on around them, what was happening to their world.

All over For us, at least. I ought to have been relieved. Instead, I felt empty.

"So," said Bruce, wryly, "what d'you want to talk about?"

Emily pinned him with a look. "First question: Do we believe him?"

"It sure seemed very..." Stan began—but at that moment, we were all distracted by a nearby table lamp, which glowed extra bright and then flickered as we passed. "...real," he concluded numbly.

"And all that," said Emily, "about the Pittsburgh Exper–?"

"Philadelphia, "I said. "Not Pittsburgh. I've interviewed half a dozen geezers who claim they were aboard the *Eldridge*. Nobody's ever been able to prove whether or not it ever really–"

Bruce jumped in with, "You may've noticed the man's leg?"

"Could have been an injury from some other–" began Emily.

"You ever see another amputation at an angle like that?"

"Gee, ya know," Emily shot back, irritated, "I'm just so

familiar with amputations you'd think I'd have a ready answer. What—we're supposed to immediately accept that it got sliced like that because his leg melted into the deck of—"

"Probably not the deck," mused Bruce. "From the angle, had to be more like a bulkhead, something standing upright."

"Enough about the guy's leg!" squealed Emily. Then, calming herself down, she asked, "Do we believe him?"

"It certainly all fits," said Bruce. "At least as much as he told us."

"The Navy could be doing anything out there," I said uncertainly. "You know how many cover stories they cook up on a daily basis."

"What's his motivation for lying to us?" asked Emily.

Just what I wanted to know. But I countered with, "What's his motivation for telling us the truth?" I was supposed to be the cynic here, after all.

"He sounded—looked—proud of what he's doing," said Stan. "If they are fixing this horrible wrong they did half a century ago, I think he *wants* people to know. He's dedicated his entire adult life to it."

"Plus," said Bruce, "like the man said, we're certainly no threat."

"Benirall's the one who could make the biggest stink for them," I agreed.

"And he seemed to buy it hook, line, and sinker," said Emily.

Something was nagging at the back of Stan's mind again. "Benirall looked very relieved," he recalled, "about..." He screwed up his face in frustration, and concluded lamely, "something..."

Something was happening on the periphery of my vision. A phalanx of interns, naval officers and SPs, were moving across the lobby—and in their midst: Weist. We watched as they swept through the glass doors to the caravan of dark blue vehicles waiting outside. Emily looked at her watch. "Guess we'll know for sure at eleven o'clock tonight," she remarked.

"What d'you think happens?" asked Stan. "I mean... after? We wake up tomorrow morning—are we going to notice anything different?"

"Yeah," I quipped, "we're all suddenly missing a foot." Nobody chuckled.

Emily looked around the lobby, at the other guests chatting and laughing. "None of them knows," she breathed.

Then, suddenly, Bruce leapt as if he had been stung. "Wait a second," he cried, and his eyes were alight with excitement. "Wait a... I know exactly what happens to us tomorrow." He looked at us, astounded that we hadn't seen it yet. "*We get our five million dollars!*"

It says a lot about what we'd all been through, how much had changed in so short a time, that none of us knew what to say to that. Certainly, if it hadn't been for the money, none of us would have been here—and yet, it seemed like the least important detail now.

But Bruce was determined to infect us with his enthusiasm. "We did it," he crowed, "what we were contracted to do. We brought Benirall his answer! Well, *led* him to his answer... C'mon, people. It's Miller Time!"

And slowly, very slowly, it began to sink in on me, what Bruce was saying—what that money could do for my life. My real life. The one I had almost forgotten.

"We could wake up tomorrow," Bruce continued, "our crazy visions gone, the Triangle gone, everything back to normal."

"Not normal," said Emily, the ghost of a smile pulling at her lips. "Stable."

"Whatever. Except" And Bruce was waving his hands for emphasis. "We're five. M*illion*. Dollars. Richer. Each!" He grinned. "The world is definitely going to change tomorrow. Talk about stability."

And I tried to focus on that thought, tried to think about all the things I could buy for Traci, all the making up I could do but it was no good. It was no good, because, deep down, this didn't feel right. It just didn't *feel* like it was all over yet.

Not until eleven o'clock. Not until six minutes and forty-three seconds past.

Not until the tear had been sealed, and the world was changed. For the better.

Or...

CHAPTER 24

"...truly qualifies as a freak storm. The National Weather Service isn't copping to having missed predicting this one, especially one this big—but they are recommending that day sailors and pleasure boaters stay off the water today. And, typically with weather like this, the roads are very, very ugly out there right now..."

What do you do when you think the world might be coming to an end?

When you think it might be about to change, at least? When you're afraid that something terrible might happen, but it's only a feeling in your gut—nothing you can prove? When you keep telling yourself that your fears are unfounded, that everything will be okay, but you just can't quite believe it?

Meeno Paloma had stayed on the breakwater till the storm hit. He had half expected it to bring with it a revelation, perhaps to whisk him away to another place where everything would be clearer. Instead, it had just hammered at him like any natural storm, like it was mocking him.

And then he had turned, and he'd seen that ceiling

of black clouds sweeping inland, as if with a purpose. Sweeping toward the metropolitan grid of Miami.

And he had thought of his family, and run for his car.

The storm had beaten him back to town, darkening the streets and slowing traffic to a crawl. Meeno had taken side streets and back alleys, made illegal turns, even mounted the sidewalk at one point. He had no time for sitting in the never-ending congestion. He was on a mission.

By the time he had reached the school, the rain was slamming down so fast and hard that the car's wipers couldn't keep up. He had pushed through the main entrance doors, raced down the corridors like a man possessed, dragged his son from his classroom. Ruben had protested as his father had bundled him out into the school grounds, in front of the astonished eyes of members of staff who didn't know whether to intervene or not. There had been no time to explain.

"We've got to pick up your mother!" Meeno had insisted. "We got to get out of here! Out of Florida! As far away as we can!" And he had tried to ignore the nagging voice in his head that had told him there was nowhere he could go. Nowhere far enough to escape what was coming.

"...*Zoo officials say it began around three o'clock today. The animals just began, quote, 'losing it.' Doesn't seem to matter whether it's mammal, reptile, or bird. For some inexplicable reason, they're all in a highly, highly agitated state...*"

Meeno raced through the front door of his house, dripping wet, keeping a grip on Ruben's shirt, afraid to let go. He was shouting to his wife—but as he started toward the stairs, he saw somebody else at the kitchen table, and he froze.

It was Dylan. Little five year-old Dylan. Sitting there. Drawing.

He was thrilled, at first—thrilled that the boy was back.

But terrified, too, that it was happening again.

Then he sensed something odd, and he realized that his balled fist was closed around... nothing...

...Ruben was *gone*...

Too late. Meeno's blood turned to ice, and that nagging voice was telling him, *You can't outrun it... Nowhere you can go...*

And he looked toward the kitchen again, praying that at least he might still be able to save his wife and his *other* son, and...

...Helen was there, doing the dishes, as if she'd been there all along—and maybe she had, though Meeno hadn't seen her. It didn't matter. She was *there*. And he opened his mouth to call out her name, but then everything changed again.

Everything changed—and this time, it wouldn't stop changing.

The room before Meeno began to segment. It was like he was looking at his own kitchen through a prism—multiple views through its door fanned out before him, one right beside the other. In one view, Dylan was drawing, Helen was doing dishes. But in the one beside it, Dylan *and* Ruben were gluing model airplanes. In the one beside that, Helen was engaged in a frenetic sexual encounter with a guy in shorts—she was clawing his back wantonly as he pressed her against the counter, ripping her clothes. In the next, she was in mourning black, seated at the kitchen table, sobbing...

Meeno stared at this nightmarish kaleidoscope of possible realities, and he knew that the voice in his head had been right. There was no escape. Not for him. Not for any of them. He couldn't save them.

He stumbled backwards, groping for the door handle behind him. He almost fell down the porch steps as he backed out of the house.

He ignored his car, just found his feet and ran...

...knowing that it would do him no good at all...

And Stan Lathem just stayed indoors and watched the TV.

"Dad... what are you doing here?"

I couldn't blame Traci for being surprised to see me. I didn't often drop in on her unannounced, wasn't often I could make the time. But then, what else *do* you do when you think... well, you know.

I tried to reassure her with a smile, though there were butterflies in my stomach. "I wanted to check in," I said. "See how you're doing."

"Okay, I guess." Traci glanced back over her shoulder, as if afraid of what her mother would say if she found me here. "You could've just called..."

"No," I said firmly, "I couldn't 'just call.' I wanted to see you." She tried to hide it, but behind her eyes I could see how much this pleased her.

"Have you talked to Mindy or her mom?" I asked. Smart move—making it seem like I was worried about Traci because of what had happened yesterday, not because of what might happen tomorrow.

"I left messages," she said. "They haven't called back."

"That the pizza?" Sally appeared, in shorts and a tank top. She had just showered, and she was toweling her hair. She stopped dead in her tracks as she saw me.

"Mom..." pleaded Traci, needing almost as much as I did to head off another row.

"Pizza, huh?" I said with a weak smile, trying my hardest. "Botelli's?"

My ex-wife's expression remained very carefully neutral. But the act got me inside the house, and for that I was grateful—because there was nowhere else I could have imagined being that evening.

The night came quickly, the storm bringing an early darkness. Our—I mean, Sally's—apartment was rocked by bright lightning and thunder. I was sitting at the kitchen table with Traci, a pizza box and an antipasto container open between us. Sally stood at the bar, letting me have this time but keeping her distance. She had a glass of wine and a slice of pizza on a plate.

I was trying not to think about the storm—but, more and more, I found myself thinking about the money. About what it might mean—for us. For all of us.

"Like I said," I mumbled through a mouthful of food, "I can't give you all the details—it's too much. And without the details, you'd flat out think I'm crazy. But it's actually pretty credible. Credible enough..."

There was no mistaking the look in Sally's eyes—the one that said I was chasing dreams again, that she'd heard all this before. I can't deny that smarted. "Maybe more than just credible," I persisted. "I don't know. But the concept itself is huge. This could be the big one. The big story."

"And it has to do with what happened to Mr. Granger yesterday?" asked Traci.

"That, and a whole lot more."

"So what do you mean 'credible enough'?" she asked, with an edge of hurt. "We were there. Both of us. We saw it. Together."

Sally shifted her weight and fingered her wine glass. "Howard," she said. "Why are you here tonight?"

"Because..." I hesitated for a moment, "...something may be happening tonight. Nothing bad. Probably. But... I just wanted to spend some time with the two of you."

And, with that, I had said too much. I had unsettled them both—though Sally tried to hide it behind another crack at me. "Something happening tonight? Can you be more cryptic? What—?"

"Nothing," I said quickly. "It's nothing." I took a breath, and tried to lighten my tone. "On the other hand, after tomorrow—miracle of miracles—because of this story, there may be, possibly, some money coming my way. *Our* way."

"Howard..."

"I'm not positive. But it's a possibility." I studied my hands. I hadn't begun to say all I'd wanted to say. I didn't know how.

"One of the aspects of the story," I said, feeling awkward, avoiding their eyes, "it has to do with... temporal displacement. The idea of multiverses..." I glanced up, then. Neither Sally nor Traci knew what I was talking about. Guess they didn't read my work. "Alternate paths," I clarified, "life paths...? All the different directions a person's life can go...?"

How best to explain it? How to find the words that they

might accept? "For example," I said, "if you choose to drive down a certain street, you get in an accident, but if you pick a different street, or leave your house one second later, you miss the accident and everything's fine. Or..." I looked straight at Sally. "You decide not to go to a frat party, instead you go to a movie, and at the last minute you buy a Coke, and you end up spilling that Coke on the girl sitting on the aisle." The way we met. I saw her expression shifting.

I continued, "Or you choose to spend so much time working, you don't listen, you don't share yourself, your life, as much as you should..."

I could read Sally's eyes. She didn't know why I was doing this, saying this, now. I had hurt her too bad, it'd been too long... and yet... and yet...

"The lesson is, I guess—if there are all these different paths, maybe it isn't always too late to change the one you're on."

Her arms were crossed, wine glass in hand. Talk about defensive body language. But in those eyes, I was sure there was a hint—just the tiniest hint—of something... something not quite dead...

"Anyway," I said, defusing the moment, "there's maybe some money. And this story..."

More thunder. The house lights dimmed for a second, and it seemed a struggle for them to come back up.

Meeno had taken refuge in the boatyard again. But there was no hiding from the storm.

The hangar-like shed was locked—no one working late tonight. He pressed himself against its side, taking what shelter he could—but the crashing of the rain on the roof was relentless, like a drill to his skull. His eyes kept flicking to the shapes of the boats around him, including, he noted, his own cigar boat, presumably hauled out here at last by an impatient Yarrow. He almost expected the dead whalers to rise from behind it. Or Don Beatty. Or something worse...

He couldn't go home—couldn't face that—couldn't do anything. But then, nor could he do nothing. He had tried running from it, and it hadn't worked.

Then, his idle hands found something in his pocket. A piece of paper. He pulled it out, unfolded it, recognized the creased newspaper clipping. BERMUDA TRIANGLE 'FACTS' AND FALLACIES. My photo and byline.

Meeno stared at the clipping for a long time, until the rain had drenched it and made the words run together. And finally, he made a desperate choice that was really his only choice.

And Stan was still watching the TV.

"...at thirty-seven thousand feet when their plane just began to drop."

He had changed into a pair of well-worn warm-ups, heated up some soup. Tried to act like tonight was a normal night.

"Although still unconfirmed, an airline source told us that the plane might have dropped almost the entire distance to the ocean below..."

They were reporting live from the airport: a line of shaken, sobbing passengers being ushered into the terminal.

"...free-falling for over two minutes before the crew was able to regain control and level off the massive Airbus A330..."

Another channel. Another news report, from a street intersection where the power was out. *"...what has officials so baffled is that power is failing throughout the entire southern half of the state in a pattern that defies explanation."*

He couldn't deny it any longer. He couldn't pretend that the headache was psychosomatic, just a product of stress.

"In most cases, it isn't complete grids that are failing, but only sections of grids..."

He had to do something.

Stan left the TV playing to an empty apartment as he grabbed his coat and made for the door.

The *Observer* newsroom. Not that much news was being gathered right now. Most of the staff were at the windows, mugs in hand, watching as the crazy weather pounded and rattled the glass.

The storm appeared to be worsening. The lightning was

now daylight bright, each thunderclap a mini-earthquake that was greeted by giggles and "Whoa!"s from the staff like they were kids at Magic Mountain.

I sat alone at my computer, writing, trying to keep my concentration, trying not to think about how the story would end. But I couldn't keep my eyes from straying to the UFO statue clock on my desk. A gag gift from a colleague.

8:09.

"Eleven-oh-six," I muttered to myself. I'd stayed with Sally and Traci as long as I could, as long as they'd let me. It hadn't been long enough. "Three hours..."

"Three hours what?"

I'd forgotten that Ben was at the next desk. One of the other reporters. He'd been sitting with his feet up, watching the TV news. Now, he looked at me—and as I returned his gaze, he performed a double-take. "Jeez, Howard, you okay?"

"What do you mean?" I covered.

"You look, I don't know, like something's really eating you."

I was still trying to think of something to say, some way to get out of answering at all, when someone else caught my eye.

He was standing in the doorway, looking around. Looking for me, I realized as our eyes locked onto each other. He was wet, bedraggled. I thought he was a homeless guy for a moment, come wandering into the building in search of shelter, but there was something familiar about him.

I rose to meet him as he came toward me, and I realized: "You're that guy I interviewed. The Greenpeace guy."

"I don't know where else I can..." stammered Meeno Paloma. "You're the only one..." And he stared into my eyes for a long moment, before he pleaded, "Help me!"

I was struck dumb. Nothing like this had happened to me before. None of my "nutcases" had ever come to me like this. But Meeno, I recalled, had seemed more rational than some. More cynical. Like me, he hadn't wanted to believe in the Triangle—and yet, perhaps he had had no choice.

And I'd written him off because he *did* believe.

Perhaps he thought he could talk to me. Perhaps he thought I would understand. He was the last person I needed to see right now.

No, scratch that. The *second* last—because the very last person had just appeared in the doorway behind Meeno. Stan. And I could tell from his expression that he wasn't the bearer of good tidings.

So suddenly, I had to play Mother Theresa to these two losers. Right when I was having enough problems just trying to keep myself sane. That was my first thought.

The second was worse. It came from deeper inside— and it was the one I'd been denying all day. The gnawing realization that something really *was* wrong here. And that—holy shit—maybe it was up to me to step up and do something to fix it.

CHAPTER 25

What do you do when you think the world might be coming to an end?

Emily went shopping.

Like Stan, she was just trying to maintain a semblance of normality. Running through the rain toward her condo complex, with a couple of bags of groceries in hand. Like Stan, she soon learned that tonight was anything but normal.

There was a light in the window. Up on the second floor. Her apartment.

And the shape of a figure, moving across the glass.

She was startled at first. But then, she realized what might be happening—who that figure had to be—and she felt a far more complex cocktail of emotions.

She stood for a long time, staring up at that window, as the rain pelted her eyelashes.

Bruce went to work.

Normality, again. And company. Life going on around

him. Same reason I'd gone into the newsroom. To absorb himself in what he knew, and just hope that, when he looked up again, the Navy's deadline would have passed.

Oh yeah, and he'd brought an armload of pamphlets with him—for cars. Big cars. How better to while away a few hours than in deciding where to spend some of that five million bucks?

As Bruce peeled off his windbreaker, he hardly noticed the activity around him—his students, still working with super energy and intensity. He'd almost forgotten the task he had set them—almost forgotten that they didn't know what we now knew.

"Dr. Gellar?"

"Yes, Marie?" he murmured, wiping off a wet pamphlet with his sleeve.

"Some really unbelievable stuff here." The strain in the girl's voice pricked Bruce out of his daydream. He looked up to see that his best grad student was struggling with a stack of ring binders, all of them bulging with paper.

He hurried to help, and they half-lay, half-dropped the binders onto his workstation. "We've been pulling data from multiple sites and sources," Marie enthused. "Darrin started... you know Darrin?" Bruce gave a non-committal shrug. Truth was, he had no idea who Darrin was. "Well, Darrin started—accidentally started—entering incorrect positional coordinates. Before he realized, he'd pulled satellite data from several other continents around the globe."

"Look, Marie," Bruce tried to interrupt, "I really appreciate the work you've been doing here. *Everybody's* been doing—"

But Marie was too enthused to stop there. "Most important, he also didn't clear the ambit settings after each array shift—"

"Super job, super job. But we can start dialing back some. In fact—"

"—so he was getting overlapping readings. Normally a bad thing, but you should see what he found—"

"—basically, we can stop."

"Stop? But..." Marie looked stunned, as Bruce's words began to sink in at last.

"You'll all get credit," he promised. "Tell me what you think is appropriate and you'll have it. No sweat."

"You should look at Darrin's data," she insisted.

"I don't need to," said Bruce. "I've already got my answer." With a little self-deprecating smile, he confessed, "Had it handed to me, actually." But Marie looked so disappointed that he couldn't help but feel sympathy for her.

"Which one's his data?" he relented. She indicated a green binder, and he promised to take a look at it.

"So, I should just send everybody home?" she asked.

Bruce nodded, and Marie moved off, the air gone out of her.

He watched her go, then looked down at his pamphlets. He made to pick up the top one, but something was gnawing at his conscience.

Yeah, I was surprised, too. Bruce has a conscience.

He looked at the green binder. Took a long moment. Then, with a sigh, he pulled it out of the stack and opened it.

"There you are."

Emily's mother—the woman who *said* she was her mother—was in the kitchen. She was carrying a steaming pot to a waiting trivet on the table. She'd laid out place settings for two.

When she saw Emily, dripping in the doorway, she approached her and gave her a casual peck on the cheek. The touch of her lips was electrifying. "How about this weather?" she said, going back to her serving, oblivious to her daughter's reaction. "Hungry? I know how you feel about eating with your boring old mother, but I was hoping you weren't planning to go back out on a night like this."

Emily just stared at her, not knowing which of the myriad emotions that were pulsing through her she should deal with first. The way she described it to me later, she was afraid to move, almost afraid to breathe, for fear of doing anything to make the stranger in her apartment vanish.

She *would* vanish, sooner or later. Emily knew that. She ached with that horribly tenuous feeling that comes with a good dream, when you know you're about to wake up and you can't stop yourself and it's all going to be gone.

She wouldn't get this chance again. She had to make the most of the dream while it lasted—accept that the Triangle had given her a gift, if she had the courage to accept it.

Slowly, tentatively, she stepped up to the table, finding her voice.

"I... I'd like that very much..."

Bruce was on the phone, talking breathlessly, his heart hammering against his ribcage. He had hardly noticed how much the storm had worsened—that the roof of his research lab had begun to leak.

The power to the whole building was out.

Emily just sat there in the dark, staring at her untouched dinner, as her mother rooted out and lit an assortment of mismatched candles, finding all of Emily's little hiding places as if she had lived there all her life.

"There," she said as she placed the final pair on the table and retook her seat. "That should do us. Actually, it's rather nice... Where was I? Oh, bridge. So Donna bids three no trump. Well, you know, it's Donna. Janet thinks it's her hip medication. Makes her kind of spacey..."

Emily sat rooted to her chair, letting the onslaught of gossip wash over her.

"...Emmy, honey, what's the matter with you tonight? You haven't taken a single bite. You're not back on that crazy diet?"

Still, Emily couldn't speak, though she was yelling at herself inside. "Can't be the dinner," said her mother. "I know how you feel about lamb chops."

"They've always been my favorite," said Emily in a small voice.

Another roll of thunder from outside.

"Heavens," gasped the older woman. "What is it with this weather?"

"By tomorrow," said Emily distantly, "it should all be over."

And she would never see her mother again.

"Over? Really? Did you hear that on the radio? Because

everything I've heard, the weather people have no idea when this is going to end."

"I heard it from somebody in authority... seemed to know what he was talking about."

"Seemed?" Emily's mother smiled. "Never known you to listen to anyone—especially somebody in authority—if it went against your own instincts. What do your instincts tell you?"

This made Emily think—and she was surprised to realize that the answer was, "That he may be wrong..."

"That sounds more like my Emmy," said the older woman with a grin.

"I... I'm going to ask you a question," Emily blurted out suddenly. "You'll think it's strange, but... What's your name?"

Her mother chuckled. "My name? What do you mean, what's my—?" But she stopped as she saw the deeply earnest look on her daughter's face.

It had taken all of Emily's courage to get this far. She held on to it, and forced herself to repeat, "I need to know your name!"

"Laura. My name is Laura."

Emily absorbed this, almost physically. Knowing her birth mother's name, at long last—it was a kind of an epiphany for her. She looked deep into the woman's eyes—soft, kind, loving eyes—and she asked simply, "Why?"

"Why what, dear?"

"Why would you give me up? Why did you—?"

"Give you up? What on earth has gotten into you?"

"For adoption. You gave me—"

Laura put down her fork with a loud clang, almost angry. "Emily, now you're scaring me. I never, ever—"

"When I was a week old!"

And now her mother's expression shifted. Slowly. As if it had been decades since she'd thought about this. "My God," she breathed, "how did you?"

Emily maintained her steady gaze. She wasn't trying to be judgmental, she just needed to know, hungered for it so deeply.

Her mother took a few moments, steadied herself, then:

"When your father abandoned me just before you

were born, I had no way to care for you. The nuns at the hospital—and my father—they wanted me to give you up. I almost did. Almost. But I...I just couldn't bring myself to do it."

Emily felt tears pushing at the backs of her eyes. Laura was still confused, but her response was natural and instantaneous. She rose from her chair and moved to her daughter. Emily, too, managed to find her feet—and for the first time in her life she felt the arms of her mother closing around her, holding her, and the tears were rolling freely from her closed eyes now.

It took several moments before she could raise her own quaking arms and close them around this woman. Then she virtually melted into the embrace, and into the soft voice that reassured her that her mother loved her so very much.

And then, she was standing alone, holding on to nothing, beside a table set for two. Listening to the storm as it crashed against her windows.

There were buckets and bowls set up around Bruce's lab, catching the multiple leaks from the roof. And the room was bustling again, his students a blur as they rushed about with sheaves of data in hand, tearing scrolls of up-to-the-second charts and graphics from the printers, calling out updates to each other.

Bruce's hair was mussed, a fine sheen of perspiration on his forehead. He was standing at his workstation, too juiced to sit, working mouse and keyboard, his monitor a patchwork quilt of weather graphics and scrolling data from around the globe. The piles of paper around him were increasing by the second, as students tossed new reams of printouts onto them.

"I've tried to get everybody back," explained Marie as she hurried up with more data.

"Great, good," said Bruce. "What's this?"

"It's the latest from the Pacific Rim."

"And?"

"They're registering a mind-boggling increase in tropospheric ozone," said Marie. "Presently in the two hundred range, up over fifty points in the last hour."

"They're in daylight. That should help mitigate any significant damaging effects."

"Fifty points in the last hour?"

Bruce just nodded, accepting Marie's point but too busy with the big picture to address it right now. "Where's the latest from the poles?" he asked. Marie didn't know, so Bruce called out, "Who's got Amundsen-Scott Station in the Antarctic?"

Marie was trying to get his attention. "*What is happening?*" she pleaded. Her expression stopped even the juggernaut Bruce in his tracks. She was scared out of her wits—and now that he stopped to think, now that he really thought about what he was learning here, what his students had discovered...

...thought past the hard science of it, to the actual consequences, to what it might mean, for the world, for everybody...

Bruce blinked—and Emily was there, soaked to the skin, moving through the cross traffic of students with a definite purpose. She stepped up to him, a little out of breath, and met his eye. And with typical directness, she said, "What if they're wrong?"

Something passed between them as they held that look. Then Bruce scooped up a fistful of papers, and said gravely, "*Way* wrong?"

CHAPTER 26

And what if, in the end, there was nothing? Nothing at all...

"...never laid eyes on the boy before in my life. But he was my son. And there were bodies in my shower. And the scuzzball whalers..."

The streetlights and the traffic lights were out. Many of the stores were ominously dark, too. Meeno's car inched along in the frustrating bumper-to-bumper traffic. I was driving, because he was in no state. He was in the back, unloading to Stan, who was watching him in the rearview mirror with an expression of deep concern. I was half listening, while talking to Bruce on my cell. "He's a Triangle survivor. Like the little girl. We might be able to learn something from him—something we can use. Based on the story he tells, he's a damn poster child for everything that's going on."

I was hardly surprised to learn that Bruce and Emily were back on the case already. I told Bruce that Stan and I would be with them as soon as we could.

"...just as I was getting used to him," moaned Meeno, "to care about..."

In the end, we couldn't have timed our arrival better.

Bruce had just made a discovery—one that had made him instantly excited. One that he'd had to tell Emily about right away, but she'd been too busy with her own data. Bruce had had to literally take her head in his hands and twist it to face his screen, to break her concentration.

"*Look!*" he insisted.

"What?" she snapped impatiently.

"See these?"

"Of course I see them. What—?"

"Pressure waves."

Emily didn't get it at first. Bruce had to repeat, "Pressure. Waves. *Waves!* Waves aren't linear. They're a pattern phenomenon."

Now it was starting to sink in. "But that can't be. Mr. Big Shot Navy Guy said his Philadelphia thing caused a tear. That's a wedge phenomenon, not a pattern..."

She'd got it. Bruce grinned wide, and spread out his hands as if to say "Aren't I brilliant?" It was at that moment that Stan, Meeno, and I stumbled into the room, marveling at the frenetic activity that suddenly surrounded us.

Emily and Bruce hurried to meet us, and I tried to introduce Meeno but there was no time for pleasantries. "We think the Navy may be operating under a set of wrong assumptions," said Emily, talking almost as fast as Bruce did when he was off on one. "Very wrong assumptions."

"We've got data here," added Bruce, "that suggests— strongly suggests..." He decided to just say it "...*irrefutably* suggests—the events that are taking place all around us right now cannot be caused by a tear like Weist told us. It has to be something else."

A new drip from the roof hit the floor beside Emily. She used her foot to ease over a bucket that was already catching another leak.

Stan protested, "But the Navy's had their people, certainly brilliant people, on this for decades."

"The fact they've been on this for decades may be exactly why they're wrong now," conjectured Emily.

Bruce agreed. "'Decades' means lots of turnover of staff. Newbies coming in on an established project tend naturally to accept the assumptions of their predecessors as fact."

I noticed that Emily kept glancing back at that bucket, at those ripples. "If you're coming in on a sixty-year-old project that you've been told is about a 'tear,'" she said distractedly, "that's where you're going to focus your own work."

"You wanna know how we know what we know?" grinned Bruce. "Because a first-year lab assistant named Darrin screwed up. He got us to look at some data that anybody who's brilliant would never think to look at."

And now, Emily's breathing had grown fast and shallow as a thought coalesced in her mind.

"Sure," Bruce continued, "they're all geniuses out there. But what they probably don't have are any Darrins." And he let out a yelp of pain, as suddenly Emily grabbed his hair and unceremoniously pulled his head around to look at the bucket. Turnabout is fair play, after all.

"Ow! What are you—?"

"Look!"

Bruce frowned down at the bucket. I looked at it, too, but I couldn't see what the fuss was about.

"Your pressure waves," prompted Emily. And slowly, Bruce's eyes focused on the drips hitting the water in the bucket. Drip. Drip. Drip. And his expression changed.

He looked up at Emily, wide-eyed. "A ripple?"

"A ripple!" she said.

"What—?" I began.

"Not a tear at all," breathed Bruce.

"The Triangle effects," said Emily, "could be *rippling* out from 1943!"

"Totally fits with our new data," announced Bruce, satisfied.

"Toss a pebble in a lake, the effects ripple outward from the point of origin."

"The Navy?" piped up Meeno. I'd almost forgotten he was there. If I thought *I* was having trouble keeping up with all this, I could only imagine what it must have been like for him, ten pages behind the rest of us. It must have been like trying to leap aboard a runaway train.

"You're saying they caused everything that's happening out there? Everything that's happened to me?"

"Because of a failed experiment they performed back in the forties," Stan filled in quickly.

I was still trying to get my head round what Emily and Bruce had been saying, working through their ripple metaphor—and something had jarred with me. I was no scientist, but...

"Whoa, wait," I said. "Wrong. You can't be right. The effects are getting stronger. Pebbles in a lake: the ripples diminish, they don't increase. If this is the result of the forties' experiment, it should have been stronger back then. Not—"

"We're not talking about something that's only moving in three dimensions!" said Bruce. "It's traveling in—"

Emily finished his sentence for him. They were doing that for each other a lot, it seemed, "—four."

"Four dimensions?" echoed Stan.

"Time," said Emily.

To my surprise, I could see where they were going with this—and, perhaps even more surprising, I couldn't help but be intrigued. "So," I said, "what we're experiencing may not be the effects of the Philly Experiment in 1943—"

"—but the effects of the backblast thing the Navy is about to set off!" Now, Emily was finishing *my* sentences, too.

"But how can there be any effects at all," said Stan with a frown, "from something that hasn't even happened yet?"

"Ripples are concentric," said Emily, "they travel outward in all directions—"

"—so the effects of this more powerful event," said Bruce, "would be moving forward *and backwards* in time—"

"—and the closer we come to the moment it's triggered—"

My turn: "—the stronger it is!" I concluded. "If this is true... then what the Navy's about to do isn't going to stop anything—"

"—it's going to cause it!" exclaimed Emily.

"Sheedy's worst case scenario," I realized. "Everything could just... cease to exist."

And Meeno, who had been looking from one of us to the other, trying desperately to follow all this, leapt in again. "What do you mean," he demanded, "'cease to exist'?"

I looked at Emily and Bruce and Stan. They looked at each other. We were all thinking the same thing: how far we'd come in such a short amount of time; how ridiculous all this would have sounded to us just a few days ago. How it must sound to Meeno now. And Stan's earlier question still had a resonance with us: Why should it be us who had discovered all this, when nobody else had?

But there was no doubt in our minds that this was it. This was where it had all been leading. That feeling I'd had in my gut since Weist had told us his story. The end...

"Whatever's been happening to all the ships and planes over the years," said Bruce quietly, "it happens to everything..."

And it was only now, hearing it said, that I really started to think...

...and then I had to spend the next few seconds trying *not* to think...

"Okay," Stan ventured in a quavering voice, "so what do we...?"

"We gotta tell them!" said Emily.

"Great idea," I said, my smart-ass side coming out to paper over my anxieties. "Somebody get me Secretary Weist on the phone. He's probably out at his top secret underwater lab right now, but, hey, it's the four of *us* calling."

"Screw you!" growled Emily.

"We call Benirall!" cried Bruce. "He got through once."

Emily shook her head. "He's right," she admitted reluctantly, shooting a glance at me. "We'll never get through to Weist. Not now."

"So we go public," said Stan. "We tell the TV news."

"Sure," I said, "because we've got just so much credibility."

"With everything that's happening, maybe they'll listen to us." But even Stan sounded doubtful. He knew, more than any of us, that people didn't like to listen.

"So, what," said Emily, "we do nothing?"

I held up my watch for her to see. "We've got less than two hours! How do we convince anybody of anything in—?"

"You can't convince them."

Meeno spoke softly, but that in itself was such a contrast to the histrionics of the rest of us that we all fell silent, and turned to look at him. "You don't have to convince them," he said—and I was impressed by his absolute confidence, coming from someone who, a second ago, had looked like he was a step away from being committed. "You've just gotta buy yourself some time. With more time, you might *then* be able to get them to listen to you."

"Great," said Bruce, "wonderful. And how do we do that?"

Meeno was in no doubt. "You get up in their faces. Make it so they can't set off their... whatever it is. Confront them. Head on. Stop them."

And so it was that, with minutes to go until there was nothing, I found myself in Meeno's cigar boat, blasting across waves into the pitch black storm, holding on against the wind and the rain with a white-knuckle grip, trying not to look too hard as the occasional lightning flash provided a snapshot of the insanely tall swells around us.

I wasn't even sure our captain was fit to pilot a boat but considering what we were out here attempting to do, it probably didn't matter much. The boat itself didn't look like it should have made it out of the harbor—the paint job was still unfinished. But Meeno had shown me the engine—an immaculate monster—and reminded me that looks can be deceptive.

I joined the others below deck in the tiny forward space where they were tucked out of the rain. "We almost there?" Bruce wanted to know. I just shrugged.

Emily looked at her watch, her expression darkening. "We're really cutting this close."

"If this works," began Bruce, but he faltered. He was thinking the same as the rest of us—that now we were out here, faced with the reality of our decision, it seemed like such a lost cause. He forced himself: "If this works, what do we do first? We need to be prepared."

What none of us expected, right then, was to hear laughter. And the last person we expected to hear it from was Stan.

He realized we were all staring at him, and explained, "I finally... I've finally seen... That other person I saw in the mirror, standing behind Benirall..."

Emily and Bruce had no idea what he was talking about, so Stan directed his words toward me. "Winston. It's a brother. Benirall's brother. Winston Benirall. Some years ago, he... he disappeared on one of the family's ships. Disappeared into the Triangle." He was smiling, shaking his head to himself. "That's what this has all been about for him. For Benirall. It's all been about finding his brother."

And then, Meeno's voice came drifting down to us. An urgent shout: "You better get up here!"

"The Navy—the *scientists*—have to see that!"

Emily wasn't wrong. Every time I thought I'd seen everything, that I couldn't be surprised again, it seemed there was something else. And this time, it was the nucleus of the storm itself. A swirling vortex of dark, roiling, low-slung clouds from which whole clusters of lightning bolts came stabbing downward into the sea. It was hundreds of yards in diameter, with a power that defied description.

But Bruce voiced the awful truth: "They still think that's what they're going to stop!"

And suddenly, Meeno wrenched the wheel hard, forcing us to grab frantically for anything we could reach. And even as Emily was demanding to know what he was doing, we saw them: A trio of V22 Ospreys coming in low across the mountainous swells, backlit by staccato lightning flashes.

"Okay, Mr. Greenpeace," shouted Bruce over the clamor of winds and engine noise. "What happens now?"

"Get below!" ordered Meeno. "We've got to get close enough to where they're—"

And then there was a tremendous sonic boom, and the wind—already hurricane level—seemed to gain astronomical velocity.

I was the first to do as Meeno had said, but Emily was right behind me. We were fighting the wind to reach the hatch, and it didn't register for a moment that, even below deck, I was still fighting it. It was only when I turned to the others that I realized—when I saw Bruce, caught halfway through the hatch, Emily pulling at him frantically.

Then I knew that the 'wind' wasn't blowing against us. It was *pulling* us.

"Give me some help!" yelled Emily—and I started back, but Bruce was shouting at us to forget him, to shut the hatch and save ourselves. And that suction force was steadily gaining in power, and I looked past Bruce, past Stan and Meeno, and there was something on the water. A pinpoint of light. So intense, so blinding, that I couldn't look at it directly.

And it was growing. Growing fast.

A lot of things happened at once, then.

The engine of the cigar boat just cut off. Two of the Ospreys spun out of control and slammed into each other. The explosion lit up the sky, and I had a fleeting impression of an engine whizzing into the cockpit of the third plane to create another blossom of flame. Fire and debris rained down on us, and the light was a ball now, doubling and redoubling in size, so fierce that it was almost silver. It was rippling outward, coming inexorably for us, and the suction force was increasing.

Everything was flying, the seats of the boat tearing loose along with everything else that wasn't part of the vessel's superstructure—and over it all, the rending and the howling, I could hear Stan's mournful voice: "We're too late..."

And then, just like that, he was gone, ripped away by the storm, his body instantly shrinking into a dot and then engulfed by the light.

Emily and Bruce were clinging ferociously to the stair rail, and I was trying to get to them, trying to reach them without being snatched away. By the time I made it, I'd had time to ask myself why, what had I thought I could achieve. I was holding on to the hatchway, and watching as the world came apart before my eyes. The silver light was upon the bow of the boat now, whiting out everything, and I knew it wouldn't stop with us, that it wouldn't ever stop.

And my eye went to the brightest point of it—what looked like the epicenter—and don't ask me how, don't ask me where it came from, but I was filled with some primal instinct. With all the light and the noise and the chaos swirling around me, I suddenly knew what I had to do it. And I did it.

I let go, and I ran. I charged the light. I, Howard Thomas, hard-bitten, cynical journalist, made the ultimate leap of faith. Into the heart of the phenomenon.

And there was nothing. Nothing at all. Just infinite white.

Until the white faded to black.

CHAPTER 27

My hearing was the first sense to return.

I could hear a rushing of wind, as if from some distant place but getting closer. And mixed with it: a high-pitched squeal that was growing in intensity.

It was like waking from a deep dream, my mind suddenly empty, grasping for what was real and what fiction.

A voice in my ear, distorted: "You still there? Hello?"

And I was in my car, rocked by the sudden change of time and place, feeling a stab of fear in my chest. *I'd fallen asleep at the wheel!*

My foot went to the brake, but there was no reason to press it. The wheel was straight. I was in no danger. I must only have closed my eyes for a moment, but it had felt like an eternity. I blinked as I recognized the Overseas Highway, the waters around it sparkling in sunlight.

"You want to leave a message for Dr. Gellar or not?" The phone. My cell phone, pressed to my ear. And, in the rearview mirror: Stan and...

...Karl Sheedy.

I was just staring, memories—impossible memories—flooding back into my head. I knew I hadn't been dreaming. But...

What if I was dreaming now? People say your life flashes

before your eyes when you die. But why this part of it? What was the dream trying to tell me?

"My God!" cried Sheedy. "What is that? What's happening?"

And Stan screamed my name.

And I realized that, somehow, this was real—that it was happening, it was happening again, and I had to deal with it or...

Cars were disappearing at random, just like before. And construction cranes were materializing at the sides of the road... which was dissolving... and the end of the road caught up with us, reached the underside of my car, and there was nothing at all beneath us...

...the ocean growing larger through my windshield...

I couldn't believe I was reliving this. I felt numb.

All I could do was hold on.

We hit... like being smashed into a concrete wall... I was thrown forward, arrested by my seatbelt, dazed. Glass shattered; airbags erupted. Seawater gushing in, pooling around my feet. I fumbled with my seatbelt, turned to the backseat.

Stan was unconscious. His head bobbed on the water.

"Help him!" yelled Sheedy. But I couldn't move. The water hit Stan's face, waking him, and he was panicking. My eyes held on him for an agonized moment.

I clambered over my seat, hampered by the airbag, catching my foot, plunging under, feeling for Sheedy's seatbelt release. I found it, wrestled the old guy through to the front of the car and shoved him out through the smashed driver's side window.

Stan was still struggling, submerged now. The car lurched, and I was thrown back, jammed up against the windshield. I stared helplessly at him.

He was terrified. Every instinct I had screamed at me to go to him, to save him, but I knew there was no time—and I couldn't afford to go down with the car.

I made the hardest decision of my life, right then, down there in the freezing water, and I tried to convince myself I hadn't made it for selfish reasons. The world needed me. Incredible as that sounded, it was true. It needed my knowledge, and it needed Sheedy. It didn't need Stan.

THE TRIANGLE

I wished I could explain. I thought he would have understood why I had to abandon him. Why he had to be the one to die. Or maybe I was just fooling myself.

All I could do was tear my eyes away from him, pull myself out of the broken window. Strike out for the surface, and be sure not to look back. Explode into fresh air, gasping and spluttering, to tread water beside Karl Sheedy and to wait for Highway 1 to return as I knew, this time, it would.

Along with the storm...

I didn't bother with dry clothes, this time. We ran straight from the taxi to Bruce's research lab at the university. He and Emily were working urgently, fresh from their adventure in the *Weather Seeker*. I didn't have to imagine how disheveled we looked; I could see it in Emily's eyes.

"My God," she exclaimed, "what happened to you?" I didn't answer. No time to recount another bizarre Triangle experience—what did it matter, anyway? I had the answer in my head, and the proof standing right there next to me, and the sooner we acted on both, the better our chances.

"This is Karl Sheedy," I began—but Bruce interrupted me.

"Where's Stan?" he asked. And this question, I couldn't avoid.

"Stan's dead," I said quietly.

Emily and Bruce were both slammed by this, but there was no time to explain, or even to mourn. That would come later. I hoped. "I've got something I've got to..." I began. Then I faltered, groping for the words. "I know what's going to happen. Everything..."

I saw Bruce's cell phone on a workbench, and I grabbed it. I'd dropped mine in the car, underwater. I dug in my pocket, and pulled out a wilted business card. Emily and Bruce were just staring at me, still whipsawed by the news about Stan. They'd never seen me like this. Nobody had seen me like this.

I knew exactly what I looked like. I'd seen it from the other side too many times. "I'm not crazy," I insisted as I dialed. "I'm not making this up. And I'm not hallucinating.

Stan died over this. I'm not going to let him down."
Then, as the phone was answered: "Akerman. It's Howard
Thomas. We've got something. We've got to see Benirall,
right now."

Akerman tried to say something, but I cut him off. No
time. "I know he's not there. He's holed up in his yacht,
won't see anybody. Doesn't matter how I know. Tell him we
want to see him. He'll see us. I know he will."

We were in Bruce's SUV, but I'd insisted on driving. I
was darting around, past and through the gridlocked traffic,
breaking a zillion laws. We were slamming around in our
seats like pinballs, as I explained about the ripples. Emily
and Bruce didn't know whether to believe me or not—their
own theory—but they hadn't seen the evidence that had
birthed it yet. They hadn't spoken to Weist.

In that respect, Sheedy's presence was a blessing. He
didn't know—none of them knew—where my sudden influx
of knowledge had come from, but he knew it made sense.
Keeping himself, and his voice, calm, he said, "But atoms
aren't really solid at all. They're loaded with space. In fact,
they're mostly space. The only reason I can't put my hand
through this car door is because the door's atoms and mine
are operating on a mutually interactive frequency."

Emily saw where he was going. "But if you could
somehow change the frequency of the atoms in your hand,
your hand would, could—theoretically—pass right through
that door—"

"—and since we also see along same-frequency visible-
light wavelengths," Bruce took up the baton, "the door
would also seem to disappear."

"Any body would," confirmed Sheedy.

"Like a ship," said Bruce, "or a plane—"

"—but it would continue to exist," said Emily, "only in
some other... some other dimension."

"That's what the Navy was trying to do in 1943," I said,
"turn a ship invisible! Only they screwed up. And they're
using the same process now to try to fix things. Only they're
using much, much more powerful technology. And, by the
way—they're completely wrong."

"So all the planes," said Emily, "the ships, all the people, over all these years... they aren't gone. They may've simply been knocked out of... out of phase... with our world. And actually continue to exist—"

"—in some parallel dimension," said Bruce.

"Theoretically."

I took my eyes from the wheel long enough to give Emily a sidelong glare.

I almost ran Akerman down at the yacht berth. He was yelling at me as I leapt out of the car and made for the gangplank, but I just pushed past him. The others slowed down to explain, and I heard Akerman demanding to know who Sheedy was. "Mr. Benirall isn't going to allow somebody he doesn't know to—"

No time.

By the time Emily and Bruce reached the stateroom, I was already settling Benirall into his chair in the adjoining galley. They were taking in his condition, reacting with alarm to the black-painted windows and mirrors, as I kneeled in front of him and stared him right in the eye. "Sir. Mr. Benirall—I need to tell you something... something that's going to sound incredible, but..." No, that wasn't going to do it. I knew what would.

"We have your answer," I said. "We know what's causing the Bermuda Triangle."

Benirall blinked, and focused on me for the first time. Then he turned to Emily and Bruce, and Emily gave me a look—an appraising look—as she tried to decide whether she could commit to everything I'd told her. I pleaded with her, with my eyes. "This could be the answer," she conceded, finally. "It all fits."

"The theory has to do with space-time," said Bruce. "A ripple that may be traveling backwards through—"

No time. "Sir, you have to believe us," I urged. "There isn't time for you *not* to believe us. I—"

Akerman and Sheedy had been hovering in the background, but now Akerman stepped up with a glass of water for Benirall. "Put some Glenfiddich in that," he said, "and—"

"—Glenfiddich in that and I might drink it." Everyone

turned to look at me. I was a spitting firework of emotions, struggling to find some measure of detachment, not to sound crazy. "I've experienced this before! We've been here like this before! In a very few hours, the Navy is going to trigger something out in the Atlantic—something that sets off some sort of massive chain reaction..."

Oh yeah, I knew how this sounded. Never thought I'd be the one to utter these words.

"...that changes the world forever..."

Benirall still hadn't spoken. He was studying me, and I met his gaze, unblinking. Emily spoke up, almost apologetically. "We do have reason to believe that there's some kind of facility that's been built out in the Atlantic—"

"—some enormous device out there," said Bruce. "Underwater."

This was Sheedy's cue. "I know for a fact that it has—"

"Who are you?" asked Benirall.

"He's Karl Sheedy," I said.

"My partner and I," Sheedy explained, "we developed the core principles that the Navy—"

"I don't know you," said Benirall curtly, and he turned back to me. "And you expect me to believe—?"

"Mr. Benirall, listen to me, please. The Secretary of the Navy—Weist—is here, in Miami. You have to get us in to see him!"

Benirall reacted to that with an incredulous chuckle. "I what?"

"He's here in Miami—I know he is! *You* know he is!"

"You truly have lost your mind."

"Weist can stop this!" I insisted. "We have to explain it to him. Get Sheedy to him." Our physicist. The missing member of our team. He had to believe us, this time.

But Benirall gave me a look I knew too well, although I'd never been on the receiving end of it before. The look I must have given to every ranting madman who'd ever come to me with a crackpot story. And despite his tired and frayed state, despite the emotional tumult I knew he was still feeling, he told me clearly and firmly, "I'm not letting you anywhere near the Secretary of the Navy."

"You did it before!" I yelled—and before I knew it, I'd grabbed Benirall and I was shaking him, and if a part of me knew that that was the worst thing I could have done it was subsumed by the greater part that didn't care because there was just *no time.*

Anyway, I had a trump card. I'd only just thought of it, but it would change Benirall's mind for sure, make him see. "You told us you were worried about all your ships disappearing," I ranted, "but that isn't the real reason you wanted an answer to the Triangle! The real reason is Winston!"

Akerman and Bruce had waded in, were pulling Benirall and me away from each other, but I kept talking. "Your brother disappeared into the Triangle, didn't he?! And you've been having hallucinations of your own! You and he were very close, weren't you? It's all been about your brother!"

Bruce was muscling me out of the room—as much, he thought, for my own good as for Benirall's—but it didn't matter. I could get through to him. I knew I could. "Winston might still be alive! That's what you've been sensing, isn't it? Stopping what's about to happen could be your only way of knowing for sure! We have to stop this!"

And then I was outside the stateroom—we all were—and I felt a plunging sensation in my stomach as I realized what I'd done.

I had to calm down, had to put my case more reasonably—but with Bruce and Akerman all but carrying me away, it was impossible to be heard. And then we were outside, at the top of the gangplank, and I pleaded with Akerman, "You've got to talk to him! He's gotta get us in to see Weist!" But Akerman just glared at me with an expression like thunder, and he slammed the door in my face.

I stood there in the pelting rain, my chest heaving, knowing there was no way in hell I was getting through that door again, unable to believe what was happening because I'd been so sure—so sure that, because he'd taken us to see Weist once, Benirall would do it again. Like it was fated, somehow. And I'd blown it.

The others were all staring at me. I don't think they knew how to react. They knew me. They wanted to believe. But.

"Was that real?" asked Bruce, finally. "The stuff about his brother? How'd you know?"

"Stan," I said numbly, staring up at the yacht as if I might find another way on board, think of something I could say.

"Look," said Sheedy, "let me try to reach Victor. If I talk to him directly—"

"He's not exactly down the street at a Motel 6," I snapped. "If he's anywhere, he's out at Ground Zero. You think the Navy's going to let you talk to him now?"

No, there was only one thing to do now, one person we could talk to. One person who could change everything. It would have been easier with Benirall on our side, but we didn't need him. After all, I knew where to find our man.

"We gotta get to Weist," I said.

The dark blue vans and SUVs were just pulling up outside the Four Seasons Hotel. Uniformed drivers were climbing out, stretching their legs. We were here about an hour earlier than last time, and the Navy hadn't packed up yet.

I avoided the eye of the Hummer driver as I barreled toward the hotel entrance, deaf to Emily and Bruce's pleas from behind me. "Howard. Wait." "C'mon, mate—let's do this smart. We need some sort of plan."

In the hotel foyer, I sent a bellman's cart flying and nearly bowled over an elderly couple. People were frowning at me, but I didn't care. I should have cared. I should have noticed that a pair of hotel security men had started to keep a very close eye on me. Instead, I was making a beeline for a familiar face: the female lieutenant who'd met us at the entrance, first time around.

I should have known how she'd react to me; to be fair, I'm sure I wasn't making a great deal of sense by then. I remember deciding she was unimportant, like Benirall—that I only had to convince Weist. I remember darting around her, trying to jump into the elevator. And I remember that she was on me in a flash. I tried to hold her off, but she knew her stuff. She put me right down—and the security guys were on me a half-second after that, driving my face into the elevator floor.

I could feel a knee in my back, hear the crackle of

walkie-talkies. And I remember wondering where my friends were—Emily, Bruce, and Sheedy—why they had just stood back and let this happen to me.

Should have known that, in their shoes, I'd have done exactly the same thing.

CHAPTER 28

I'd done all I could.

When they'd brought me into the police station, I'd shouted and struggled and demanded to speak to somebody in authority. It had done me no good. I'd been thrown into the holding cell, surrounded by drunks and thugs—left to sober up or come down, whatever it was the cops thought I had to do. Left here and forgotten about.

I was sitting on a wooden bench, surrounded by noise: people yelling abuse or protesting their innocence as I'd protested mine to begin with; sirens blaring from outside the building as cop cars raced off on urgent calls. The sounds filled my ears, and merged into one sound: an endless, toneless crashing like the breaking of waves on a beach. Life was going on around me, but none of it meant a damn thing.

I'd done all I could—and it hadn't been enough.

That realization, that sense of futility, had brought about a remarkable change in me. I was calmer than I'd been in hours, able to think clearly despite the petrifying fear that lay at the end of each train of thought. A week ago, I'd have been mortified to have been here. I'd have worried about what Sally might say, what Traci might think, what this might mean for my career. Now, it didn't matter. It didn't matter where I was when the end came.

I wondered if it had been like this for the crews and the passengers of all those ships. The *USS. Cyclops*, the *Mary Celeste*. I wondered if they'd seen it coming, like we had. I wondered if they had tried to get away.

I thought about the *Witchcraft*: A pleasure yacht with two men aboard that had run into engine problems in Miami Harbor less than a mile from shore, a few days before Christmas 1967. It had taken the Coast Guard less than twenty minutes to reach the stricken boat. Less than twenty minutes—and yet, in that time, the *Witchcraft* had disappeared without trace. Disappeared, despite the fact that it'd been drifting in only forty feet of water. Despite the fact that it had a flotation device, which purported to render it "unsinkable." Despite the fact that its captain had flares prepared to lead the Coast Guard to him, and yet he never had the chance to fire them.

I thought about the two lighthouse keepers who disappeared from their post in Bimini in 1969, and were never seen again. And I thought about all the hundreds of ships whose names I would never know: the dozens listed as "overdue" each year by the Miami Coast Guard, and those that took to the sea without notifying the Coast Guard at all. I once spent weeks trying to compile a definitive list of the missing, only to surrender in the face of incomplete and misleading records. In the end, the only evidence for most of the more recent incidents was anecdotal, easy to dismiss.

Yeah, the spooks had done their job well.

I wondered if those lost souls, wherever they were, knew what had happened to them. I wondered if they knew what was *about* to happen—if they were happy or sad that the rest of us were about to join them.

"Anybody know what time it is?"

They'd taken my watch from me. I'd asked the question before—several times, I think, as the minutes had turned into hours, or maybe just endless minutes—but no one had answered me. It could have been late afternoon, still. It could have been eleven o'clock, with minutes to go before the end.

"The time!" I said, louder, my voice close to cracking. "Anybody?"

"Will you shut up about the damn time?" snarled a tattooed, pierced bruiser three times my size. "Nobody in here's got no damn watch, okay?"

"Howard!"

My head whipped around to the bars, and I saw it: my second chance. Actually, my third or fourth chance, but who's counting? My last chance...

Bruce. Bruce Gellar, striding toward me like an angel, escorted by two cops. I pushed my way to meet him—to the bars, at least—ignoring the protesting squeals and snarls of guys who could have pounded my head into papier-mâché without breaking a sweat. "Emily is posting your bond," said Bruce. "It's taken us this long to—"

"What time is it?"

Bruce checked his watch. "Almost eight."

So much time lost. "I thought you were going to just leave me here."

"We seriously considered it."

"What convinced you—?"

He looked me squarely in the eye, and he said, "What if you're right?"

The storm had built to full force. Outside in the parking lot, I noted the inordinate number of police cars that had apparently stalled, officers fiddling under their hoods at a loss to explain their sudden power failures.

Emily was waiting for us under an overhang. I couldn't help myself. I ran to her and hugged her, gratefully, emotionally. "Thank you," I almost sobbed.

She extricated herself from my grip, touched but uncomfortable. "The Grinch grows a heart," she quipped awkwardly. "You're squishing me!"

I looked around, saw Bruce's SUV waiting nearby with Sheedy inside.

"What time is this thing supposed to—?" asked Emily.

"Just after eleven," I said. "Eleven-oh-six."

"That's less than three hours," said Bruce.

"We tried to talk to Benirall again," Emily said to me,

"but he's gone under. He's done talking to us."

"If we can't get to the Navy..."

A thought hit me. I looked at my newly-returned watch, glad that the makers hadn't exaggerated their claims of its waterproof qualities. "The Greenpeace way!"

"What?" said Emily.

But I was already racing into the rain, toward the car.

The *Observer* building was only a few blocks away. We arrived dead on time, for once—and I started to think that maybe, this time, it would work. Maybe I could get it right.

Meeno was heading up the steps to the main entrance door. I raced across the street, and shouted his name—once I could remember it. He turned, and squinted through the rain at me. He had no idea what was happening. "I was just... just coming in..."

"Coming in to see me," I panted, robbed of breath as much by tension as by my brief exertion. "I know."

Meeno looked at me, then at Emily and Bruce who were running up behind me. I reminded myself that he wasn't prepared for any of this. He didn't know anything about the Navy project, the Event—he was just a man at the end of his wits, looking for somebody to make sense of everything he had experienced. And I was about to make it all much worse.

"At your boatyard," I said, trying to sound reasonable, trying not to make the same mistake I'd made with Benirall, "you've got this cigar boat, this really hot cigar boat..."

And so, to the Atlantic again, blasting across the waves, trying not to look too hard at the insanely tall swells around us; Meeno at the helm of his boat, probably wondering how his already screwed-up life had taken this turn—and yet doing what I'd asked of him, believing and trusting me in a way that I'd refused to do for him at the hospital. For that, I'll always be grateful to him.

To the others, too. I sat with them below deck, tucked out of the rain. Emily, Bruce... and Sheedy. "It's all about getting inside," I was insisting. I motioned to Sheedy. "Whatever we have to do—get him inside, get him talking to his old partner, to anybody who'll listen."

"I can't believe we're doing this," said Emily under her breath.

"Hey," I said wryly, "this is my second go."

"What makes you think this time will be any different?" asked Bruce.

"We're earlier than we were last time."

"How much earlier?" asked Emily.

I looked at my watch, and grimaced. "Twenty minutes."

And then, Meeno's voice came drifting down to us. An urgent shout: "You better get up here!" Déjà vu all over again.

"The Navy—the *scientists*—have to see that!"

The nucleus of the storm. Hundreds of yards in diameter. But was it a little smaller, a little less powerful, than the last time I'd seen it? Or was that just what I wanted to believe?

"They think that's what they're going to stop!" cried Bruce.

I grabbed the wheel from Meeno and wrenched it hard, forcing the others to grab for anything they could reach. Emily demanded to know what I was doing, but her voice tailed off as she followed my pointing finger and saw them: The three Ospreys, coming in low across the mountainous swells. Twenty minutes earlier than before, but reacting to our intrusion right on cue.

"We've got to get around them!" I yelled. "Get close enough to where they're going to set this thing off." Meeno was doing a slow burn at me, and all I could do was shrug and say, "This was your idea!"

I'm not sure he heard me. The Ospreys were hovering in formation around us, the whup-whup-whup of their propellers deafening as they closed in, looking like giant metal insects. Spotlights snapped on, and the bright harsh light seemed to galvanize Meeno into action. He took the wheel again, and slalomed the cigar boat through the chop. We were being hammered by the spray from the Ospreys' prop wash, holding on with all we had.

And suddenly, I saw something igniting under the lead Osprey's wings. They were firing on us. They were actually *firing on us!*

Two missiles streaked toward us. I didn't have time to scream at Meeno, but luckily he'd seen them already. Or maybe they had just been warning shots. Either way, they slammed into the sea, only just missing us as we sliced between them. Two thirty-foot plumes of water erupted into the air, jolting our boat. But the Ospreys were still closing, and now the other two released their payloads.

We had a split-second to see the inevitable; to follow the trails of smoke as they converged upon our position, to realize that these were no warning shots and that no way could even Meeno avoid all four of these babies.

Then Meeno leapt overboard, and Emily and Bruce weren't slow to follow his lead. Only Sheedy hesitated, and I shoved him over the side myself—and followed, as the missiles hit their target and a series of explosions ripped the boat apart.

I was buffeted by a wave of hot air, then plunged into cold water, spinning end over end, disoriented, not knowing for a second which way was up.

I broke through the surface, unexpectedly, and forced my legs to start treading, concentrating on staying upright, aware of the others doing the same around me. The flaming wreckage of the cigar boat was raining down around us, and I really thought this was it for me—third time unlucky— that the Navy were just going to let us drown out here.

I tilted my head back, and immediately felt the sour taste of ash in my mouth. That vortex of clouds was immediately above us now, and it looked darker and more ominous than ever.

I didn't know it was possible to be so cold.

We were huddled against the wind, in a Navy Assault Boat that was fighting its way through the swells, escorted by the Ospreys flying low overhead. All five of us, present and correct. I couldn't help but wonder how Stan would have coped with being dumped into the freezing water as we had been—whether he'd have survived.

We'd been fished out by Navy Seals, all dressed in black like those who had snatched us from Captain Jay's sub. They were standing guard over us, though I think it's fair to say that none of us were planning to go anywhere. They were taking us where we wanted to go, anyway.

The Ospreys peeled away, and we were yanked toward the gunwale. The boat had pulled up alongside a platform, about thirty feet square, barely above the waterline and painted in sea-surface camouflage. A plane or ship passing nearby would never have noticed it.

As we were escorted forcefully onto the platform, I felt a nudge in my ribs. Bruce had spotted something out in the ocean. I followed his gaze, but wasn't sure what I was looking at. Some sort of framework, stretching out for yards—no, for *hundreds* of yards—just below the surface. From the way its metal surfaces curved away into the depths, I was sure it had to extend a good deal further downward.

I remembered what Bruce had said, what he'd seen behind that sealed door: "*... some big mother of a superstructure. All underwater.*"

The Ospreys and the Assault Boat were speeding away from us, getting the hell outta Dodge. There was a hatch set into the platform, like a submarine hatch, and one of the Seals threw it open. As we were shoved through it and herded down a long ladder, I lost any doubt I may still have had that we'd been brought this way before. Of course, last time, we hadn't been awake to enjoy the view.

The dark and mysterious corridors felt familiar, this time—as did the uniforms and white coats that hurried past us, up and down the intersecting passageways. Only now, their urgency level was at maximum. As well it might have been.

The Event was only minutes away.

Time to start talking. "We know what you're about to do!" said Emily to our grim-faced escorts. Her words fell on deaf ears.

"You've got to let us talk to somebody," said Bruce. One of our guards gave him a firm push. "Somebody whose job isn't just to shove me!" he protested.

There were more lab-coated people moving past. They didn't look military-intimidating, more accessible. I rocketed out of line, cut off a couple of them. "Please! Get to Osserman! Tell him Karl Sheedy is here!" I jerked my head toward Sheedy, and repeated his name.

Then the guards were upon me, yanking me away from the nonplussed scientists—but Sheedy himself was joining in: "Tell Victor I'm here. Tell him he's got it all wrong!"

"Tell Osserman! Sheedy is here!"

The scientists just stared at us and moved on, as the guards closed in around us all, denying us the chance to go after them.

A minute later, we were bustled into a small, windowless storeroom. The same room, I was fairly sure, in which we'd been locked the last time. The door slammed loudly, and we all heard the thunks of locks being thrown on the outside. Bruce hurled himself at the door as if he thought he could batter his way through it, and Meeno—who'd been silent up till now, letting those of us who thought we knew what was going on do the talking—was right beside him.

I knew they were wasting their time. I just stood and breathed hard, fighting down a panic attack, beyond frustration. To have come so far, so close—and now I was right back to Square One. I'd just swapped one prison cell for another. And I knew that, this time, there'd be no one coming to get me. No way we'd be let out of here, even get to speak to another human being, until after the Event had been triggered.

Except, I knew there wouldn't *be* any "after."

Bruce was tearing open supply boxes, and Meeno joined him. Sheedy asked what they were looking for, and Bruce said, simply, "Anything."

They found machine parts—mostly small, no use to us—but they kept looking, frantically. I didn't want to hope, couldn't allow myself. Half of me was thinking I'd made the wrong decision—that the Triangle had given me a gift and I should have used it, spent the final hours with my family. I remembered Traci's face when I'd called on her, eaten pizza with her, how pleased she had been. I'd done the right thing for once. And now, from her point of view, none of that had ever happened—because, second time around, I'd squandered that time on a fool's errand. She was about to die, and she would never know...

They'd found something. A sort of rod, tapered at one end. I didn't know what it was meant to be, but I knew what it *could* be. I joined Bruce and Meeno, and the three of us tried to wedge the wrench into the almost invisible seam of the door frame.

"This is just a damn storage room with extra locks!" Emily pointed out. "Forget the lock side! Try the hinge side!"

We did as she said, dislodging the wrench and jamming it into the other side. Still, it was a hell of a struggle—and, focused on this, I didn't see what Emily and Sheedy had seen at that moment.

The nail heads in a crate had begun to crackle with an odd, intermittent silver-white energy. There was a metal screen over the air vent in the ceiling, and this too was crackling. Sheedy must have felt something funny, because he reached into his pocket and pulled out a bunch of coins. They'd fused together into what Emily later described as a kind of mini-modern art sculpture.

No time.

She threw herself across the room, and joined the rest of us as the door hinges splintered away from the frame in a shower of wood shards. The combined strength of the four of us succeeded in breaking the door open the rest of the way, and we rushed out into the corridor.

I couldn't miss it now. There were flashes of spontaneous energy sparking white in the very air. Emily let out an exclamation as she dodged one frighteningly close to her head. "Where do we—?" asked Meeno. He was one of us now. He'd seen enough.

Bruce was looking up and down the passageway, trying to remember. "Big-ass control room..." He was the only one of the five of us to have seen it. "I think... dammit... I think this way..."

And he charged off, leaving the rest of us to exchange looks for a heartbeat. Isn't it great when the guy guiding you is just so damn confident?

As if we had a choice. We raced after him.

Our last chance.

Our *last* last chance.

CHAPTER 29

More energy flashes peppered the air. We were running down passageways that all looked the same. Sheedy's age had caught up with him—he was ready to drop—but I forced him to keep him moving. We couldn't do this without him.

Suddenly, Bruce seized up, and the rest of us almost ran into his back. A moment later, I saw the reason why. They were right ahead of us: a phalanx of beige-suited security people. Marching our way, with a purpose.

Our group started to backpedal, but the guards parted—and, between them, I caught sight of the unshaven, sixty-year-old scientist I'd glimpsed during my first stay in this facility. The man I now knew to be Victor Osserman—and if I'd had any doubts about that, it would certainly have been dispelled by Sheedy and Osserman's reactions to each other.

"My God," whispered Osserman.

Only later did I have time to wonder what someone so important to the project was doing outside the control room at this crucial stage. I think maybe he was coming to find us. Maybe my message had made it to him, after all. The security team hadn't known about our escape, I don't think—they seemed as surprised as we were—they'd just been providing an escort.

They reacted quickly to the new situation, though. They fanned out, overran us, and pinned us hard to the walls, even Sheedy. Making sure none of us could threaten Osserman as he moved cautiously into our midst.

"Karl. I couldn't believe you'd actually..." Osserman was at a loss for words. "How did you... what in blazes are you doing?"

No time for this. "Doctor!" I spoke up. "We've got to talk to you!"

"What you're about to do," said Emily through a mouthful of wall, "you have to stop!"

"Listen to them, Victor," pleaded Sheedy.

And Osserman stared at him with an expression of pure incredulity. "Is that what this is about?"

He had another scientist with him—a slightly younger man, who tugged nervously at his sleeve, addressed him as "sir," and reminded him that he had to get back to the project. But Osserman was still staring at his one-time partner. "You voiced your reservations years ago when you left the project. And you're here, now, like this... My God, Karl."

"Sir, please..."

And, to my horror, Osserman allowed his assistant to pull him away from us.

I started shouting, and so did the others. I'm not sure what I said. I remember Emily pleading for just five minutes; Bruce insisting that we had new data. But the guards were herding us back down the passageway.

Our last last chance...

"You're here because the Navy thinks there's a tear!" I yelled—and suddenly, my voice was the only voice, my words the only words. "You're trying to repair a tear! But it's not a tear—it's a ripple! A ripple! You think you're going to fix things! But you're going to cause the Triangle! You're about to end everything!"

Osserman just kept walking.

Reached a bend in the passageway.

Started his turn.

Then...

He stood there with his back to us, for several moments. And there was silence—even from the guards. Until Osserman turned to face us again. Frowning.

I'd done my part. I'd brought Sheedy and Osserman face to face, made Osserman listen. It was up to them now. It was up to Sheedy. All I could do was hold my breath.

Sheedy spoke with a composure I could only envy. He could have shouted, screamed; instead, he kept his voice low-key but incredibly intense. "Victor," he said. "You and I—we argued, always, over everything. Our Vaughn-McAfee paper—remember? I thought we were going to kill each other. But, in the end, you were right and I was one hundred percent wrong. One of us was always right."

A short silence, then, but it seemed to stretch into an eternity.

"Well, this time," said Sheedy, "you're wrong."

And Victor Osserman just stared at him—at all of us—and his internal struggle was written large upon his face.

"We are now at Stage Four! All departments, we need real-time data from you! Ladies and gentlemen, this is Stage Four of Five!"

I recognized the door from Bruce's description. "1-1 SECURITY AREA—AUTHORIZED PERSONNEL ONLY." The cavernous control room beyond it, I could hardly have imagined.

It reminded me of NASA Mission Control, only more shadowy—and way, way cooler. Dozens of technicians were rushing about, bathed in the glows of ultra hi-tech workstation screens, calling out readings.

And Secretary Weist was here. He was standing at the back of the room with a cluster of high-level VIPs. I recognized some of them: cabinet members, naval officers—and Lieutenant Commander Landon.

But all this was dwarfed by what I could see through the IMAX-sized window that fronted the room. As Bruce had said, it looked out onto an underwater scene—where floodlights cut through the ocean depths to illuminate the framework of a construct like nothing I'd set eyes on before. It was a gargantuan device, ten stories tall—and I realized

I'd been right, that I *had* only glimpsed the tip of it out on the floating platform.

It was spinning. Spinning madly—massive interlacing ceramic Podkletnov Rings rotating around each other like some huge Discovery Store perpetual motion desktop puzzle. They span faster and faster, igniting energy flashes like those out in the passageways, only larger and more intense, discharging glowing veins of silver-white into the seawater. An unsettling whir-cum-whine permeated the control room, and the VIPs were fumbling with polarized goggles and noise-canceling headgear.

Not so Weist. I caught a glimpse of his face as Osserman and his security contingent led us through that door. I saw his expression of sublime satisfaction, and I realized that, for him this was more than just another project. This was the culmination of a lifetime's endeavor, and he wanted to revel in the full sensory experience of it.

Weist was doing something no one else had ever done—at least, no one outside the Bible. He was saving all humankind. Or so he honestly believed.

That satisfaction drained from his face as he saw us: five civilian intruders—strangers to him—wet and disheveled. Other heads were turning toward us, too. Technicians were freezing in their tracks and staring, just as most of us were frozen and staring through the window at that gargantuan superstructure.

One of the Navy VIPs made a beeline for us. A captain. I could practically see the veins pulsing in his neck. "What the hell is this?" he demanded.

The head of the security guys spoke quickly, apologetically. He knew how bad this was. "On his authority, sir." He indicated Osserman. "He said it was project specific. And his orders when related to the project are—"

"Get them out of here!" the officer yelled. "Now!"

"No," said Osserman, not quite as firmly as I would have liked.

Weist was moving our way now, as quickly as he could with his cane, and his expression had darkened. "For God's sake, Victor..."

"Mr. Secretary," mumbled Osserman, looking positively vertiginous, "there's something—"

"Are you the guy in charge?" interrupted Emily. "Cuz whoever's in charge really has to listen to us!"

Weist's eyes flashed to her, and then to the rest of us, without a flicker of recognition. "Sir," I said, talking for all our lives, praying I could find the right words this time, "we know what you're hoping to do here. We don't have time to make you understand how we know, but–"

Those energy flashes were getting brighter and closer together. A couple of tech panels around the room were picking up the charge, silver-white electricity rippling along their edges. And that whine was rising.

"You gotta put the brakes on this thing!" insisted Bruce. "Give us a chance to explain!"

Weist looked like he'd just fallen through the looking glass. Not that he was buying our story—not for a second—he just couldn't believe we were here, that this was happening. And Osserman...

Osserman was in his own insecure little hell. "I know it's crazy, sir," he said, glassy-eyed, "but... I think it's possible, *possible*–"

"Wait just one..." Weist spluttered. "You... Now... you're suggesting *now* that..."

And one of the technicians called out: "Sixty seconds to Stage Five! Stage Five in sixty seconds!"

I'd never known pressure—or frustration—like it. To believe in something—in your heart of hearts, to know it to be true—and yet to be unable to open the eyes of the people who mattered "Mr. Secretary," I stammered, "God... we know you were on the *Eldridge*. Your leg, we know about your leg."

And Weist turned to stare at me, completely flummoxed.

"What you're about to do here," I told him with as much passion, as much sincerity, as I had in me, "it isn't going to stop the Crux Event you're so afraid of. It's going to cause it!"

"Forty-five seconds!"

Through the IMAX glass, the superstructure was reaching what had to be its peak. The whine was almost overbearing; more electricity was crackling along control panels and beginning to arc between them. I could tell the techs hadn't been expecting this, but they stayed bravely at their stations.

"The device is beginning to expel its charge," insisted Emily. "It isn't contained! Look! *Look!*"

Osserman was staring at the silver-white discharges, and Bruce read his face. "You weren't expecting this in here, were you?! You trigger the main event and it's everything we've said. It's the entire world!"

And finally, Osserman said it. He said it under his breath, so I could hardly hear him, but he *said* it. He said, "We have to shut down."

And then, louder: "We have to shut down!"

But Weist was resolute. "No!"

"Thirty seconds!"

And everyone was staring at the Secretary of the Navy, and he was almost shaking with frustration. "Thirty years, we've known what's coming! We must countervail the Crux Event or we lose everything!"

"But, sir," ventured Osserman. *"We may be wrong!"*

"You are wrong!" I yelled.

"Twenty seconds!"

And there was silence, but for that penetrating whine.

A long, long moment—Secretary Douglas Weist's face unreadable as he pondered what we'd told him, holding the fate of humanity, of existence itself, in his hands.

A long, long moment...

Then Weist said firmly, "We go."

And the silence ended.

We were all shouting: "No!" "Look at what's happening here!" "We know!" "You can't do this!" I think I might have physically thrown myself at Weist if it hadn't been for those security guys closing in around us again now that the Secretary had made his decision. I was feeling like the bottom had dropped out of my world, like whatever I did, whatever I *had* done, Fate had been determined to work against me all the way. Fate... or time. Perhaps you couldn't change your destiny after all.

Then Landon spotted something on a bank of security camera monitors and sensor data readouts—and she let out an exclamation, and called for the captain who had intercepted us on our way in. He rushed to her side, and

Landon highlighted something on her screen for him. "We got a bogie out there!"

"Sea or air?"

"Sea!" she said. "A ship! Big."

"Where the hell'd it come from?"

"Our sentries have all pulled back to green-line safety positions—"

"What's its registry?"

Landon was already typing, and as the information came up on her screen she read out loud, "A 138k m3 LNG carrier. 138k—that's aerosol tank capacity. She's a methane tanker."

"What's her goddamn registry?!" the Captain demanded.

"Registry is... domestic. Owner/operator... Benirall Shipping."

Emily was the first of us to find her voice. "It's Benirall."

"We are at Level Five! Five out of Five! We are ready to go!"

But the tech's voice was almost drowned out by that mind-melting whine—and the superstructure was flashing an insane staccato rhythm, and now the captain too was doubtful, rushing up to Weist. "It's square in the zone, Mr. Secretary."

"I don't give a damn about one ship!" snapped Weist.

"It's methane," Osserman pointed out. "If it goes, it takes this whole facility with it!" In less critical circumstances, I might have smiled. I could just picture Benirall on the deck of his tanker, his back set against the unrelenting storm. Determined to do this, to stop the Event. For his brother. Back to his old self at last, perhaps.

"We're not talking about just this facility," I said, "we're talking everything."

"Don't trigger it," pleaded Emily.

"Don't," said Bruce.

And then there was something else on Landon's readouts. Something that really walloped her. "I got..." She took a deep breath. "I got more bogies!"

And everyone looked at her, wondering what the hell was happening now.

"Sea or air?" asked the Captain again.

"Both," reported Landon, astonished. "There are dozens of them. Maybe... hundreds... And they're not approaching."

"What do you mean 'not approaching'?"

"They're just... appearing. All around us."

"All the ships," I gasped, "planes that have been taken by the Triangle—that's what's out there now." I don't know where the idea came from—but once I'd said it, it made perfect sense. In a weird kind of a way.

I looked at Weist, and I predicted confidently, "You aren't going to do it."

The storm had passed.

The Navy captain—Saunders was his name—led the way up the ladder to the floating platform. Weist was right behind him, followed by me—then Emily, then Bruce, Meeno, Sheedy, Osserman, and a clutch of security people.

I heard them before I saw them. The rushing of ships and the humming of aircraft, layered one atop the other, strangely distorted as if filtered through... well, space-time itself. And then I emerged into the cold sea air, and I saw:

The platform was surrounded by a green haze, and within that haze were the ghostly signatures of all of them. On the water: large ships and small private craft, coming and going, not fully corporeal, crisscrossing each other's paths, sometimes passing right through each other. In the sky: The ethereal signatures of commercial liners and military transports, private planes and helicopters. It was like, just for the moment, this little patch of ocean had become Grand Central Station.

I couldn't help myself; I let out a whoop of excitement—and the others joined in, laughing and hollering. Emily and Bruce's eyes met, and she abandoned her reserve and hugged him, tightly and wantonly. I shouted over the noise to Weist, who was still trying to fathom all this. "You did it, Mr. Secretary! Exactly what you wanted to do! You closed the Bermuda Triangle!"

"More to the point," cried Emily, "the Triangle never happened at all!"

"Never happened at all" repeated Bruce.

And slowly, I began to realize what this meant, and my

brief exaltation faded.

I was only a few seconds ahead of reality. Even as I looked at the green fog again, its ghostly inhabitants were fading. A moment later, the fog itself began to dissipate—and then there was only the calm ocean at night. And one ship: Benirall's methane tanker, I realized, standing a hundred yards away. But then, this too shimmered white and vanished.

"What's happening?" cried Meeno.

Another white shimmer, and now Saunders and Osserman were gone, right from our midst. "If the Triangle never existed," breathed Emily, "then nobody disappeared! A zillion things change!"

It wasn't fair.

Meeno was next, blinking out on us without warning. Then Weist, before he could say a word. The security people. And Sheedy.

All we'd been through, everything we'd done—and all I could think was that nobody would know. Would we even remember?

Bruce suddenly cried out in pain and clutched at his leg. Emily reached for him. Their eyes met, and I could see their fear—that if the Triangle never existed, they would never have met. So much to say, no time to say anything.

Bruce shimmered and went. Emily looked at me, helpless, afraid, and then she was gone, too. And I was alone.

Alone on this platform, in the middle of the ocean, knowing that the light would take me, too, terrified of what I might find on its far side this time.

Then the platform itself began to shimmer, to dissolve beneath my feet, and I felt a greater fear: That somehow I'd been overlooked, abandoned out here. That there was no place for me in the new reality we'd made.

And then, just like that, there was nothing again.

CHAPTER 30

Where the hell am I?

Pastel colors. Morning sunlight through windows. Almost idyllic.

A room—familiar, and yet not familiar.

I was lying on a bed—and as I started to adjust to my new surroundings, to remember my all-too-recent fears, I realized I was lucky to be alive at all.

If I *was* alive. Pretty much every perception of reality I had was up for grabs at that moment.

A body shifted on the mattress beside me. I turned quickly.

Sally. My ex-wife, sleeping beside me. Had I gone back? Further, this time?

No. The room—it was our room, the room I remembered, but at the same time different. Redecorated. This wasn't the past. It was the present day. A different day.

I studied her face. She was so very beautiful—and at that moment, so peaceful. Without thinking, I reached out and touched her cheek.

Sally's eyes opened. They focused on me. Then they darkened.

"As if!" she snapped—and she flopped over away from me, angrily.

"Hi, Daddy."

I was still trying to get my bearings, walking in a daze in my sleep T-shirt and shorts. But Traci seemed to expect me to say something, so I said, "Your mother's... still sleeping."

"Yeah. So?"

She was still fifteen. Sitting at the kitchen table, eating cereal, reading the back of the box. As if she wasn't at all surprised to see me here. A normal morning. And my own words came drifting back to me, from a time—from a world—that no longer existed. *"Alternate paths... life paths...maybe it isn't always too late to change the one you're on."*

I'd been given a gift.

Back in the bedroom, I watched Sally sleeping for a while, then found myself moving to the walk-in closet. I stood in the doorway and looked at her clothes lining one side, mine on the other. A world where we hadn't separated. But it was only a matter of time.

Behind me, she was getting out of bed. I looked at her, and wondered how different her memories of our marriage—of me—were to mine. I wondered if I knew her at all any more. I wondered if I ever had.

Sally headed for the bathroom, saw me looking into the closet. "You thinking of packing and moving out?" she asked. "Good."

I knew one thing.

I rushed to cut her off, and she glared at me. "What the hell do you think you're—?"

"I... don't want to move out." I took a deep breath. I felt like I had when I'd confronted Weist, and Osserman before him—like I was talking for my life, like I had to find the right words or it was all over. This time, they came easily.

"The problems we've been having," I began.

"*All* the problems," said Sally archly.

"I want us to work them out. I'll... do whatever I have to this time."

I knew her well enough to read her expression. I'd caught her by surprise. I guess that, even in this reality, she'd never heard me talk like this.

Sally eyed me warily—but there was also that tinge of

something else in her eyes. Something I'd glimpsed when I'd visited her and Traci a few hours before the end of the world. Something that made my heart surge with hope.

Then she frowned, and with a gentle challenge, she asked me, "What do you mean 'this time'...?"

This time...
Emily was disturbed by the ringing of the telephone.

She'd been standing in her kitchen, looking out through the window. The sun was shining, and her neighbors were going about their morning routines. Everything seemed perfectly, impossibly normal.

She looked at the phone for several seconds, not ready to face the outside world yet. In the end, though, she gave in to its shrill tone, and picked up.

A man's voice. One she didn't recognize. "Hey, babe. Look, I know, I know—I'm running late. Egregiously late."

"Who is this?" asked Emily.

"Okay," said the stranger, "I totally deserve that. I'll be there as fast as I can. Faster. I promise. Hope this means you still love me."

Emily just plopped into a chair and stared at the wall.

A few minutes later, she was on her feet again, rushing into the bedroom, rummaging in the closet until she found the strongbox she kept at the very back. She opened it, and pulled out her birth certificate, adoption decree, photos of her as a baby. She spread them out on the bed around her. Her only link to her past. Until now.

She paged through the phone book with trembling hands. Found the name she was looking for. She'd half expected her to have moved away from the area, but there it was. Patterson, Laura. She dialed the number before she could talk herself out of it, listened to her own breathing echoing in her ears over the sound of the ring tone.

The voice that answered was instantly familiar. "Hello?" Then, a few seconds later, "Is anyone there...?"

"Is this... Laura?" asked Emily, although she knew the answer.

"Yes. Who's this calling please?"

She took a trembling breath. "I'm calling about... your

daughter."

"My daughter?"

A pregnant moment. Then, sounding a little flustered, Laura Patterson said, "I'm sorry, I'm afraid you've mistaken me with someone else."

Emily felt tears brimming in her eyes. It was no more, no less, than she had expected, but still it hurt to hear the words said out loud—to know that, in this reality as in her old one, her mother was a stranger to her.

"I'm sorry to have disturbed you," she said finally. "I won't be bothering you again."

And she put down the phone.

This time...

Bruce woke on a fully reclined green Naugahyde Barcalounger, in the family room of somebody's suburban home. He looked around, disoriented, at kids' toys and beanbag chairs, and his first thought was that he'd been condemned to Domestic Hell.

He started to get up, and immediately felt a shooting pain in his leg, like the one he'd felt on the platform. More shocked than hurt, he crumpled back into his seat.

There were children playing and laughing outside, and Bruce picked himself up and limped to a bay window. Two kids—a boy and a girl—dangled precariously from a jungle gym in a tiny, cluttered yard, and he watched them for a moment, hardly daring to believe what he suspected to be true.

"We're going to be taking both of those kids to Emergency."

Bruce span round at the sound of a woman's voice. He hadn't heard her sidling up behind him—about his age, and certainly attractive, dressed in a cute sleep shirt. He had no idea who she was, but she flung her arms around him from behind and smiled.

"Well, what do we expect?" she continued happily. "After all, they're just like their father..."

This time...

Meeno woke in his own bed, and his first thought that

STEVE LYONS

it was happening all over again. Reality becoming illusion, illusion becoming reality. He didn't dare move. He just let his eyes rove over the room, taking in every detail, bracing himself for the one detail that might have changed this time.

This time. The last time. The life he would be stuck with. Somehow, he knew that much to be true.

He was relieved to find Helen, sleeping in her usual place beside him—and between them in the bed, his son Ruben. Back to normal, then? Meeno had been through so much, he couldn't quite believe...

And there was something else. Some*body* else. The crown of a tiny head just poking out the top of the covers. He peeled down the sheet, hardly daring to hope...

...and there, snoring lightly, was his younger son. Dylan.

Meeno's eyes filled with tears. He felt overwhelmed. This was more than he could have wished for. He was hardly aware, at first, of the telephone at his bedside ringing. He reached for it, trying not to disturb his sleeping family. He found his voice. "Hello?"

"Hey, Meeno. Hope I'm not calling too early."

Meeno caught his breath, recognizing the voice at once. "No, Don," he said hoarsely, "it's okay."

No Triangle. No mysterious force. No whirlpool sucking at the Greenpeace raft. No deaths on his conscience. What the sea had taken away from Meeno, it had returned to him.

"I was thinking about the Greenpeace meeting this afternoon," said Don Beatty. "There're a couple of items I'm thinking of adding to the agenda and I wanted to run them past you first. You got a minute?"

Meeno looked at his family, at the familiar room around him, as if he expected it all to disappear—but this time, he knew it wouldn't. Little Dylan snuggled closer to him, and he smiled as he turned back to the phone and announced, "I've got all the time in the world."

Meeno Paloma was finally home.

Two weeks passed.

THE TRIANGLE

Two weeks before we were together again—though I'd spoken to each of the others many times by phone in the meantime, comparing notes. It had taken us that long to get an appointment with the man we wanted to see. We'd also needed time to adjust to our new lives, to discover all the little differences, the things we didn't know—about our partners; about ourselves.

Two weeks, and then the four of us were reunited on the harbor outside the offices of Benirall Shipping. The original four. Benirall's team of so-called experts.

It was a shock to see Bruce walking with a cane—almost as much as finding he was a family man in this changed timeline. That electricity that had sparked between him and Emily was gone now; they were awkward around each other, and when their eyes met they were filled with melancholy. Emily had ended things with her boyfriend, realizing that he wasn't what she wanted. But Bruce...

He had decided to give his new life a chance. It wasn't what he had expected or planned for himself, but it was the path he'd apparently chosen in this timeline—and Gina, his wife, is a good woman. He hadn't wanted to let her down. As for the kids—well, last time we spoke, he said they were "growing on" him. I think he might just make a success of this, after all.

And Stan...

Stan was back, none the worse for wear for his temporary death and rebirth. For the fact that I let him die... He still ribs me about that sometimes, but I got my chance to explain and he does understand. I know he does.

Stan doesn't have those psychic flashes any more, though he does have the satisfaction of knowing his gift helped save the world. I think he's happier, now.

One final surprise awaited us in the conference room of Benirall Shipping. We'd been shown in and told to expect "Mr. Benirall"—but the Benirall who entered a few minutes later was a stranger to us.

Winston Benirall. Eric's brother. His twin; I hadn't realized that before. Looking at this Benirall was like looking at the other, the most prominent difference being that this version sported a small, precise moustache.

Winston glanced, but only glanced, through the folder that Bruce presented to him. Our final report. Then he closed it, and shrugged. "I'm afraid I must admit," he said, "I only comprehend perhaps one percent of what you've set down here. But if I understand your basic claim—you say my company entered into some sort of arrangement with the four of you. That if you were to discover the secret behind something called the... the Bermuda Triangle... you would each be paid five million."

It was a lost cause. Stan, Emily, and I had known it all along; there was no evidence, no contracts any more. Bruce had been the one to press it. "We really should be talking to your brother," he said. "He's the one who made the offer. If anyone were to remember, it'd be—"

The door opened at that point, and somebody entered. I didn't recognize Aron Akerman at first, dressed in a neat suit, clean-shaven, his hair cut short. Obviously, with two Beniralls at the helm, a few things had changed around this company.

Akerman handed Winston a sheaf of papers, then left, showing no sign that he recognized us at all. Winston got to his feet, evidently deciding we'd taken up enough of his time. "I'm the company's Chief Financial Officer," he said stiffly. "If my brother were ever to make such a... remarkable arrangement, it would still require my approval first. I agreed to meet with you because, collectively, your credentials and reputations—"

"If we can only see your brother!" interrupted Bruce.

"I've allowed you to waste my time," said Winston Benirall, "specifically so you wouldn't waste my brother's. Good day."

And he marched toward the door.

"The only reason you're even here today," Bruce shouted after him, "is because we..." But Winston was gone.

Bruce's voice dropped, and he continued to himself: "... we changed the world..."

"Hey," said Bruce defensively as the four of us stepped outside into a gorgeous sunny day, "*we* remember. It was worth the shot to see if Benirall—"

"We don't know why we remember," Stan pointed out. "Maybe it was all that we went through. Maybe—"

"You were dead," Bruce shot back. "You got nothing to complain about. Me? I've got responsibilities now." He made it sound like a dirty word—and I didn't miss the quick flash of his eyes toward Emily. "I also got a bum leg."

"You ever find out what—?" I began to ask.

"I got it caught on a diving trip in the Aleutians many years ago." Bruce looked at Emily, who nodded. She knew this story from before. "Only in this reality, I wasn't so lucky."

"'In this reality,'" sighed Emily. "Are we ever going to get used to saying that...*living* that?"

"This is our reality now," I said. "Permanently. Eventually we'll get used to it."

Eventually...

"So," said Stan, "I guess that's it then. This is... goodbye. I mean, considering the fact that we never actually met..."

"It isn't over," I said doggedly. "Not really. Remember what Weist said? That area of the Atlantic has always been home to strange phenomena."

"Plus," said Bruce, "everything the Navy was attempting— the science still exists. We stopped it this once, but Mankind is going to have to avoid the temptation to ever attempt it again."

"Mankind never avoids the temptation," said Emily with a hint of resentment.

"We're just going to have to make them," I said. "Make them see. Make them..." And I stopped as I realized what I was saying, how strange the words must have sounded coming from my mouth. But the others were all looking at me, so I bit my lip and I finished the sentence.

"...*believe.*"

CHAPTER 31

In fourteen hundred ninety-two, Columbus sailed the ocean blue...

Some things haven't changed.

History's most famous seaman still ground to a halt in the Sargasso Sea during his Atlantic voyage. He still watched helplessly as his old enemy Bobadilla sailed off to his death, a decade later. Nowhere in his logs, though, does Columbus mention an encounter with a twenty-first century cargo ship called the *Winston Pride* II. At least, not in any logs I've been able to find. No great surprise there, given that no such ship exists—or has ever existed.

I'm typing this on my computer, in my home office. My new home. My *old* home. I spend a lot more time than I ever used to working from here. I see a lot more of my family, despite my latest obsession.

I've told them everything, of course—Sally and Traci. I think they want to believe me—but I know, perhaps better than anyone, how hard it is for them. I know that most people will dismiss my story as a delusion, the rantings of a nutcase, and it would be hypocritical of me to blame them. The things I saw, the events I lived through—by their very nature, they're impossible to prove.

THE TRIANGLE

Few people have even heard of the Bermuda Triangle.

So, I've been reading books, surfing the Net, talking to people. Not just to those who remember—Stan, Emily, Bruce, and Meeno—but to those whose experiences and expertise, even in this reality, might still prove relevant. People who might be able to help.

Scattered across my desk are a hundred photographs: pictures of the Atlantic, of the Overseas Highway, of the USS. *Cyclops*—taken in 1923—and of the Torpedo Bombers of Flight 19. There's even a recent photo of little Heather Sheedy, six years old again, with her parents and grandparents. And letters—from various luminaries in the scientific community, among them Doctors Sheedy and Osserman. I haven't talked specifics with either of them yet, but our correspondence is full of theories about exotic matter, electromagnetism, and time vortices. And ripples. If it *were* to happen again, I'd like to think we'd be a little prepared for it now.

Douglas Weist is no longer Secretary of the Navy. He never was. I tracked him down to his retirement home in Malibu, and wrote to him on the pretext that I was putting together an *Observer* article. I asked a few pertinent questions about the Philadelphia Experiment, and in return I got a two-sentence brush-off. The Navy's official line: No such project existed. I wrote a second time, making reference to Weist's service aboard the USS. *Eldridge* and the injury he suffered. Never heard back.

Another person reluctant to talk to me is Eric Benirall. I've tried, many times, to get a face-to-face with him, but he doesn't return my calls. Not surprising, you might think, given the apparently preposterous claim the four of us took to him not so long ago. But there's one thing I never mentioned to the others; one thing I can't be sure of myself.

As we left the offices of Benirall Shipping, that last time, I glanced back over my shoulder and I thought I saw him: Eric Benirall, looking down at us from the mezzanine floor. Watching us as if he *knew* who we were and what we were doing there. As if he remembered after all. As if he remembered everything.

If that's true—if he's avoiding me, avoiding all of us—then I doubt it's about the money. Twenty million dollars is small change to him. No, I think Eric Benirall—for all that has happened, for all that's changed—is still a haunted man.

Or maybe I was mistaken. Perhaps it was Winston I saw, just making sure we left the premises. They do look very much alike.

I thought it would be difficult for me to write all this down, to open myself up to ridicule. In the end, it was easy. It was just something I had to do.

I go out to the breakwater, sometimes, or the harbor, and I listen to all the people going about their business around me, blissfully unaware. I listen to them, but I don't watch them. I look out across the water instead. The mighty Atlantic. I look for the beginnings of storm clouds—and sometimes I find them, and have to convince myself that they're natural, that I can't see the ghost images of lost aircraft in their random formations.

Most days, the ocean is quiet and peaceful. For the moment.

If you were to drill straight through the world from the center of the Bermuda Triangle—or rather, from where it once was—you would come out in the only *other* place on Earth where compasses point to true north and magnetic north at the same time. Another area famed for its mysterious disappearances, of many ships and planes. A larger area than the Triangle, but familiar in shape. Local fishermen refer to it as "the Devil's Sea"—the same name that was first given to the Bermuda Triangle by E.V.W. Jones in 1950—and it's said to stretch from the southeast coast of Japan to the northern tip of the Philippines to the island of Guam. Three sides...

In October, 1492, the very day before he set foot in the Americas at long last, Columbus saw a row of greenish lights dancing on the horizon. They seemed to flit from one spot to another. He never did find their source.

Some things haven't changed.

It's still out there.

It's waiting.